SHIPWRECK IN PARADISE

Først publisert i Norge i 2023

Første opplag

Omslagsdesign: Trond Kulterud
Satt med Garamond Premier Pro 10,5/14 av Per Høyer-Steffensen, potatodesign.no

ISBN: 978-82-303-6245-7

KONSTANTINOS GUSTAD PADAZOPOULOS

SHIPWRECK IN PARADISE

"Life is a daring adventure or nothing at all."
CLIVE CUSSLER

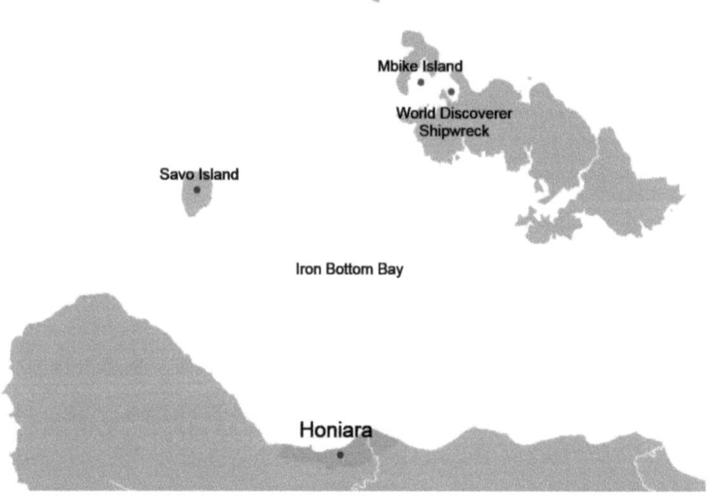

I

A REFRESHING BREEZE hit Captain Oliver Kruess's face as he emerged onto the port side of the deck. It was a welcome change from the cool, air-conditioned atmosphere inside the bridge. He adjusted his tortoise brown Wayfarers and took a deep breath while savouring the view. His ship, the World Discoverer, was about to enter Sandfly Passage after setting sail from Honolulu Harbour seven days ago.

The journey had been exceptionally smooth until now, with calm seas and warm weather. Oliver and his crew were in high spirits, eager to lay anchor in a few hours. He couldn't wait to stretch his legs in Honiara and unwind. This time of the year was always special for him after enduring a long winter sailing through the polar regions. Antarctica stood out for him, and he relished the challenge of navigating his ship in that region. The sunrises while sailing the Strait of Magellan could be glorious when the sky turned indigo.

For now, though, he was ready to embrace the warm weather and the tropical beauty of the Solomon Islands. He instinctively glanced at his white dial Omega Seamaster. 4:45 pm – perfect. 'We're on schedule, Dennis. Make sure we have the right course on approach,' he called out as he walked back into the bridge.

'Roger that, Captain. The course is plotted on the chart, and we have everything under control,' Dennis responded confidently.

Dennis was Oliver's first mate aboard the ship. They had been travelling together for many years and functioned seamlessly in tandem. Although Dennis was younger than Oliver, he garnered almost as much respect from the crew. While Oliver had a more no-nonsense approach to leadership, Dennis preferred to be more smooth around the edges. He always strived to be the voice of reason in difficult maritime situations.

Oliver picked up the phone from the wall and dialled the cruise director's number. 'It's almost time now, Niklas. Spread the word to the passengers. We will soon sail through the passage. I'll bet many of them are eager to see some land again.'

'Consider it done, Captain,' Niklas responded before hanging up the phone and switching over to the ship's speaker system. He cleared his throat and took a sip of water before addressing the passengers onboard.

*

Down on the Explorer deck, Antonio was checking himself in the cabin mirror. An announcement over the ship's speakers had abruptly cut his siesta short. It didn't help that his fiance, Julia, had shaken him hard to awaken him before dashing out of the cabin, excited to get a taste of what the Solomon Islands offered. Antonio couldn't help but smile while splashing some water on his face. Her enthusiastic spirit was one of the many reasons he had fallen in love with her. He combed his black hair, donned his sandals, and locked the door behind him.

This was their first trip together after being engaged for a month. He had proposed on the Santa Monica Pier, next to Maria Sol, the restaurant where they had first met. At first, Antonia feared the proposal would be awkward, but Julia said yes immediately. It was an unforgettable moment, with the Californian sunset creating a magical backdrop for his proposal on the pier. All those memories and his feelings for Julia gave him an instant boost of confidence and an extra spring in his step. You know what? Let me get a shot of tequila on the way up to the deck, he thought.

He pressed the elevator button that pointed upward, but when the sliding doors opened some seconds later, it revealed an elevator clogged with people. Antonio smiled politely and walked away to take the stairs. The hallways and main staircase were teeming with people making their way upwards. Antonio had to zigzag through the crowd until he reached the entrance to the Fire & Ice lounge. With all the people moving outside to enjoy the view, the bar was empty, save for him and the two bartenders behind the counter.

'Good evening, sir. How can we help you?' asked one of the bartenders.

'I'd like a shot of Pepe Lopez Gold.'

'A fine choice, sir. Isn't it a bit early for tequila by yourself, though?' the bartender asked while preparing the shot.

'No, not at all. I recently got engaged and wanted to grab a shot before going out to find my fiance.'

'Well, in that case, I will pour myself a shot too. Cheers!'

They both smacked their glasses hard on the counter after finishing their shot.

'Good luck with finding your fiance out there. It's quite chaotic out on the observation deck now. Everyone wants the perfect photo,' the bartender added, pointing to the window.

'Trust me, if I can find her while she's shopping at The Grove on a Saturday in LA, this should be a walk in the park,' Antonio replied with a chuckle.

However, locating Julia proved to be much trickier than expected. Feeling slightly guilty for stopping to have a drink before meeting her, he began to believe in the law of instant karma. Suddenly, he felt a tap on his shoulder, and he quickly turned around.

'What took you so long, honey? I thought you fell asleep again,' said Julia with a laugh.

'I just made a pit stop and refuelled myself with some tequila before looking for you.'

'You and your silly motorsport jokes. I found a spot where we can enjoy the last leg of the trip. Follow me.' She led the way to the ship's stern. After walking for a while, she froze and turned around. 'Did you bring the camera?'

Of course. I had to forget the one thing I was supposed to bring with me.

'I'll be back in five minutes. Sorry, my love.'

He planted a quick kiss on her forehead and hastily retreated towards the cabin. How could he, a full-time professional photographer, forget the one thing he always carried with him? Vacations sure tend to make you absent-minded.

He pushed open the swinging double doors of the observation deck and turned right to consult the ship's layout map. After scanning for the quickest way to his cabin, he broke into a jog. He contemplated sliding down the handrails like in his high school days, but quickly scrapped that idea. As he sprinted down the ship's main staircase, a deafening sound pierced his eardrums. It sounded like someone scratching a blackboard but it magnified greatly. The floor rumbled, and the ship abruptly slowed to a crawl. Antonio lost his balance and flew off his feet a short distance before landing nastily on his shoulder. His ears were ringing, and his view was blurred. He slowly felt the ship listing as he lay on the floor, grappling with the pain. I have to check if Julia is safe, he thought, his senses slowly fading. The muted screams from the passengers on the decks above were the last sounds he heard.

*

'What the hell just happened, Dennis?' Oliver yelled, trying to pick himself up from the floor.

'Captain, we must have hit an uncharted reef. There's no other explanation,' Dennis replied in a composed manner.

'We need to assess the damage and get a status report from the engine room. Thomas, please send a distress signal to nearby ships and the port of Honiara. I'll handle the steering and wait for your update, Dennis. Can someone keep Niklas in the loop in case we need to evacuate? He's on the deck at the moment with most of our passengers.'

All the crew at the bridge nodded affirmatively and got to work. After the initial shock of the impact had waned, people began following Captain Oliver's orders and trying to handle the situation. However, the gradual tilting of the ship and the persistent alarm sounds from the various displays were dampening their spirits. Oliver sensed the tension in the room but remained locked in, knowing it would take a lot for his ship to go down.

The ship had received a reinforced double hull from Rauma Shipyard in Finland, classifying it as an A1 ice-class ship. This had been a necessary upgrade for conducting cruises and expeditions in polar regions. Oliver was counting on his ship's resilience and was hoping it would still be seaworthy. Everything would be alright if they could get to Honiara. However, he was keeping all options open, mentally preparing alternative plans in case the status report from the engine room was dire.

Dennis returned to the bridge, catching his breath before delivering the update to Oliver.

'Captain, we got a reply from the chief engineer. We have a four- to five-metre gash on the starboard side. The sealed doors will contain the water in the watertight compartments. Power output to the engines is reducing substantially, and we estimate the ship will continue to list further.'

'Ok, we've listed by eight degrees now. Before we cross nineteen, we need to abandon the ship and start evacuating the passengers. It's safe to say we cannot reach Honiara and have to think of an alternative plan. Is there any shallow location in the vicinity to which we can try to steer the ship for easier evacuation?'

Oliver knew that time was of the essence and that all the lifeboats would be useless if the ship continued careening to its side. Dennis walked to the GPS display screen and scoured the map for a suitable location. Only one place stood out – Roderick Bay. It had shallow waters, and the Roderick Bay Yacht Club could assist in the evacuation with the pleasure boats that were moored there.

'Captain, we could sail into Roderick Bay and try to evacuate the ship there.'

After calculating the distance, the speed at which they were moving and the ship's condition, Oliver gave the order.

'Affirmative. It's our only viable plan to avoid sinking. Let's focus on the passengers' safety and minimising damage to the ship. Sound the alarm and initiate our ship evacuation routine.'

Like a well-oiled machine, each of the crew members started doing their respective tasks under the stoic gaze of Captain Kreuss. They needed a minor miracle, but he was certain they could make it. The weather was on their side, and the crew had responded well and seemed up to the task. While he was making some minor adjustments to the steering, Chief Radio Officer Thomas barged in, interrupting his thinking. His usually slicked-back hair and cocky demeanour had been replaced by a messy hairdo and a worrisome look. Sweat was trickling down his forehead, and his face was flushed like a Brandywine tomato.

'Captain, I got a response from the port of Honiara. A local ferry has just disembarked and is on its way to Roderick Bay to assist with the evacuation. The yacht club will house our passengers until we get everyone off the ship.'

'Copy that, Thomas. Keep your cool and return to your post.'

Thomas nodded without uttering a word and headed back to his office, trying to pull himself together. Communication was key, and he needed to keep his head in the game for the sake of everyone around him.

*

After donning her life jacket, Julia grabbed a second one for Antonio. She scanned her surroundings to ensure no crew members were near the swinging doors. She had patiently waited for Antonio to sprint through the doors, but he still hadn't shown up. That was very uncharacteristic of him. Now was her chance to sneak in and look for her fiancé. She walked through the groups of people congregating on the deck, checking once more if any crew members were watching. The coast was clear, and she slipped through the doors silently.

Inside, Julia had to immediately adjust her centre of gravity to compensate for the ship's heeling. After six days onboard, she had a good idea of the inner workings of the ship. She had explored the ship well and knew exactly which way Antonio was likely to follow. However, navigating her way through the lounge was tricky, as she had to use her hands to lean on tables to maintain her balance. Broken glasses, bottles and overturned chairs were strewn across the floor, slowly sliding to the side.

Even though Julia's everyday life as a bank clerk lacked the high stakes of her predicament, the way she handled the situation surprised her in a good way. The only thing she needed to do now was get to the lower decks and find Antonio.

Spotting the main staircase that connected all the decks, she hastily grabbed the railing and increased her pace. Right before reaching the Explorer deck, she began calling out for her fiancé.

'Antonio! Are you there? Please answer me.'

She tried multiple times to hear from Antonio but to no avail. Her vocal cords hurt, and her despair increased as complete silence loomed over the nearby corridors. Suddenly, she spotted Antonio lying on his side, totally unconscious. She let go of the railing and frantically ran down the last steps.

Crouching beside him, she tried to awaken him. Antonio's eyes slowly opened, and he seemed to regain his senses. Just as relief washed over her, Julia felt the water around her feet. She turned around and noticed water seeping through a door marked 'For crew members only'. This discovery put her into overdrive, and she immediately got up on her feet. She grabbed Antonio's left arm and tried to lift him.

'Come on, baby. We need to get a move on.'

He responded by painfully forcing himself up and trying to get his bearings. Julia put his arm around her shoulder and began walking upwards. The first metres were agonisingly heavy. Then, Antonio summoned some energy and slowly mumbled some words.

'What's wrong? Why are we in a hurry?'

Frustrated by the questions, Julia snapped, 'Now is not the time for small talk. We need to move up.'

Just then, a crew member who was doing a last sweep for passengers emerged from the 'Crew members only' door. He offered to help Julia and tried to place Antonio's right arm over his shoulders. But as soon as he touched Antonio's right arm, he yelped in severe pain, clenching his teeth and emitting some painful groans.

'I think your right shoulder is dislocated, sir. Please stand still and let me push it back into your shoulder socket.'

Antonio complied and relaxed his muscles. He closed his eyes as he braced himself for the adjustment. The crew member moved swiftly like a military paramedic and got into position behind Antonio's back. Crack! He instantly felt as if he could move his arm again and thanked the crew member.

'Feeling better now, drama queen?'

Julia always knew how to make him crack a smile, no matter the circumstances.

'Of course, never better. Last one to the top orders room service at the hotel.'

They shook hands and followed the crew member upward. Julia looked closely at the cabin crew member's suit. He was wearing a white tuxedo that the waiters had worn on a formal night. She wondered what on earth a waiter from the top deck restaurant was doing down in the cargo and engine rooms? Upon closer inspection, his suit looked like he had been involved in a serious scuffle, with his jacket and pants full of stains and creases.

Upon exiting the lounge, the crew member turned right and blended into the myriad of tourists on deck. Julia decided not to alert her fiancé about her observations, so she turned her focus elsewhere. As she looked towards the yacht club, she could easily see how close they were to land. They couldn't be more than three hundred metres away.

Surrounding the ship were numerous small fishing boats and some recreational yachts. The entire scene, set against the spectacular tropical landscape of Roderick Bay, felt surreal. Just then, a message blared from the speakers, drowning out the murmurs of the people on deck.

'Passengers, please brace yourselves for impact. We are about to ground the ship in less than twenty seconds. Please remain calm and follow the crew's instructions.'

Antonio hugged Julia, mentally preparing himself for the impending crash as he counted down the seconds in his head.

*

A deep metallic screech emanated from the bottom of the sea as the World Discoverer grounded itself on the shallowest part of Roderick Bay. Captain Kreuss had slightly turned his ship before grounding it, estimating that it could stay upright for more hours in this position. His strategy was to use the underwater rock shelf of the bay as a sort of bicycle support for the ship. Now, the hard work of offloading the passengers onto land was about to begin.

'Dennis, can we use our lifeboats for the next hour if the ship maintains its current state?' Oliver asked.

Dennis quickly cross-checked with Niklas on deck before replying to the captain. 'It seems doable, yes. Both the port side and starboard decks can safely lower the lifeboats.'

A small celebration erupted among the people on the bridge. Only one remained silent and cautiously optimistic, and that was Captain Kreuss. He was feeling calm regarding the passengers' safety, but his mind was preoccupied with many new thoughts – how did this happen? Will they be able to salvage the ship? Did everyone get out of the lower decks safely? How will the authorities and company react to this accident? Was he about to lose his job?

The floodgates of his mind had opened, and it would keep him awake throughout the humid night.

2

NICK CLOSED THE bathroom door behind him and gave his thick, black, luscious hair a good rub with his towel. He tied the belt of his bathrobe and walked across the living room of his Frogner apartment. The rising sun cast a rosy hue across the morning Oslo sky, promising a perfect early summer day.

Turning around, he checked on his light blue Ariete espresso machine in the kitchen. It had finished its task, so Nick added froth on top from the milk steamer. He always preferred a thicker cappuccino, from top to bottom.

While taking the first sip, he switched on his sound system and put on a vinyl record by The Temptations to play in the background. The groovy bass line of 'Papa Was a Rolling Stone' set the mood for the day with rhythmic cymbal strikes, dramatic violin screeches, a funky guitar riff and a buttery smooth trumpet solo. The next step in his morning ritual was ironing his white shirt for the day. On Fridays, he liked to spruce up his outfits, and today, he would be donning a cream-coloured cotton suit with white leather Velasca sneakers. Maybe he could out-style his CEO, Mario Santini, for once.

Santini had single-handedly impacted Nick's career the most and was probably the flashiest person he had ever met. He was a loud and flamboyant Italian in his mid-40s from Napoli with a fine taste and dapper lifestyle. Having previously worked for the Guardia Costiera as a commandant and a security consultant for various European shipping companies, he knew how to balance demanding work with the finer things in life.

A chance meeting the previous summer in Greece was the start of their professional cooperation. Nick had just wrapped up his career in the Norwegian Navy and was eager to turn a new page in his life. While taking up odd jobs, one of them was as a certified diving instructor down in Zakynthos.

While taking a break from a diving session at Shipwreck beach, he found himself mesmerised by a boat close to his. A vintage 1979 Riva Aquarama Special was rocking back and forth on the calm turquoise waters in the bay. It had recently been waxed and was glowing under the scorching Greek sun. Immediately, Nick wanted to give his props to the man climbing up the swim step. He appeared to be a gentleman with many interesting tales. Nick sparked up a conversation, and the rest was history. One thing led to another, and after a few more meetings, which included a significant amount of negotiation, wine and seafood, Santini offered Nick a job at the Okeanos Marine Investigation Agency in Oslo.

The company was run by Jacques Rousseau, who was Santini's good friend in Norway. Rousseau was a legendary French–Norwegian marine biologist and maritime law specialist whom he had linked up with on the Costa Concordia case back in 2012. Nick's role as a marine investigator focused on investigating accidents at sea, the operational logistics around it and doing the dirty work of the company. Until now, though, most of his cases had been run-of-the-mill jobs, and Nick was feeling the pressure to land something big to repay his boss's belief in him. If not, he would struggle to find any motivation to go to work because, in all honesty, he didn't know whether this was his dream job or not. This was also the reason he had resigned from his role in the Norwegian Navy almost a year ago.

For the time being, Nick was enjoying the perks of the job, which included a snazzy apartment in downtown Oslo, an interesting job description to win over the ladies and the possibility of globetrotting, if he was lucky enough to find an interesting case – an opportunity he had been anxiously awaiting for almost a year now. The money was an excellent incentive for him to stay at OMIA, enabling him to fund his bachelor life, but if nothing else motivated him, he would have to look for something else to do. Just working and going through the motions was his ultimate nightmare. He didn't want to end up like most people his age who sat like immovable passengers on the train of life, speeding past any memory worth stopping for and numbed by the corporate rat race. No, he wanted to do more, but first, he had to put some food in his rumbling stomach.

Before leaving for work, he made a quick and tasty breakfast. He finely chopped some chives, parsley, tarragon and chervil before cracking three eggs in a bowl, adding some seasoning, piercing the yolks and whisking them together with a fork. Nick used his knife to drop the finely chopped herbs into the mix before intensifying his whisking. When the butter had almost melted, he poured the well-blended mixture into the pan. A few minutes later, he removed the pan from the heat and used a fork to roll it like a carpet while tilting the pan. With a gentle smack on the pan's handle, channelling his inner Jacques Pépin, the omelette dropped on the plate in a torpedo shape.

This right here was the reason Nick loved to wake up early in the morning. It allowed him to awaken his senses and fuel himself for the day without stressing about rushing out of the house like most of the people in the city.

He slipped into his attire, picked up his leather bag and locked up the apartment. Inside the elevator, he made the last adjustments to his hairstyle – a classic slick-back side part to the right. Exiting the elevator, he pressed a button on his keys to awaken his Alfa Romeo 4C, revelling in the Rosso Alfa colour, which always put a childish smile on his face. Placing the bag on the passenger seat, he turned the key in the ignition, letting the Italian inline four-cylinder turbocharged engine whirr in the parking lot. Music to my ears, he thought and put the car into gear.

3

OSLO WAS NOT a city built for fancy cars, but he could not care less. Manoeuvring the tight streets and driving without power steering gave Nick a rewarding sensation. He felt alive driving the 4C, and every time the opportunity arose, he would press his foot a little harder on the gas pedal. Those Italians sure know how to make a sports car with an old-school feel.

He wrestled the car around the block and got into Bygdøy allé, the primary avenue of Frogner. The car was itching to go faster as Nick headed towards the E18 interchange, next to the Bygdøy allé marina. As soon as he entered the E18 highway, Nick increased his speed and started shifting with his paddle shifters.

Nick watched as he sped by countless recreational boats docked at the local marina on his right. He knew he was quickly approaching Oslo's downtown when the Color Line port terminal came into sight. He had to do some delicate navigating again in the tight streets of downtown Oslo before he whizzed by the city's pride and tourist trap, the National Opera. Nick quickly downshifted, admiring the accompanying sounds, and turned into the company's underground parking facility.

OMIA's headquarters was located in one of Oslo's most bustling downtown hubs, the Barcode. Inspired by modern architecture, this neighbourhood had turned into a staple of the city's skyline. Overlooking the fjord of Oslo from the 15th floor was a privilege few employees enjoyed.

'Good morning, Mr Diamantis,' greeted Emma, the company's receptionist.

'How many times do I have to say it, Emma? Please call me Nick.'

'A request I have to deny yet again. OMIA's company policy.'

'That Frenchman needs to time travel back to the modern world.'

'That won't happen soon. What needs to happen ASAP, though, is your report on the Russian fishing boat sinking. Requested by Mr Santini himself.'

'Consider it done. Don't want to disappoint the boss,' Nick said, flashing her a big smile.

As Nick made his way through the main office hub, he noticed an unusual silence. This usually happened when something big was about to occur. Santini and Rousseau would lock themselves in the soundproof board room to discuss critical matters before breaking the news to the rest of the team. Nick couldn't fathom what could be happening on such a wonderful day.

After hanging his blazer in the office, Nick stepped out into the corridor. Maybe his new field partner, Jason, had some notion of what was going on. He knocked two times on his half-open door before opening it.

'Hey! Morning, Nick, all good?' Jason stretched out his arm and gave Nick a high five.

'Not much, man. I was wondering if you knew where everybody's gone?'

'I don't really know, to be honest. I was the first to arrive today, so I thought little of it,' he replied nonchalantly.

'Oh... Then they've probably taken the day off and left us to do the report. Come on, let's work in my office.'

Nick's office was much more spacious and had all the required amenities. It was situated in the corner of the 15th floor and exuded the Art Deco aesthetic, with floor-to-ceiling glass windows that provided the room with ample lighting. Nick had opted for a vintage cherry wooden desk and an Eames soft pad chair. Visitors could sit in one of two black Barcelona chairs that were separated by a small coffee table. A stack of carefully selected Gentleman's Journal and National Geographic issues was placed on the table, and a handcrafted Zoffoli globe drinks cabinet, with an array of expensive booze, was strategically placed in the room's corner. The two walls were decorated with retro marketing posters of different cruise lines from Nick's second home, Greece, and a medium-sized bookshelf stored most of Nick's document folders and case files. Crammed in between the folders, the shelves were decorated with various models of vintage Italian cars and famous historical ships.

'Make yourself comfortable, Jason. I think we can wrap things up in four hours and grab lunch outside.'

Nick booted up his computer and settled down in his chair. Arranging some paperwork in front of him, he pulled himself closer to the desk. In his email inbox, he found some files sent by Jason.

'Alright, let's break down the sequence of events,' Nick began, rubbing his hands with excitement. 'Time to find out why this fishing boat sank.'

4

THE FIERY RED fishing vessel, Onega, was preparing to sail from Kirkenes with Novaya Zemlya as its next stop. Led by Captain Nikolai Volkov was a crew of nineteen people, and their mission was to fish in the northern Norwegian Sea before heading to the Russian Rogachevo Air Base to deliver canned fish rations. They would then complete their trip by offloading the rest of the fish at the nearby settlement of Belushya Guba before returning to their last port of call in Murmansk.

Constructed in Norway in 1979, the Onega was a workhorse of a ship, having sailed in the rough northern seas for many years. The crew did not lack experience either and were a hard-nosed group of Russian sailors working for the Krasnoye Znamya Fishing Collective. After completing the preparations in the evening, the captain ordered the anchor to be weighed.

He slowly steered the ship out of the port of Kirkenes, deftly adjusting the rudder. The wind had picked up since the morning hours, with the ship's anemometer registering wind speeds of up to seventy-seven kilometres per hour. Nikolai could easily discern the six- to seven-metre waves on the horizon while approaching the last stretch of Bøkfjorden. This was shaping up to be a long day for the crew, as they would have to sail into these waves throughout the night.

'Nothing new for us Russian sailors,' Nikolai said to his first mate after taking a vodka shot to warm himself up.

The air temperature had dropped to minus ten degrees, and he had to rub his hands to restore warmth to his fingertips. It felt like sailing through Niflheim, the misty and cold world of the dead.

When the Onega cleared the fjord, the high waves welcomed the ship into the open sea with wide arms. The eastern winds were hammering the ship on its starboard side, making it shake violently. The spray, generated from the foam of the seven-metre waves, was hampering Nikolai's vision from the bridge. Each time the ship crashed into a wave, more spray would cover the bridge's windshield, and the wipers did not operate fast enough to clear the water.

Reducing the speed to five knots, Nikolai tried to navigate the ship to slice through the waves to maintain their course. After half an hour of fighting the waves in the open sea, something did not feel right to Captain Volkov. The ship felt significantly heavier to steer compared to earlier. However, neither had the waves increased in height nor had the wind speed changed. Nothing on the bridge indicated a problem with the ship. Maybe he was just overthinking. He tried to push aside those thoughts and focus on maintaining the charted course through the tempestuous sea.

Suddenly, an enormous wave crashed with a deafening thud on the starboard side of the Onega, pushing it violently over to its port side. The crew members on the deck were thrown around like rag dolls. Two of them were hurled over the railing and into the freezing sea. Nikolai could almost see the left side of the bridge being submerged under the sea. He feared the worst, fully aware of what would happen next.

A second wave followed, pushing the ship even further down the sea this time. Nikolai and the rest of the crew went completely silent and exchanged sombre, resigned looks as they accepted their fate. They were at the mercy of the sea, and they could do nothing to cheat death this time.

The next wave sealed the Onega's fate, causing it to capsize. In a few seconds, the forty-metre vessel was swallowed by the pitch-black, sub-zero waves, claiming the lives of all nineteen souls aboard. The Onega's lights flickered underwater as the generator gasped one last time for mechanical energy. The lights went off at the same time as the last surviving crew member succumbed to death. This sinking went on to be the deadliest civilian accident in the Barents Sea since the military submarine Kursk sank in August 2000, claiming the lives of all one hundred and eighteen crew members.

5

NICK STOOD UP from his chair to stretch his back and headed to his drinks cabinet.

'So, let me get this straight, Nick,' Jason began. 'How did you conclude that this was not simply a case of a rogue wave taking down an old ship? We had a difficult time collecting clues when we examined the wreck with our underwater Remote Operated Vehicle.'

'Allow me to explain, Jason.' Nick was busy mixing two negronis for them. 'As the wind blows over the sea, energy is transferred to the sea's surface itself. When strong winds from a storm blow in the opposing direction of the current, the forces might be strong enough to generate rogue waves.'

'Exactly! That was my initial thought when trying to investigate this shipwreck.'

'What you did not take into consideration, though, is that our tech guru and CTO, Gus Johnson, has some pretty insane software at hand in our HQ. Let me show you.'

Johnson was indeed a tech wizard. He had made a name for himself while working for big corporations in New York during the tech boom in the 90s. All the companies wanted him because of his ability to develop custom technological systems tailored for any company. No one could match his level of expertise, and he had gathered tons of experience from various industries in that decade. However, in the early 2000s, feeling homesick and drained from life in the Big Apple, he moved back to his hometown, Cape Cod, to work from home and follow his passion for maritime technology and whales. Universities in Canada and Northern Europe were among the first customers of his software. Johnson eventually connected with Rousseau, who was doing his master's degree in marine biology. When the idea of setting up

OMIA in Oslo came up with Rousseau and Santini, he immediately accepted and moved overseas.

Nick took a sip of his negroni before continuing with his explanation. 'First, I pulled out all the data from the ship's Automatic Identification System transponder. I extracted the specific data from when the ship weighed anchor in Kirkenes until it sank and its signal went dead.'

Jason was like a sponge, absorbing all the minute details from Nick's analysis. Nick recognised that look as the same one he used to have in his first couple of months in OMIA when working alongside Santini and Rousseau. He could sense that his partner was eager to learn and had a good work ethic.

It didn't hurt either that Jason was a former Rockport mercenary, specialising in combat, maritime piracy and the commandeering of sea, land and air vehicles. However, the mercenary business proved too draining for Jason's loyal and principle-oriented lifestyle. When he took a sabbatical from mercenary work, he met his Norwegian wife, which led to his relocation to northern Norway. His career took a complete turn, and he used his savings to start a fishing company. As fate would have it, he ended up rescuing a few marine biologists from a research ship with engine issues in the Northern Sea. Word quickly got to Rousseau, who immediately looked into this brave American. Intrigued by Rousseau's job pitch, Jason agreed to work with OMIA, where his unique skill set could be utilised.

'Ok, Nick. After all this data scavenging, what was next?'

'Then, I got Johnson to cross-check the weather and sea data with the Onega's. I wanted to see if your rogue wave theory was valid. Unfortunately, the wind patterns and sea currents did not align with the ship's course to generate rogue waves.'

'I see. Close but no cigar. Something must have sparked your interest to further look for an answer.'

'For sure. I leave no stone unturned. Next, I looked into the Voyage Data Recorder of the Onega. I had to request a translator from the Russian Embassy in Oslo to assist me.'

Jason burst into laughter. 'You sneaky devil, I knew it! Don't tell me they sent you a translator who could easily be mistaken for a runway model. That would be typical Nick Diamantis stuff.'

'How did you know? Am I that predictable?'

They both had a good laugh, clinked their glasses and finished up their negronis.

'So where were we?' Jason asked, lowering his glass.

'Ah, yes, the translation,' said Nick, readjusting himself into a more upright position. 'The translator's trained ear picked up on a minor exchange of words between the captain and his first mate. We pinpointed it to be about twenty minutes before the ship went down.'

'Interesting. What did he say?'

'Captain Volkov made a passing remark about the ship feeling heavier when steering. Mind you, they had already filled the ship to the brim with fresh fish, canned fish rations and fishing equipment.'

'There was no damage to the hull, where water could have entered. We had thoroughly examined it. So the extra weight must have come from somewhere else,' Jason mused.

'Bingo! Ever heard of the phenomenon of icing?'

'Never. I grew up in Florida. The last time it was cold in Miami was back in January 1977. My father speaks about it to this day.'

'I figured that much,' Nick said, stroking his chin. 'Icing can happen on ships when temperatures are below freezing, combined with strong wind. This causes the spray blown off the sea to freeze when in contact with the ship. Such ice makes the ship heavy, posing a serious hazard. In combination with strong wind, gigantic waves and heavy cargo, icing significantly increases the risk of a ship capsizing.'

'Seems to me like the report is almost complete. This right here ticks all the boxes.'

'You said the right word there – almost. I have one more detail to back that theory up.'

Nick turned his computer screen to show Jason a virtual map on OMIA's system. The map clearly showed the Onega's course as it set sail from Kirkenes. Nick zoomed in on the ship as it approached the spot where it sank.

'I will now add an overlay to show where the waves hit the ship as it sailed. Right before it capsized and sank, the Onega was hit by three waves on the starboard side. Watch closely.'

Jason leaned in to get a better look at the screen. The visual representation was crystal clear. He could clearly see the waves battering the ship on its starboard side. Soon after, the ship's blip disappeared from the map.

'I compared the characteristics of these three waves with all the other previous waves the ship had encountered that night. These three were the highest and most intense waves they faced that night.'

'I'm sold, Nick. It makes total sense. I think we have everything we need to file the report.'

Nick nodded, and together, they began typing the last pages of their report. After reviewing it, Nick finally uploaded it to the company's cloud system.

Checking the time on his blue dial Squale 1521, Nick saw that they were on schedule. Nearly four hours had passed, and the orange minute and white hour hands were about to align at the lumed arrow indices at twelve o'clock. Everything was falling into place. Maybe they would end up finishing earlier and leaving the office before four o'clock.

Nick's mind was racing as he caught himself appreciating the view from his office. His focus slowly shifted from the boats in the Oslo fjord to the translator's raven hair, styled in a chin-length bob, and her fiery dark brown eyes. It was all he could think about. He had felt those eyes penetrate his soul every time he had made eye contact with her at the Russian Embassy. She exuded the aura of a Russian empress and had a certain mystique Nick would have liked to explore. He couldn't help but wonder what outfit and perfume she would wear if they ever went out for dinner. Judging by her silver Cartier Santos and black Valentino bag, she was a woman of good taste, and that was one thing he didn't have to worry about.

6

'NICK... NICK,' JASON nudged him to get his attention.

Nick gave his partner a confused look before apologising for drifting into his thoughts. As a romantic dreamer, Nick was used to these instances where his stream of consciousness took over and he just existed. Although people perceived him as a superficial, rough-around-the-edges playboy, he believed he was a deeply sensitive man with a complex emotional register.

Going out and dating new women all the time has its fair share of fun, but Nick wanted to find someone to settle down and share a life with. He needed only one to two encounters to determine if the relationship was worth pursuing and building upon. Some called it a spark; he called it kapsoúra. The Greek language has an eloquent way of describing feelings that the Norwegian and English languages cannot.

For Nick, kapsoúra is the love that burns so ardently that it threatens to consume itself. If a woman could evoke that feeling in him, he would instantly know that she was the one. The key, he believed, was to attract that feeling and not go around chasing it and trying to convince himself that he had found the one. Should his next encounter be the one, amazing! If not, he would learn a thing or two about the female mind from her, give her an unforgettable experience and move on.

One of the aspects Nick appreciated about women was their innate desire to nurture and protect the ones they love. When you are with a woman who's fully smitten with you, she will jump through fire to be by your side. For reasons unknown to him, he hadn't experienced that connection yet with a woman. But he was fine with it, considering he was too young to have everything figured out. Being in his late twenties, he believed he had plenty of prime years left in the tank, despite contrary opinions from his friends and family.

Maybe his perpetual singleness had something to do with his views on masculinity. Up to this point in life, he had always felt compelled to go out into the world. To go to battle, to face the fire and to protect his family, colleagues and loved ones. He had to do all this while taking it in stride. It was hard and tedious at times, but out of respect for his loved ones, he downplayed his everyday life. All the male figures in his family tree shared a similar mentality. Plain and simple, he did not want to gloat or boast about what he was doing and accomplishing. He sure had his fears of losing his life in the vast abyss of the seven seas, but he always tried to use his wit and charm to sweep those grim feelings under the rug.

In an age where emotions often overtook rationality, Nick embraced them and practised self-control. He would never allow his emotions to cloud his decision-making process – a useful mindset when most of his free time was spent hundreds of metres underwater.

A pair of aggressive knocks on the office door caught both him and Jason off guard. Nick's philosophical state of mind completely shut down as he tensed up in his chair. Before he could utter a word, the door swung open and Mario Santini bolted into the office holding a black dossier.

'Gentlemen, we have an extraordinary issue at hand. We need to meet Rousseau in the meeting room ASAP. Follow me.'

Nick and Jason sprung up like two space rockets from their chairs and tried to keep up with Santini's brisk pace. His Paolo Scafora oxford shoes clicked rhythmically on the office's marble floor.

Finally, some action again, Nick thought. He was ready to crack on with a new case.

In the meeting room, Rousseau had dimmed the lights and was fiddling with something on the big TV monitor. The grey curtains blocked out all-natural light, enshrouding the soundproof room in darkness akin to the cinemas. Santini beckoned them inside the room and showed them to their seats around the oval table. Once they were settled, Santini whispered in Rousseau's ear to signal they were ready.

Rousseau was an expert orator – a skill honed through all of his studies, conferences and maritime expeditions with the University of Oslo. He had a particular interest in shipwrecks and uncovering their causes. To him, each shipwreck was an open history book, frozen in time since the ship's sinking and waiting to be read. One could say that the idea of forming OMIA was born after his first expedition in Svalbard, where he helped to map out the locations of fifty-seven shipwrecks. His favourite quote was, 'The world's oceans are the biggest underwater museums in the world.' It was a phrase he lived by.

'Messieurs, thank you for assembling in the meeting room on such short notice,' began Rousseau, his gentle voice filling the room. 'Mr. Santini and I would like to show you a case that landed in our laps this morning. BEWA Cruises from Norway owns a cruise ship called the World Discoverer, which is currently grounded in the Solomon Islands. The accident happened a couple of hours ago, and they feared the possibility of completely losing the ship. We have been tasked with launching an independent and unbiased investigation to determine the cause of this accident, assess if the ship is salvageable and coordinate with the local authorities to sort this out.'

As Rousseau pressed a button on the controller, the TV screen came to life, showing footage captured from a helicopter. It was circling a cruise ship that was grounded and listing close to land. Nick's mind raced as he tried to break down everything he needed to do once he touched down in the Solomon Islands. The case was going to be demanding, but he knew this was the moment to step up and work harder than he had ever done before. He exchanged a determined look and a silent nod of approval with Jason before switching his focus back to their boss. Jason reciprocated with the same reaction, indicating he was ready for the colossal task ahead.

'Due to the country's financial situation, we will receive technical help from the Royal Australian Navy and the Royal Solomon Islands Police Force. I have arranged for a research vessel that will serve as our floating HQ. It's on its way from Brisbane to the Solomon Islands as we speak.'

The chosen vessel was RV Solander, a 36-metre-long ship painted in blue and white – colours reminiscent of the houses that dotted the Greek islands. It could house a crew of eighteen and was commandeered by a hard-nosed Australian, Captain Spencer Clark. The stern of the ship was designed to store submersible ROVs, a RIB boat and most of the diving equipment. For the first time in the ship's fifteen-year history, it would deviate from its usual oceanographic duties to assist in the investigation of a marine accident.

'Thankfully, all the passengers and crew have been evacuated from the ship with zero casualties. I already shipped our equipment via a cargo plane three hours ago, including a new and custom-made Fifish OMIA PRO W6 ROV, our manned submersible Viperfish II and our Goldfish X9 RIB boat. Gus Johnson and Chief Engineer Morten Bakke are travelling with this plane and will help load the gear onboard the RV Solander.'

Nick appreciated how there were no budget constraints for this case. Rousseau was ensuring they had everything they would need. It was nice to have the support of Bakke and Johnson as well – two savvy experts in their fields who complemented one another and could provide valuable feedback during this investigation.

Bakke was the ying to Rousseau's yang. Having been childhood friends since elementary school, they were inseparable. The first time they followed separate paths in life was when Bakke moved to Trondheim to pursue his master's degree in maritime engineering. In OMIA, he was tasked with maintaining and continually improving the diving equipment and tools they were using while working offshore and underwater. Bakke also worked closely with all the suppliers and manufacturers of the equipment they used in OMIA. He was introverted most of the time, but he had moments where he showed off his quirky personality. Nick, in particular, enjoyed his dry humour compared to Johnson's old-fashioned American humour.

'As you are aware, BEWA Cruises is owned by our Norwegian multimillionaire golden boy, Gustav Breland. This accident will make headlines in the world's biggest news outlets in the following days and weeks. Be prepared to work under immense pressure, gentlemen.'

'I was made under pressure, Boss; my name is Diamantis,' Nick confidently replied. Santini tried to keep a serious face on, even though he wanted to make a facepalm and slap Nick. Jason, on the other hand, lowered his head and covered his mouth to hide his huge smile.

'Thanks for clarifying that, Nick.' Rousseau was clearly unphased by Nick's pun. 'However, this is not the time for jokes. This, right here, is the biggest case in the company's history. Santini has specifically paired you guys up for this case, and I demand that you deliver. Questions before we round up this meeting with your travel itinerary?'

Both Nick and Jason shook their heads.

'Very well. You guys will leave from Oslo airport on a business jet, courtesy of Breland, in approximately two hours. Santini has organised accommodation for you at the Coral Sea Resort in the capital city of Honiara. On your first day, you will be meeting up with the local authorities and combating jet lag before setting sail the next morning to Roderick Bay with the crew of RV Solander. Santini will join you as your liaison. Anything you want to add, Mario?'

Santini nodded and stood up beside Rousseau.

'I've prepared a folder for you with information about the ship, blueprints from the shipbuilding company, nautical charts of the Solomon Islands, initial statements from the crew and intel on the country itself. Everything is available in our system, so I suggest you use your time on the jet wisely. Familiarise yourself with the intel and brush up your combat skills.'

Nick felt slightly uneasy hearing Santini's last words. It wasn't that he was uncomfortable handling a gun, but it was the first time he'd received such instructions in an investigation briefing. Maybe this case was more complex than he thought. Gustav Breland was a filthy rich businessman who worked mainly with his green energy company, GEOrganic. After his father's untimely death, he took over the family's cruise liner company, BEWA Cruises. He was the poster child of modern Norway, but why would his cruise ship raise so much attention, especially when it was on the other side of the globe?

'Boss, why would we need a gun in this investigation?' Jason asked bluntly.

'The boat is in an area where many smugglers and pirates operate. I'm guessing a lot of them would like to sneak into the ship and loot it as soon as the rescue crews leave the area,' Santini explained. 'I don't think we'll have to use them, but it's a good precautionary measure.'

The answer put Jason's mind at ease, but Nick was still a little sceptical about having weapons in this investigation. Should push come to shove, though, he would not hesitate to open fire on some local pirates.

'Time is money, gentlemen. So, if that's all, I suggest we pack for our journey. Meet me in two hours at Hangar 13 of Gardermoen Airport.'

After saying their goodbyes, Nick took the elevator down to the garage to pick up his car. As the elevator descended, he visualised himself being lowered into the crystal clear waters of Roderick Bay. The initial nervousness from the meeting had worn off, and he was pumped to work. The only thing he did not look forward to was being stuck in a flight cabin for twelve hours. Hopefully, the folder Santini had prepared would keep him entertained for some time before he resorted to cold drinks, food and a vintage paperback.

7

BACK AT HIS apartment in Majorstuen, Santini was packing the final pieces of clothing he needed for the trip. After checking off the last few items on his list, he looked back at his private office to see if he had forgotten anything. Satisfied with the state of his office, he grabbed his navy linen field jacket hanging from the coat stand and headed to the door. Just then, his phone started buzzing in his pocket, displaying Jacques Rousseau's name on the screen. Santini let go of his duffel bag and answered the call.

'Mario, do you have a second? I won't slow you down,' Rousseau said.

Santini could instantly tell something was off from the tone of his voice.

'Sure, Jacques. What's up? You sound a bit stressed.'

'I'm good. Don't worry about me. Long week at work and the university, you know how it goes. There's something I wanted to give you a heads-up on.'

'I'm all ears. Go on.'

'I just got off a call with Gustav Breland,' Rousseau explained. 'He wanted to check on our plans and your ETA in Honiara. He and his entourage are on their way to the Solomon Islands to show face.'

'Sounds like a normal reaction to me. A chance to transform this accident into a positive PR campaign for him and his company.'

'I just don't want him to slow your work down or get in your way. You know how possessive rich businessmen are about their property.'

'Don't worry, Jacques. I've dealt with a fair share of rich shipowners over the years. I assure you that his micromanagement will not affect us.'

'Glad to hear that,' Rousseau said and froze.

Santini picked up on his hesitation as the line fell silent.

'Anything else you wanted to share with me? I'm kinda on my way out of the apartment.'

'Yeah, there's something else on my mind, but I'm not sure how exactly to put it in words.'

'Just fire from the hip and let it all out,' Santini said, his jovial attitude easing the tension.

'I was honestly just wondering if Nick is the guy we need for this job. He hasn't led a major case yet, and it's also the first time we're sending him abroad with Jason.'

'I see what you're saying, but think of it like this. Personally, as his closest leader, I believe it's time for him to show us if he's really made for this role. And you've seen how restless he gets back at the office. We can't keep giving him our most basic tasks any longer. It will bore him in the long run, like every other job he has tried until now. Would be a shame to lose someone with his talent just because we didn't manage him right.'

'Fair enough. We'll see how it goes then. I would never doubt your judgement, Mario. Have a pleasant flight with the boys.'

'Thanks, Jacques. We'll be in touch throughout the trip. Ciao!' Santini hung up the phone and slipped it back into his pocket.

He shared the same concern as Rousseau. Many of the most successful and richest people in the world were idiosyncratic individuals. Success on such a massive level did not come just with hard work. You had to be a different type of animal to come out on top in any industry. Such was the case with all the shipowners Santini had dealt with in his career. They were a group of proud people who always garnered the respect of their countrymen.

However, the world has evolved since shipping tycoons commanded celebrity status. The time when Aristotle Onassis and Gianluigi Aponte ruled their countries has become part of a bygone era. Now, everything is controlled by conglomerates, corporations, investment groups and people with new or old money.

Gustav Breland was a peculiar case in this industry. He had not set out to be a shipowner like his father but had carved his own path, focusing on renewable energy. He took the mantle from his late father to carry the legacy of BEWA Cruises with him into the next generation. Compared to his father, who was a humble businessman, Gustav had a more pompous approach to his work. His name was a typical fixture in the media, and the public adored him. Santini had never had the opportunity to link up with Breland, but he had a good opinion about him. He reminded him of the larger-than-life shipping tycoons of the old days. No wonder Rousseau was stressed about him being in the Solomon Islands with them. He would bring the whole media circus with him, adding to the chaos surrounding the ship. Sending in a rookie investigator as well was also a ballsy move considering the circumstances. But Santini liked to occasionally take risks and bet on someone's abilities. That's how a CEO could and should separate the wheat from the chaff.

Even though Gustav's company was bankrolling the investigation, Santini knew how to keep him away from the proceedings. If anyone messed with their investigation, they would get a small taste of his Italian temperament. Santini did not discriminate on that front, no matter how high someone's net worth may be.

He popped the trunk of his Blu Emozione Maserati Levante Gran-Lusso and placed his duffel bag inside. As soon as he sat in the front seat, he adjusted the rearview mirror slightly. The drive to Gardermoen Airport usually took him about forty-five minutes, but today, he would have to cut down the drive time by some minutes. It was a flight he couldn't be late for. By the time Santini hit the highway, he unleashed the three hundred and fifty horses of his six-cylinder Ferrari-powered car on the asphalt.

8

'WELL, WELL, WELL...WHAT do we have here?' Nick muttered to himself as he turned the corner towards Hangar 13.

Lo and behold, Breland's private supersonic jet was parked there. A group of five ground handlers were diligently working on the jet, preparing it for its long-distance flight. Two tall and buff security officers in black suits were standing by the ramp, ready to inspect the OMIA crew.

Most people would likely overlook the jet as a normal Learjet, like the ones used by any Fortune 500 CEO. This one was special, though, and Nick knew that. It was a one-of-a-kind supersonic business jet called the S-512, built by Spike Aerospace. They had commissioned only four in the world, and Gustav was one of the first to jump forward and pay the hefty price of eighty million dollars.

Cruising at a speed of 1.6 Mach, without producing a disturbing sonic boom, the S-512 could halve the travel time compared to regular jets. It was a pocket-sized Concorde for the world's elite, something highly convenient for a man like Breland. He could start his day off in London, attend a Global Economic Summit in New York by lunchtime and finish the evening with a round of golf at the Oslo Golf Club.

'Welcome on board, Mr. Diamantis. We wish you a pleasant flight to the Solomon Islands with us,' the chief purser greeted, offering a glass of Veuve Clicquot when Nick entered the cabin.

He was an amiable old man in a navy suit with a vest and tie. His short stature and warm smile reminded Nick of his late grandfather back in Greece. Nick would do anything to have one more conservation with him down by the sea like they used to. His heroic tales from his days as an officer of the Greek merchant fleet had inspired Nick to follow his passion for the sea, scrapping the idea of a regular nine-to-five job.

'Food and drinks will be served throughout the flight,' the chief purser explained. 'If you would like to stretch your legs and catch some fresh air, we will have a short refuelling stop at the Dubai International Airport in approximately three and a half hours.'

Nick thanked him for the welcome drink and took a seat. What immediately caught his eye inside the cabin were the expansive, high-definition screens lining each side. These displays could show any view the passenger wished, whether it was the real-time aircraft surroundings, a favourite movie or a mission briefing. All one needed was to connect their devices to the jet's internet.

'Pretty high-tech stuff, Nick. How can I ever go back to flying commercial with my wife?' Jason asked.

'You simply don't. Unless we rack up Diamond status on some airline or our boss right here gets us our own OMIA-branded jet.'

'Keep on dreaming, boys; we're not the CIA. Consider yourselves lucky this time,' Santini said while looking over his emails on his laptop. 'May I remind you we need to go through the technical logistics of our operation and try to come up with a game plan before we land in Dubai? After refuelling, we can conserve our energy and get some shuteye.'

'Yes, Boss. You got it,' Nick replied.

When their meeting was finally done, they were airborne and cruising at supersonic speeds. Santini disconnected his laptop from the multimedia display, and the cabin lit up again with the blue sky displayed on the screens. The surreal feeling created by those screens still mesmerised Nick. It felt like they were floating on a cloud – that is, if a cloud could serve you a negroni, offer plush reclining leather seats and have a Michelin chef dish up a sumptuous four-course Scandinavian-inspired meal.

All the technical details from the meeting had worked up Nick's appetite. From the way he completely devoured everything that was served to him, one would think he had clean plate syndrome. He then chose to relax and read around a hundred pages from his travel companion, Ian Fleming's Thunderball, before the S-512 lowered its wheels, landing on the blazingly hot Dubai runway.

Santini indulged in a cigar break, while Nick and Jason decided to stretch their legs and check out the VIP lounge at the airport. They had to dash out of the lounge as soon as Nick felt his phone buzzing in his pocket – probably Santini wondering where the hell they had disappeared. Luckily, their boss was not interested in scolding them and only ushered them into the jet. Both Jason and Santini fell asleep effortlessly after their take-off from Dubai, but Nick was struggling. No matter how many times he tried to reposition himself in his seat, he could not get his mind and body to switch off. He stood up and paced slowly in the cabin until the chief purser, who had reentered the main cabin area, inquired if something was bothering him.

'I think I'm just jittery about this investigation. Maybe working on this case will ease my mind and get me out of my head,' Nick said to the kind gentleman who introduced himself as Einar Iversen.

'This shows you take pride in your job. That's a rather good thing, young man. Reminds me of my younger days when I worked at sea.'

'Oh, really? You don't say. How many years have you been working for the Brelands, if I may ask? I could visualise you as a hotel manager in one of their BEWA cruise ships.'

'You can read people – impressive! That's right, I was in fact a food and beverage manager for over thirty years at BEWA Cruises. I worked closely with Gustav's father, and I have seen his son grow up before my eyes. It's amazing how he has elevated his father's company.'

'Don't hype me up too much now,' said Nick with a laugh. 'Reading people is just part of my job as an investigator. How come you work on his private jet now? I haven't met a lot of seamen who become chief pursers on planes, let alone supersonic jets.'

Mr. Iversen smiled with a hint of bashfulness.

'I was one of the longest-serving crew members of BEWA. When Gustav's father passed, may God rest his soul, he reached out to me because he knew how close his father and I were.'

He teared up, and Nick touched the old man's shoulder comfortingly. 'It can't be easy losing someone close to you.'

'It's the worst thing. Especially now when more people from my generation are passing away.' He dried his tears and gave Nick a sad smile. 'Every other week, I learn about a recent death. Thankfully, I have a job I can keep myself occupied with, two beautiful grandchildren back home, and I'm healthy enough to travel the world.'

'Sounds like a dream, the way you put it, sir. Don't forget to treat them to an extra big ice cream when we return to Oslo.'

'I will. That is a mandatory expense as a grandfather.' Iversen's face lit up again.

'Do you think they can salvage the ship, Mr. Iversen? You've seen your fair share of incidents at sea.'

Iversen leaned back in his chair and stroked his chin, pondering Nick's question. 'I can't really tell, to be honest, based on the limited footage I have seen on the news. I hope so for the company's and Gustav's sake. His five ships mean the world to him.'

'I can tell. Rarely do shipowners actively partake in this process, let alone travel to the country where the accident happened.'

Iversen leaned in closer to Nick and lowered his voice.

'To be honest, Nick, I think Gustav is really stressed about this accident. It will be a big dent in his company's reputation if the accident is proven to be the crew's fault.'

Nick sat up straighter, listening intently.

'The mid-size luxury cruise market is a booming niche right now,' Iversen continued. 'The competition from Seabourn, Ponant, Silversea, Windstar and Regent Seven Seas is at its peak. Everybody wants a piece of the pie.'

'I can imagine. A misstep from any of them will be capitalised on.'

'Exactly! Money talks in the end,' said Iversen, leaning back into his chair. 'and if there's something Gustav values more than anything in this world, it's money.'

Their conversation soon shifted into one of those fragmentary discussions men like to have late at night. They discussed women, love and travel destinations, exchanged maritime stories and talked about dive watches. Nick could listen to people like Iversen talk for hours. He had a charismatic way of storytelling, making it impossible not to admire the guy. Things got heated when Iversen tried to defend his choice of wearing leather straps with his dive watches. Nick couldn't fathom why anyone would choose to wear a dive watch in such a manner. Dive watches were meant to be worn at all times, inseparable from their wearer. Using them like dress watches went against their purpose, design and heritage. Realising they would never agree on this topic, Nick decided to retire to his seat. He checked his Squale and noticed he could get a solid ninety-minute nap before landing in Honiara. At the moment, that sounded much better than no sleep at all.

9

THE RISING SUN was casting its hot rays over the port in Point Cruz. The containers lined up on the dock were absorbing the incessant heat, while the dock workers sought refuge in any shady area they could find. A cacophony of people and vehicles blended with the smell of sea breeze and diesel. Instead of the majestic World Discoverer being docked at the hundred-and-fifty-metre-long pier, a lot of smaller, local ferry ships were lined up at the dock. The crews on these ferries had been occupied with offloading the rescued passengers throughout the morning hours.

The Royal Solomon Islands Police Force (RSIPF) and their Fire & Rescue Services squad were tasked with helping the exhausted passengers. Most of them had not slept throughout the humid night, their fatigue evident in their bloodshot eyes. Various makeshift tents were set up along the pier, offering food, medical help and transport to local hotels where passengers could rest. Gym halls in schools had turned into temporary shelters with the help of volunteers during the night.

John Ramo, a young and ambitious police officer, had been tasked with collecting witness reports from the passengers – a mundane task given to all the inexperienced police officers by Chief Commissioner Francis Matanga. Ramo was sure that all the witness reports would be filed away and forgotten in the farthest, dustiest corners of their police station. His faith in his country's criminal justice system was completely lacking.

Most locals on the street would tell you the reason behind their failed justice system was the top brass, who were motivated by greed and constantly chased personal gain. However, Ramo believed it to be a combination of some of law enforcement's biggest sins – lack of accountability, lack of transparency and a general state of oversight. Turning a blind eye to anything illegal and getting paid for it was how most of his colleagues spent their days at work. These reasons fueled his motivation to join the RSIPF, aspiring to spark a necessary change and restore the police's tarnished reputation.

This was a typical case of an ambitious young man refusing to accept the grim reality during his three years in service. Even though his dreams of creating a change were drowning in this cesspit of corruption and crime, his wife and daughter back home encouraged him to push on.

After locking his Isuzu D-Max police car – a gift from the Australian government back in 2019 as part of their Bilateral Security Treaty – he donned his police baseball cap, covering his freshly shaved bald head, and began walking towards the tent used by the police. The three-minute walk in the sun was enough to drench his blue shirt in sweat.

After chugging down a bottle of cold water, he grabbed a seat by the desk where he would interview the passengers. As a fan placed next to him whirred on its highest setting, he flipped open his notepad and ushered in the first passenger for the day.

Three hours into the interviews, nothing of significance had come up. Most of the passengers described similar experiences, and nothing stood out in particular. All fingers pointed towards this being an extremely unfortunate event of the ship hitting an uncharted reef. That was until his next passenger introduced herself as Julia Ramirez. A bank clerk from Los Angeles, she was wearing a slim-fit white t-shirt with light brown cargo shorts and a pair of Birkenstock sandals. She took off her bucket hat and arranged her black hair in a ponytail. Ramo offered her a bottle of water, and she accepted with a forced smile, trying to fight back the lack of sleep. She gulped down two-thirds of the bottle before screwing the cap back on.

'I wish the circumstances were different, but welcome to the Solomon Islands, Ms. Ramirez.'

'No need to apologise for that. The most important thing is that me, my fiance and, of course, the rest of the people onboard the ship made it out alive,' Julia replied.

'Indeed, no truer words could be spoken.' Ramo turned over to a new page in his notepad. 'To spare you some time so that you can get back to your fiance quicker, I want to let you know that I've already taken many interviews of passengers who were on the observation deck at the time of the accident. I'm interested in knowing if you did anything different compared to most of the other passengers. Can you tell me where you were between the time of the impact with the reef and the lifeboat evacuation?'

Julia cleared her throat and began recounting her experience onboard the ship during the accident. Ramo appreciated her eye for detail. It helped him create a better mental image of what it felt like to be onboard the World Discoverer. When she got to the part where she had sneaked inside the ship to look for her fiance, Ramo was hooked and listening intently. He interrupted her when she mentioned that something felt off about the crew member who had helped her fiance down at Deck 3, the Explorer deck.

'What was different about this crew member?'

'The first thing I noticed was his uniform. He was wearing a suit that the waiters in the restaurant had used when we had a formal night.'

'When did the formal night happen during the cruise?'

'It happened two days ago. On the other days, they wore a simpler uniform.'

'Noted. Anything else you observed?'

'Yes, it looked like he had stumbled out of a saloon fight. Like in those old spaghetti Western movies. His suit was all messed up and full of stains.'

'How would you describe this person's appearance?'

Julia took a moment to recollect how he looked. 'He was Chinese – I heard it from his accent – and in his late 20s, probably. Very muscular with a short buzz cut. He had pale white skin, dark eyes, and a scar over his right eyebrow. His movements were deliberate, and he had a militant swagger about him.'

'What do you mean by that, Ms Julia?'

'I sensed he was more than just a regular crew member. He felt out of place there. Plus, I can't recall seeing him the day we had the formal night. This cruise ship was small compared to others, so you tend to remember the crew's faces.'

'Interesting... I'll have to follow up on this information.' Ramo took his baseball cap off to cool his head. 'Anything else you'd like to add? Now's the chance,' he said with a smile.

'One thing I still wonder is why this crew member was down in the engine or warehouse room, especially after the evacuation routine had started.'

'That's where I step in and try to unravel this mystery. There could be many reasons, to be fair, but I'll do my best to find out more about this suspicious crew member. Thanks for your time, and I hope you and your fiance have a good time in our country,' said Ramo, shaking her hand like a gentleman.

Julia smiled back, thanked Ramo for listening to her ramble on and exited the tent. Ramo sank deeper into his plastic chair and asked his supervisor not to send in any more passengers. This information had taken him by surprise, and his gut told him to act fast. Ramo quickly pulled up his phone and dialled his partner's number.

Meanwhile, back at the police station, his partner, Michael Kere, was submerged in never-ending stacks of paperwork lying on his desk. His ashtray desperately needed cleaning, and his coffee mug from earlier in the day had built up a rigid layer of coffee stains. Kere exhaled a large cloud of cigarette smoke as he lightly tapped his cigarette on the ashtray with his index finger. The herbaceous scent from the Solbako cigarette was dispersed by the overhead ceiling fan in the cramped office space. As soon as the phone rang, he picked it up and cradled it between his ear and shoulder.

'Officer Michael Kere, how can I help you?' he said while continuing to sign and stamp documents.

'It's me, John. Are you alone in the office? I need to discuss something really important with you.'

Kere stood up, closed the office door and returned to his desk. 'What's the matter? You sound really stressed.'

'I need you to check on a lead I have. Can you look up the crew member list of the World Discoverer?'

Kere turned toward his stationary computer and, after some loud typing, printed the list Ramo was looking for. He put on his reading glasses and grabbed a pen.

'I'm ready. What am I looking for?'

'A witness mentioned a suspicious crew member who looked Chinese. Can you check if any Asian crew members were working at the restaurant or bars?'

Kere used his pen to scan the lists until he got to the right page.

'Here we are. Let's see… We have three from the Philippines, four from India and two Indonesians. The three Filipinos and one Indonesian work in the kitchen. The rest work as waiters in the dining area.'

'Damn! Ok, could please just check the whole list then? Maybe he was filling in for someone else.'

The line went silent for two minutes as Kere leafed through the pages. 'There's nobody on the crew from China. Believe me. I've read the list four times now.'

'You know what this means, right?'

'Enlighten me, John.'

'Alright, so this is what we've gathered so far. We have a report of an unidentified person onboard impersonating a crew member. This person was in an area where he shouldn't have been, considering the crew was busy evacuating passengers. All this within five minutes of the ship hitting the reef. You see where I'm going with this, right?'

'I can see, and it's stressing me out. Have you thought about this thing though? If he was impersonating a crew member, then whose suit was he wearing?'

10

MICHAEL KERE'S QUESTION couldn't have been more on point. Ramo burst out of the tent, looking for the closest supervisor. After a quick chat with him, he started searching for any crew member who had been working in the dining area of the World Discoverer. He was referred to various people who were on the dock, and he felt like a ping-pong ball as he bounced back and forth, trying to find a crew member who could answer the burning questions on his mind.

His quest ended sixty metres down the pier, where a small group of people in BEWA Cruises uniforms were taking a cigarette break. The group of eight were standing in a circle when Ramo introduced himself, sensing palpable tension in the air as he explained what he was looking for. None of them knew anything about a Chinese crew member, and extracting any information from them was proving to be a real challenge.

It was at this moment that Rajani Hari, an Indian waiter, threw down his cigarette and stomped it with his black leather shoes. He threw a look of disgust at his fellow crew members before addressing Ramo.

'Let's cut the crap, people. We all know that nobody has seen our colleague, Luke Manik. They've had since yesterday to locate him, and he's nowhere to be found,' Rajani declared with animated hand gestures, clearly agitated. 'And they have the audacity to go out and claim that everyone has been evacuated and accounted for. Bullshit! Something has happened to my friend, and nobody's raising a finger to take action.'

Ramo found a more secluded space on the pier where he and Rajani could talk privately.

'Where did you last see Luke Manik?'

'It was yesterday around 3:30 pm. I passed him in the corridor, and we greeted each other. He was on his way to pick up his uniforms from the dry cleaners in the laundry room. I had just changed and was on my way up to prepare for my evening shift.'

'That's a little over an hour before you hit the reef. Do you know where his cabin was in correlation with the laundry room?'

'Of course, I know. His cabin was down on Deck 1, and the laundry room was on the deck above. All the lower-ranking crew quarters were on Deck 1, close to the cargo hold and engine room on the lowest deck.'

'I really appreciate this information. Thanks for taking the time to talk to me.' Ramo gave Rajani his contact information and said he would do his best to find out what had happened to his friend.

'I must kindly ask you to refrain from talking to anyone else about this until I inform you personally. The police force here is not exactly known for its effectiveness and transparency.'

Rajani nodded and shook Ramo's hand firmly.

'Please, find out what happened to my friend. It's the least you can do for his family.'

Ramo nodded and started his long walk back to his car. The pieces were there right in front of him, but could it be that simple? A mysterious passenger had assaulted a crew member to impersonate him during the accident. But why? What was the motivation behind such an action? What could he have possibly gained by doing that if an uncharted reef had caused the accident?

These questions were spinning around in Ramo's head as he navigated the jam-packed roads in Honiara. Feeling out of his depth on this case, he decided to talk to his commissioner, Francis Matanga, at the police station, even though he was dreading the thought. This matter was bigger than him, and maybe, just maybe, the commissioner would understand the gravity of the situation.

It did not take long for Ramo to understand that this was a bad idea. Matanga was fuming and slammed his fist on his desk before spit-screaming into Ramo's face.

'Your job is to just observe, file reports and pretend to do your job. I want none of this CSI Honiara bullshit you're doing right now. Understand?'

'But, sir—'

'No, no, no! Do not "but sir" me right now. Let the foreigners deal with this matter. Okay?' Matanga yelled as he sat down in his chair again. He clasped his hands and nervously swivelled his chair to the left and right.

'Roger, Chief. I'm sorry I bothered you with this matter.' Ramo said to calm him down. 'I stepped out of line. It won't happen again.'

'Attaboy. Now you're talking sensibly again,' said Matanga, standing up from his chair. He walked up to Ramo, and when he shook his hand, Matanga tightened his grip and pulled Ramo aggressively towards him. He leaned in and whispered malevolently into Ramo's ear. 'If I find out that you've done something reckless, I'll come after everyone you love. You hear me? It would be a real shame if something happened to your lovely wife and daughter. Honiara is not kind to widows and young girls.'

Matanga leaned back and gave Ramo a deadly stare before breaking into a sinister smile.

'Have a nice day, Officer Ramo. Get outta here!' He slammed the door shut.

God only knew how much Ramo despised that old man. His blood was boiling, and he felt like punching a wall. He tried to maintain composure as he walked towards his office space. When he felt his nerves calm down, he called his wife from his office phone. The phone beeped three times before his wife answered the call.

'Rose, I need you and our daughter to take the first bus to your family in Maravovo. Honiara is not safe,' said Ramo, fighting back his tears.

'What happened, love? What's wrong?'

'I have to finish something at work. I can't go into detail on this line. You'll get updates from me through Michael.' He could trust nobody in this police station except for his partner.

'But when will we get to see you? Your daughter and I need you alive. Please, just quit this job. It's not worth it if it pushes us away from each other,' Rose sobbed.

'Trust me, I'm too deep into it to quit now. Take care of our baby girl. I love you.' Ramo hung up the phone and sank deep into his chair, feeling drained.

For half an hour, he remained in his chair, judging his predicament and engaging in the worst inner monologue someone could have. His last beacon of hope was the foreigners he would meet later that night. They called themselves OMIA and would work alongside the Australian Navy to investigate the accident. Their most positive attribute was that they were not corrupt and would probably take an interest in the information that he had gathered today.

Matanga had chosen him to be their chauffeur and tag along on their dinner meeting later that night, acting as a guard. Ramo was determined to use this opportunity to see if OMIA was interested in solving this mystery or if they were just here to collect a fat paycheck.

He left the police station and drove back home without turning the radio on. Opening the door to his home was a sombre experience. The house welcomed him with complete silence as he stood at the doorway, and he realised how wonderful it was to be greeted by his daughter screaming "Daddy" each time he got home from work.

II

NICK PUSHED OPEN the sliding glass doors of his waterfront villa and strolled outside, taking in the fresh air. He and the OMIA crew had just settled into their rooms after being picked up from the Honiara airport by two RSIPF officers. The twenty-four-minute drive along the coastal Kukum highway of Honiara, sitting in the backseat of a late 90s Toyota RAV4 with no air conditioning, forced him to take a quick shower as soon as he got the keys to his villa.

He was feeling much more comfortable now, wearing a light blue linen shirt with navy blue terry cotton shorts. A pair of champagne-coloured Oliver Peoples sunglasses were providing his eyes with some much-needed protection from the sun's harsh glare. Nick closed his eyes and listened to the waves rhythmically crashing down at the beach while the palm tree fronds rustled in the wind. It felt nice being outside again, especially on ground level. No matter how luxurious the plane was, flying long distances always sapped the energy out of his body.

Since he had some downtime – thanks to Santini, who always ensured his team had enough time to recover before starting an investigation – Nick decided to explore his surroundings. He wore his dark brown sandals and began walking along the beach. Some kids were playing in the shallow part of the beach under the watchful eyes of their parents. In the distance, he could see the outlines of people's heads swimming in the deeper part of the beach. Further towards the back, small fishing boats were returning to the city to sell their daily catch. If it wasn't for the meeting later, Nick could see himself taking a plunge into the sea and spending some hours on the beach.

When he got to the beach's end, Nick turned around and walked towards the pool and dining area of the resort. All the walking had his stomach rumbling, signalling it was time for a quick lunch. As he approached the pool, a friendly-looking couple walked towards him. The man was holding an olive green Leica R3 in his arms.

'Excuse me, do you speak English?' the man asked.

'Of course. What can I help you with?' Nick replied.

'My fiance and I would like a photo together. My name is Antonio, by the way. Nice to meet you...' he said and stretched his arms out to greet Nick.

'Nick... My name is Nick. Pleasure to meet you guys. I love your camera, by the way. I've always wanted one of these safari models. Is it the 35 mm version?' Nick asked, pointing towards the camera in Antonio's hands.

'You're right,' Antonio replied, somewhat shocked that someone could recognise this camera model. 'You seem to know your stuff. They're really easy to use. You can see for yourself – just point and shoot.'

'At that, I'm great,' Nick said with a chuckle. 'I have the R6 one myself.' Nick had won many sharpshooting competitions in the Norwegian Navy. If they only knew whom they're talking to, he thought.

The couple squeezed in close to each other, and Nick started clicking away with the Leica. He complimented them both throughout the photoshoot, and Antonio's fiance really enjoyed it, giggling like a teenage girl.

'And that should be a wrap, lady and gentleman. Here's your camera.'

'Aw, thank you so much!' said Julia with a hearty smile.

'Happy to help. Enjoy your evening and take care.'

Nick continued his stroll towards the poolside restaurant and found a table with a view of the beach. He ordered a club sandwich and washed the sandwich down with a glass of local homemade lemonade. He regretted not bringing his book along; it was the perfect spot for uninterrupted reading.

He spent some minutes people-watching to pick up on any interesting individuals spending their time at the luxurious resort. The place had the usual assortment of old men in tropical shirts with younger, sexy partners in revealing outfits, couples on romantic getaways and a few rich families with kids running between their legs. When Nick got tired of sitting, he moved over to the bar.

'Do you have any good dark rums, my friend?' he asked the bartender behind the counter.

'Oh, I have just the one for you.' The bartender pulled out a bottle of Blackwell Fine Jamaican Rum. 'I can concoct anything you desire with this one.'

'I have a challenge for you. I want the best rum negroni you can make.'

The bartender nodded and turned to the bottles adorning the wall behind him. He picked out a Martini Rosso and an interesting-looking Campari bottle.

'This Campari bottle was made in Jamaica, and it has the highest alcohol percentage at 28.5%. I hope you're ready for this negroni. It will pack a serious punch.'

Nick looked at the bartender, mesmerised at his skill in mixing the cocktail.

'There you go,' said the bartender as he added a slice of orange to garnish the negroni.

Nick took a sip and immediately sensed that this negroni was infused with a tropical soul. The herbaceous, bitter Campari perfectly complemented the spicy dark rum and created a treat for his taste buds. He thanked the bartender and carried his cocktail with him as he strolled back to his seafront villa. Nick savoured these moments, knowing that in a few hours, he would have to get back to work. A shipwreck could take days or weeks, depending on the complexity of the investigation. As the sun was setting, the air began to cool down and the nearby palm trees provided more shade. His mind slowly drifted to unconsciousness as he lounged on the sunbed.

12

AT PRESENT, NICK was idly gazing out of the open window of their car as they drove through the main highway in Honiara. The sun had set, and the city's streets were lit up by the orange glow from the street lamps, swarmed around by groups of moths. Shop owners were closing up their businesses, and the city was preparing to settle in for the night.

The southeast wind from the sea brushed his face, carrying the smell of sea breeze and exhaust fumes. Nagho ni ara, as the locals described Honiara in their native Guadalcanal language, meant 'facing the southeast wind'. The city primarily focused on the trade of coconuts, fish, timber and the occasional gold found in Gold Ridge, a gold mine situated deep within the island, approximately forty kilometres from the city centre.

In the '60s and '70s, the city experienced substantial improvement in its urban infrastructure compared to the rest of the islands. Remnants of that could be seen in the types of buildings Nick observed from the comfort of his passenger seat. However, despite being a central trade hub and an attractive tourist destination in the Pacific Ocean, political unrest and ethnic violence have plagued the country from the '90s onwards. Rioting had traumatised entire generations on the islands, halting the further development of the country. This period of unrest was referred to as "The Tensions" by the local population.

Things had simmered down since the Australian government interfered and signed a Bilateral Security Treaty with the Prime Minister in 2017. The treaty gave the Australians the authority to assist in national security matters and natural disasters and offer general help with tasks that were out of the government's league. It was one of the reasons OMIA had been selected for the job. The catch, though, was that the Australians also got access to all the ports in the Solomon Islands for their navy to resupply and dock.

Nick and the OMIA crew were on their way to a dinner arranged by the RSIPF and the mayor. A local police officer, John Ramo, had picked them up in his RAV4. Santini was sitting in the front and going through his phone, probably ensuring nothing new had happened since their arrival. This man was a workhorse – not even the jet lag phased him. Jason was sitting next to Nick in the backseat, trying to engage in small talk with Ramo. Nick smiled whenever Jason attempted to crack a joke. Although it was tempting to join in on the fun, he was reserving his social battery for the dinner. Another RSIPF officer had picked up Bakke and Johnson from the port, and they were also on their way to the restaurant.

The RSIPF had booked a gigantic table at Club Havanah, a restaurant in the Chinatown neighbourhood of Honiara, boasting a menu inspired by French and French Polynesian cuisine. The establishment initially gave off a beach club vibe, with the main decor being sago palm leaves and giant clam shells. However, the wooden interior resembled a bungalow, and the lighting was appropriately soft, creating a relaxing, lounge-like atmosphere. The menu offered a fine selection of meats, fish, desserts and wines. A French flag hung on the wall close to the entrance, reminding everyone of the restaurant's heritage. Nick knew from experience that places like Club Havanah, which were off the beaten path and tucked away in secluded neighbourhoods, delivered some of the most authentic and tasteful culinary experiences.

George Paget, a French expat from Toulouse, welcomed Nick and all the guests arriving for their nine o'clock booking. He was the manager and chef de cuisine of Club Havanah. Nick immediately hit it off with him; he shared his backstory, and they reminisced about the European and Mediterranean lifestyle. The maitre d' soon showed up and directed everyone to their respective tables. Waiters went out of their way to be hospitable, even providing every table with mosquito repellent.

After the initial speeches and pleasantries from the mayor and Francis Matanga welcoming them to the Solomon Islands, the drinks and food showed up on the tables. An assortment of appetisers filled the table with tantalising colours and flavours. Nick sampled the various appetisers and was especially impressed by the crayfish tail dipped in a basil butter sauce. For the main course, he went with a medium-rare blue cheese steak and finished it with a sliced fruit platter. A pair of icy cold golden cans of Solbrew, the local pale lager, kept him company during the meal.

Santini steered the conversation with the RSIPF delegation and the Honiara mayor in a typical Santini fashion. The mayor appeared thoroughly entertained during their conversation, sporting a perpetual smile.

The delegation gathered around the table had an interesting assortment of personalities. Mayor Wilson Mamae was of short stature and dressed in a turquoise floral shirt and linen chinos. He had a neat, short afro, a mole near his right smile line and a well-trimmed grey beard. Meanwhile, Chief Commissioner Matanga's face was devoid of emotion, and it almost seemed as if the whole situation annoyed him. His thick black moustache and furrowed brows only exacerbated this notion.

Opposite the local delegation, Bakke and Johnson were geeking out over their day's work on the RV Solander and were rubbing it in on Jason and Nick.

'I hope you guys are ready to work tomorrow. Gus and I have everything lined up for you. Don't go too hard on tonight's dinner,' Bakke said.

'You don't need to worry about that. Besides, these types of meetings are just an excuse for the police and mayor to go out and feast,' said Nick with a grim smile.

'Yeah, Nick's right. And they put the tab on the poor people's tax money,' added Jason, taking a sip of his beer. 'Just look at them. They look so happy that they can skip working down by the port tonight.'

'I mean you have a valid point, but I ain't complaining,' said Johnson, turning his attention back to the ice cream sorbet in front of him. 'Tonight's dinner was magical. That French chef knows his stuff.'

'I can raise a glass to that,' Nick declared, raising his beer can. 'Let's enjoy tonight and get into our groove tomorrow. A big day awaits us.'

'Amen. Prepare to work some ungodly hours, gentlemen,' said Bakke, and the four of them clinked their glasses and beer cans.

Nick took a sip from his beer and sighed in delight before pushing his chair back to stand up.

'Boys, if you'd excuse me. This beer just went straight through me. I gotta take a leak.'

Nick began looking for the toilets. He had spotted them earlier that night in a small building next to the restaurant. On his way out, Ramo, who was standing watch at the restaurant's entrance, nodded and opened the door for him.

When Nick was almost done relieving himself at the urinal, he heard footsteps approaching him from behind. They abruptly stopped, and he sensed a presence in his peripheral vision.

'I'm sorry to bother you, Nick, but I have something to tell you,' Ramo whispered.

'Is it off the record?' Nick zipped up his pants.

'Yes, it has to do with the World Discoverer. I don't trust anyone at my police station.'

'Okay, lock the door while I wash my hands. How can I trust you, though?'

'I wouldn't be bothering you like this if it weren't true. I personally talked to this witness.'

'I get what you're saying, but still...'

'I mean, you just have to trust me on this one.'

'Alright. I won't promise you anything, but I'm all ears.'

Nick sensed that Ramo was one of the good guys. He was the only one who had taken an interest in OMIA since picking them up from the hotel. He was also eager to talk with them, and the discussion Ramo and Jason had earlier was interesting to listen to. On the other hand, the senior RSIPF officers at the table looked like a group of un-trustworthy policemen, with an air of superiority and arrogance about them. Nick's first impression of them was pretty mediocre.

'You have one minute before we have to leave separately. I don't want us to raise any suspicion. Your time starts now, okay?'

'Of course, I'll cut to the chase. I have witnessed reports from a crew member and a passenger on board, both describing an unidentified person who behaved suspiciously during the accident. The crew member also confirmed that we had an issue with an unaccounted-for crew member after the evacuation. I suspect something happened between our mystery man and the missing crew member.'

'Do the police and BEWA know about it?'

'I informed my partner and my boss, Matanga, but he quickly shot my theory down. He threatened to hurt my wife and daughter. They have omitted this information from BEWA.'

'Shit, that's not good at all. Anything else you've found out?'

'Our mystery man is likely Chinese, based on our witness, and was seen wearing a waiter's suit on the ship.'

'And, let me guess, our missing crew member is a waiter?'

'Yes, exactly.'

'The plot thickens. We have little time now. Here, take my card, and send me all the details you have.' Nick pulled out a business card from his wallet. 'As soon as I get your mail, I will take it up with my boss.'

'I'll send you my intel later tonight. Thank you, Nick.'

'Don't thank me yet.' Nick touched Ramo's shoulder. 'You look like a stand-up guy, my friend, but you better not be playing games with me. What you just said might throw this investigation in a whole different direction.'

'I won't let you down. You can trust me.'

'Alright, good man. Let me head out and return to your post in 30 seconds.'

Nick cautiously stepped out of the restroom, scanning the area for any eavesdroppers. It was all clear, except for a group of tourists who were leaving the restaurant in a taxi. As he reentered the restaurant, he noticed that the entire table had risen and was exchanging their last remarks about the dinner. Thank God, we can finally return to the villa again.

Santini signalled for him and the rest of the OMIA crew to walk towards the parking lot. He would probably try to get a last word in with the mayor and the RSIPF commissioner. Nick glanced at his Squale, estimating the time by which they would be back at the villa.

13

A QUARTER-HOUR LATER, Nick and Jason stepped into their villa and promptly kicked their shoes off.

'Jason, if you want to shower and change, be my guest. I want to check something out with Santini before we go to sleep.'

'Anything you can share with your new field partner, Nick?'

'I'm afraid it's for OMIA veterans only.'

'Come on now; you only have six months more experience than me.'

'Six months is five years in dog age.'

'Ouch, that was cold. So I'm your dog now?'

'Not really. I hope you'll be loyal like one though,' Nick quipped, mimicking the act of dropping a mic.

They both laughed as Nick went out to look for Santini. If he knew the man well enough, he would be sitting outside, looking at the stars and smoking a Toscano cigar. Indeed, Nick was right. The Italian had unbuttoned his white linen shirt and was leaning against a palm tree. His long, sun-kissed brown hair was swaying with the wind. Santini was the only man he knew who had a consistent tan year-round.

'Shouldn't you be asleep, mister?' Santini exhaled smoke and glanced at his Rolex 1675 GMT Pepsi. 'It's getting late, and I need you in top shape for tomorrow's dive.'

'I know, Boss. I wouldn't bother you like this if it weren't for something important.'

'So, what's this big news that couldn't wait until tomorrow?'

Nick shared the information Ramo had given him back at Club Havanah. The details captivated Santini, and they went back and forth, trying to figure out if Ramo was just trying to derail the investigation on behalf of the RSIPF. Santini also did not trust the local police, especially after spending two hours with Commissioner Matanga.

In the middle of their discussion, Nick's iPhone vibrated from an email notification. He forwarded the mail to Santini, and they both began reading the email silently. Ramo had outlined every piece of information he had gathered from the events prior to the ship's sinking and even included a witness report as an attachment. After allowing the information to sink in, Nick broke the silence.

'So, what do you think, Boss? Is this of any interest to us?'

'It depends on what we will find underwater. I suggest we keep it between us for now. I want the rest of the guys to have a clear mind when we start tomorrow,' Santini replied and paused, trying to process his thoughts. 'If we find something that can back Ramo's information – and that's a big if – I'll call for a meeting with the folks from the Australian Navy. Onboard the RV Solander, we'll be far away from Honiara and the influence of the RSIPF. Capiche?'

'Sounds like the smartest course of action for the time being,' Nick replied, stifling a yawn. 'I'm gonna hit the hay now, Boss. Buona notte, and thanks for your time.'

'Anytime, Nick. See you tomorrow. We leave the hotel at six in the morning,' Santini said, saluting him goodbye.

Nick returned to the neighbouring villa, only to find Jason fast asleep in his bed. This guy could sleep anywhere; he is like a dog in that sense, Nick thought, chuckling. He turned off all the lights in the villa that Jason had forgotten to switch off, except for his small bedside lamp, and brushed his teeth. Nick then adjusted his pillow to provide more support for his back. He removed the bookmark from his paperback and continued reading Thunderball. Reading helped him escape reality and take his mind off work. As soon as he had to fight to keep his eyes open, he set the book aside, turned off the lamp and placed his Squale on the bedside table. All he had to do now was hope that Morpheus, the Greek god of dreams and the son of Hypnos, would grant him a good night's sleep.

14

SPENCER CLARK, THE captain of RV Solander, was a colourful character. He was loud, confident and a perfectionist when it came to commandeering a ship. His forty-two years of experience at sea, sixteen of them as a captain for the Australian Institute of Marine Science (AIMS), showed on his face and hands. His skin was rough and wrinkled and exhibited signs of constant exposure to offshore winds and saltwater. He tried to hide these signs of hardship, along with his receding hairline, behind a thick grey beard and his favourite Paul & Shark cap.

'G'day mate! Welcome aboard my beautiful vessel.' He firmly squeezed Nick's hand. 'Your people awaiting you in the crew mess for some brekky and coffee. I know you Europeans like your coffee fancy, but onboard this ship, we take our coffee black.'

'The blacker the berry, the sweeter the juice,' Nick replied with a grin.

'Crikey! We're cracking jokes already. I think we might get along just fine. You seem like a good bloke.'

Clark patted Nick's back and showed him which door to enter to find the crew mess. Nick walked down the narrow corridor, following the cacophony of voices coming from the crew mess. He could not miss the distinct voices of Bakke and Johnson discussing the day's diving procedure. Nick knew it was a routine work-related conversation for them, while others would interpret this exchange of words as a heated debate between two sworn enemies. Jason sat alone, looking at the two, mesmerised by the back-and-forth exchange, much like watching a game of tennis at Roland Garros. Nick greeted them and grabbed a seat next to Jason.

As soon as Santini entered the crew mess, the room went silent and focused on him. Nick felt like he was back in high school when his angry maths teacher would enter the classroom and everyone would shut up.

'Buona sera, signori! Today is the big day. Hope everyone had a good night's rest,' Santini announced, crossing his arms. 'Bakke and Johnson, I need you two to show our divers their cabins and the setup onboard this ship. When you're finished with that, send them up to the bridge, where I'll be waiting for them with the folks from the Australian Navy.'

'Consider it done, boss. Alright, boys, grab your luggage and follow me.'

Nick and Jason followed them to the deck below, where the living quarters were located. They both got a small cabin, each equipped with a bathroom, a wall-mounted flip-up desk and a single bed. The interior was super spartan, and both cabins had a porthole, allowing the sun to shine through. After arranging their stuff in their cabins, Johnson's tour continued to the nerve centre, which was on the same deck as the crew mess.

It was a rectangular room, normally used for meetings and oceanographic presentations. Johnson had turned it into an ultra-modern operations centre where he and Bakke could monitor the diving in real time and process all the information Nick and Jason would collect during this investigation. They had placed two workstations side by side and a projector that turned the biggest wall in the room into a huge monitor, almost identical to the one they had back in their HQ in Oslo. A few bags were lined up next to the short wall, containing numerous spare electronics and components, in case anything needed to be serviced during the investigation, and facing the nerve centre were the medical bay and laboratory.

'What guns are we running in this operation? I can see the gun locker in the corner,' Jason said.

'Wow, thought you'd never ask,' Johnson replied, opening the gun locker. 'Voila! We have a set of Heckler & Koch MP5s and brand-new Beretta 92X handguns. We also have bullet-proof vests from Protection Group Denmark and some nifty tactical gadgets if we encounter local resistance, silencers, yadda yadda. You know the drill. Hopefully, these things will collect dust on this trip and be shipped back to Norway again.'

'One can only hope, right?' Nick responded, giving Jason a deadpan look.

'Okay, boys, you've seen everything there is to see inside. Let's go out to the stern, where all our toys await. Chop chop!' said Bakke, clapping his hands.

Bakke, Johnson and the rest of the RV Solander crew had neatly arranged their Pelican cases, with all of their diving equipment from Divesoft, MS3 and the small remote-controlled ROV from Qysea, trying to use the space as best as possible. The small remote-controlled ROV from Qysea was called Fifish PRO W6 and had a depth rating of three hundred and fifty metres. At the edge of the stern, they had also tightly secured OMIA's blacked-out X9 RIB boat, crafted by the Norwegian constructor, Goldfish. Hanging from the crane was their custom-made, manned underwater submersible, which was manufactured by U-Boat Worx in the Netherlands.

This modified C-Researcher, nicknamed Viperfish II, could accommodate two occupants and dive to depths of three thousand metres. Everyone in OMIA was fascinated by deep-sea creatures, hence the name Viperfish II. The manufacturers had also made sure the OMIA logo was proudly on display on both sides, an important request by none other than Jacques Rousseau.

'That's all for our tour, folks. We're about to weigh the anchor now. If I were you, I'd hurry to the bridge to meet up with our boss and the Australian Navy,' said Johnson.

It took Nick and Jason about half a minute to reach the bridge, where Santini was standing next to Captain Clark and two Australian Navy representatives. They introduced themselves as Vice Admiral David Anderson and Helen Chapman of the Australian Secret Intelligence Service (ASIS). Captain Clark barked a few orders to his crew in the background and was busy steering the ship out of Honiara and into the open sea.

The vice admiral looked shy of 180 centimetres in height and had a round face. He wore the white vice admiral uniform without the hat and looked to be in his late 50s. His dark grey eyes matched the shape of his face, and it was impossible not to notice his thick black eyebrows. His short buzz-cut hair was transitioning to grey from the black colour of his younger days. Nick concluded it was better to be on the admiral's good side, judging from his unreadable face.

Helen, on the other hand, was much more pleasing to the eye. Her honey-blonde hair was styled with a sleek middle part and pulled into a tight ponytail. Her face had soft features, and Nick immediately made eye contact with her hazel eyes when he greeted her. Her outfit comprised of slim-fit khaki pants, a white, breathable performance t-shirt and a black Arc'teryx Atom LT vest. Even though the outfit was specifically chosen for functionality first and style second, Nick could clearly see the contours of an athletic body under those clothes. A black gun holster, strapped with a Glock 22, was slightly noticeable under her unzipped vest. On her left hand, she wore an affordable Japanese dive watch with a black rubber strap.

After a few minutes of socialising up on the bridge and reviewing their plan for the day, Santini told Nick and Jason they had two hours to relax, eat and hydrate before their dive. Nick and Jason went for some cereal and a small bowl of fruit, and Jason retired to his cabin after their brunch. However, Nick wanted some fresh air and an opportunity to see the World Discoverer in real life as they cruised towards Roderick Bay. He walked to the port side of the ship and leaned over the railing.

The sun was shining brightly over the Solomon Islands, and the rhythmic pulse of the sea was steady and peaceful. Nick gazed down at the ship's wake, hypnotised by the colour and clarity of the sea. The gentle breeze erased all of his thoughts as he stood there, embracing the atmosphere.

'So, you're the special projects guy Santini spoke so highly of?' Helen inquired, leaning with her back against the railing.

'I wouldn't go that far. I'm more of a paper-pushing, underwater Sherlock Holmes,' said Nick, turning his head to face Helen. 'My work is to dive and fill in the missing pieces of what happened on that ship. Most of the time, though, I'm desk diving back in Oslo.'

'An interesting career choice for a guy with a promising future in the Norwegian Navy.'

'So you have read my file, huh? Cheeky. What else does it say about me?'

'Not to boost your ego any further, but it goes somewhat along these lines: stellar military service record, took part in Operation Active Endeavour in the Med, assisted in the United Nations Mission in Sudan before becoming a PADI diving instructor in Zakynthos, Greece.'

'I hear the Cyclades are really nice this time of the year,' said Nick, adjusting his body into an upright posture.

'Oh really? I bet you have. Does that line work for you at all back home?' Helen raised her eyebrows.

'It's a bit hit or miss, actually.'

'Glad to hear that. At least you're honest.'

'So, Ms Helen Chapman, since you seem to know everything about me, how does one end up working as a spy for the ASIS?'

'You're going straight for the jugular. If I were to reveal this information to you, I'd have to plant a bullet in your skull with this Glock,' replied Helen, tucking her vest to a side to show off her gun, 'and throw your rather handsome carcass into the sea.'

'I sensed a small compliment amidst all this violent energy.'

'You see the glass half-full. That's good to know.'

'It's good to know that the Australians have my back as well if I mess up this entire operation.'

'Let's hope it doesn't come to that. Well, to properly answer your previous question, I used to work as a vice detective at the Sydney Police Department. This is my first mission abroad, as I got transferred to ASIS earlier this year.'

'That's impressive. You must've been really good at your previous job to get that call-up.'

'I hope so.'

'Me too. For our own safety that is.'

They both laughed and parted ways after Nick noticed the time. It was soon time to change into his body suit and prepare his diving equipment. No matter how many times he had dived in his life, a shipwreck dive always made his heart skip a beat. In the back of his mind, the idea of a dead crew member inside the ship raised his suspicions about the whole accident and kept him focused on the task ahead.

15

BAKKE WAS STRESSED by all the multitasking, typing hard on his portable computer. He had set up an improvised office on top of an empty Pelican case, a protective case designed to carry and shield sensitive equipment from water, dust and impact. Checking all the diving equipment had him sweating profusely. Jason was suited up and assembling his rebreather beside their RIB. Santini, Admiral Anderson and Agent Helen were watching them from the deck overlooking the stern.

Nick glanced at Helen before grabbing his Pelican case from the floor. She tried to avoid eye contact, but Nick noticed her plump lips forming a small smile. A mere two hundred metres from their ship, RV Solander, Nick could see the superstructure of the World Discoverer. Seeing a cruise ship, albeit of a smaller size, so close to the shore felt odd. The only time Nick had seen something similar was back in 2007 when the MS Sea Diamond hit a volcanic reef near the island of Santorini. He still remembered that time vividly, being glued to the television as a teenager, repeatedly watching the same footage of the sinking.

Nick found a spot to sit down and prepare his equipment. He was diving using a back-mounted counter-lung configuration, his preferred configuration because it kept his chest free from diving equipment. He placed his fins and mask close by and turned his attention to the diving equipment inside his case. It lay atop a generous layer of foam, with padded dividers keeping each component separate. He then lifted out his Liberty Backmount Rebreather. All he had to do now was install each component in the correct order. Nick always liked to compare this part of the diving process to assembling a watch movement. Each piece had to be placed in the correct order for it to work properly. When he finished setting up his rebreather, he slid it onto his back like a backpack and secured it tightly on his body.

He grabbed two metal cylinders, one with diluent and one with

NITROX. Since they were diving deeper than six metres, they could not use regular oxygen in the cylinder. Nick placed the NITROX cylinder on the right side and the diluent cylinder on the left side of the rebreather. Both cylinders were attached to a pair of valves after a slight turn into position.

Next, he grabbed two weight pouches that needed to be strapped onto each cylinder. He slid both onto the top of each cylinder and secured the pouches on a central strap. Then, Nick put the rebreather aside for a moment and picked up two new items from the case.

The first thing he picked up was called 'head', which contained all the electronic components operating the rebreather. It was essentially the brain of the rebreather, hence the name. The second part he picked up was the scrubber canister, where all the magic in the rebreather happened. The 'head' unit and scrubber canister worked together to remove CO_2 through a chemical reaction with the diver's exhaled expired breath. Inside the canister, a CO_2 absorbent, usually soda lime, reacts with the exhaled breath, removing the CO_2 and essentially allowing the diver to rebreathe their own air.

Nick placed the 'head' unit on top of the scrubber canister and clicked it into position. Together, they resembled a conventional oxygen tank in a tubular shape. He attached it to the back-mount frame, between the two cylinders he had previously installed. The canister secured its position in the back-mounted rebreather with a lever locking mechanism. He then tightened the central strap to secure everything in place and connected the NITROX hose to the 'head'.

Then, it was time to bring out the two counter-lungs and connect them to the rebreather frame using a zipper and velcro strap. The inhale counter-lung went on the left side, while the exhale counter-lung went on the right side of the frame. When wearing the rebreather, the counter-lungs would sit atop the diver's shoulders.

Subsequently, Nick picked up the breathing tube equipped with a Bail Out Valve (BOV). The tube had two hoses extending left and right from the central mouthpiece, ending in two plastic 'elbows' that resembled the curved tailpipes of a car. He put those two 'elbows' inside the respective sockets in the 'head' unit, situated above the scrubber canister. A gentle half-turn locked them into position.

Each hose had a small 'T-piece' that required a push and twist to connect to each counter-lung. Nick did that and hooked up the last few cables needed to complete the setup. The final touch was equipping the 'head' with a protective case to further protect the electric components of the rebreather and linking up the heads-up display. Nick picked up the last few items and placed them in his SealLine dry bag.

'Jason, I'm good to go. How long till you're ready?'

'Give me a couple of minutes and it's go time.'

'Copy.' Nick lifted his gear into their RIB.

As soon as Jason finished loading his gear onboard the RIB, Santini walked down to the stern. Commandeering the RIB was his only way of staying directly involved in their investigations. Bakke and Johnson saluted the three of them as the RIB was lowered into the sea. They headed to the op centre to calibrate their instruments to be in sync with Jason and Nick's feedback from underwater.

Santini tightened his navy blue cap and put on his LGR sunglasses. His face lit up as he turned on the engine and pushed the throttle forward. The RIB came to life and cruised over the calm waters of Roderick Bay.

'Mamma Mia! What a place to ground a cruise ship, guys,' Santini exclaimed, his gaze fixed on the World Discoverer.

'Wow, it's a shipwreck in paradise, Boss,' Nick said, admiring the unspoiled beauty of the island. 'What's the temperature in the sea, Jason?'

'You're gonna like this one. Twenty five degrees celsius at the moment,' said Jason after consulting his heads-up display.

'That's much better than our last dive in Norway.'

Santini eased the throttle as they closed in on the ship's aft.

'Okay, guys. The gash should be on the starboard side of the ship, about ten metres underwater. I'll monitor you from the laptop and be in contact with the op centre,' Santini instructed, turning on his Bluetooth headset. 'Mic check, Gus. Do you read me?'

'We hear you loud and clear, Mario. All systems are on from our side. The cameras are up and running on our side as well,' Johnson responded from the op centre.

'Use your time wisely, boys, and don't go too crazy on this one. The ship hasn't deviated from its current listing since yesterday, but it's still resting on the underwater rock shelf. The ship could move without warning. No need to risk everything on our first dive.'

Nick and Jason nodded as they began wearing their fins. They were both on edge as they realised how dangerous this dive could be. Being trapped inside the ship would most likely mean death, which was a pretty grim thought to have right before your first dive. Nick spat inside his mask and rubbed his saliva around, trying to focus elsewhere. To prevent fogging, he quickly dipped the mask in the water before wearing it. He spun the bezel of his Squale to zero out the arrow to the distinctive minute hand before diving into the greenish-blue sea. Jason followed suit, doing the same with his orange-faced Certina DS Super PH500M.

A few seconds after the splash, everything went silent, and Nick felt like he was back in his element. The only company he would have for the next hour was the voice inside his head. The warm water was easy to adjust to, and Nick signalled to his partner that he was ready to dive deeper.

Their plan was to swim down to the ship's waterline and move along its starboard side from aft to stern. Santini was confident that the gash would be a few metres under the waterline. Their initial goal was to document the gash and check if it was big enough to swim inside the ship. If not, they would deploy their remote-controlled ROV, which could squeeze inside tight spaces.

Diving was an activity that invoked a sense of discovery and peace. It required the mastery of multitasking while maintaining a smooth and controlled pace. It was almost like floating weightlessly in zero gravity, except that you were underwater, not on the moon.

For Nick, being underwater felt like cheating nature. Humans weren't designed to be underwater, yet here he was, swimming among all the colourful marine life that called Roderick Bay home. All of his life above water had been a constant bras de fer against gravity. The fact that he could explore the underwater world and go wherever his mind wanted was a life-changing revelation to him. Nothing had ever given him this sense of freedom that diving provided. It all started when he went snorkelling as a kid alongside his father, watching the small fish during their summer vacations in Greece. That experience ignited his curiosity, a trait all deep sea divers share, and pushed him to go deeper.

The rebreather configuration allowed Nick to dive without creating bubbles since he did not have to exhale any gas into the water. This made the experience almost completely silent for him. Besides that, it did not blur his vision or disturb the local aquatic animals.

As they neared the ship's hull, Nick signalled Jason to swim deeper with him. He gently kicked his feet to propel himself towards the ship's waterline. When Jason was at the same depth as him, he began swimming alongside the starboard side as they had planned.

Everything seemed fine for the first metres as they scanned the hull for any damage. But as they approached the stern section, the light grew dimmer since from that point on, the ship was in contact with the rock shelf, and the ship's superstructure, combined with the rock shelf, blocked the sunrays, casting darkness over that part of the bottom.

They both switched on their lights to enhance their vision. A few metres away from the middle section of the starboard side, Nick could see the gash. The dark hole became clearer as they both focused their diving lights on that spot. Nick slowly swam close to it so that the OMIA crew would get a stable visual in their monitors. Jason positioned himself facing the gash and provided Nick with an extra light source.

Surprisingly, the gash was right on the ship's waterline, where the white hull met the red bottom. Nick would have paid a fortune to see Santini's reaction at that moment. They had debunked his initial theory.

Nick estimated the opening was about one and a half metres high and three metres wide. It was a significantly large opening, explaining the ship's immediate listing after the impact. As he got closer to the opening, Nick noticed that the sharp and jagged metal on the edge of the gash was pointing inwards, indicating that an external mass had put pressure on the hull from the outside. This made absolute sense if the ship had collided with a reef.

However, this discovery raised a new question: if they had hit a reef, how did an ultra-modern expedition cruise ship make contact with a reef that is so high up on the ship's waterline? An uncharted reef would have to protrude quite high from the bottom in that case, and a state-of-the-art Electronic Chart Display and Information System could not have overseen such an obvious reef. For now, though, Nick kept the possibility of a reef open since such deviations could happen in places with complex underwater biomes.

Nick turned and gestured for Jason to come closer to him. He needed him to cast the light inside the opening to see what was on the inside. He abruptly told Jason to stop when a new discovery caught his attention: the edges of the opening had a peculiar discolouration. The twisted and crumbled metal, which was once white, had turned darker. As Nick focused his light on that part, he noticed the discolouration had hints of dark grey and blue. Usually, such discolouration occurs when a painted surface makes contact with an object. It was highly unusual for a reef collision to leave such marks.

Nick glanced at his watch to check how much time had elapsed since the start of their dive. It was time to enter the opening and see what lay inside. Maybe he could uncover clues that could shed light on this accident. For now, his head was full of questions.

Focusing on his mind, he controlled his breathing and aligned his body to the opening. It would be a tight squeeze, but he could make it. Jason watched on from a safe distance, providing light, as Nick slipped inside the ship.

Based on the intel they had received from Captain Kreuss and his engineers on the ship, two out of six bulkheads on the starboard side had completely flooded. One of these had a malfunctioning watertight door, allowing water to completely flood the starboard section of Deck 1.

Nick's primary aim was to look for any clues he could find in the two bulkhead compartments. His second goal was to locate the malfunctioning watertight door and explore the submerged part of Deck 1 for any signs of the missing crew member. Time was of the essence, so he could not dwell on insignificant details.

As he adjusted to the ship's angle, Nick turned left and right, casting his light to get his bearings. He slowly swam around to see if he could recognise anything. On one wall, he noticed some signs with arrows and names. After carefully studying them, he figured out he was next to one of the engine rooms. The area he was in right now was part of the ship's storage area.

Having exhausted his options of finding anything in that area, Nick moved over to the next bulkhead compartment, which housed the engines. He continued swimming through the corridor, trying to avoid anything that could cut his drysuit or breathing tubes. It appeared that the crew had excellent control at the warehouse that day, with only a few items strewn around the corridor or floating around Nick. A few groups of small fish had already sought cover inside the ship; they swam away from Nick every time he was near them.

Nick grabbed a railing and pushed himself towards a half-open door leading to the engine room. He planted his feet on a flat surface and slowly pushed the door open, ensuring he did not overexert himself. Losing excessive air from your tanks could be fatal when navigating a shipwreck.

He circled the engine room, looking for anything that was out of place. Nick made one last effort, trying to look in more obscure places. Then, he got his first breakthrough of the day – a square-shaped device attached to the white wall behind one of the engines. It was jet black and looked like a small alarm box, with a tiny screen and four face buttons. Nick swam closer to the wall and took some photos of the spot. For all he knew, it could be insignificant. However, he tried to envision what this spot would have looked like if the ship were in its normal, afloat state. It seemed unusual to have something mounted there. He would need to cross-check with the engineer later if anything used to be attached there.

He checked the luminous dial of his Squale and figured he could squeeze in a search for clues at Deck 1 without pushing it. He returned to the half-open door and swam up the staircase that was a few metres away from it.

He was now in a long corridor comprising mostly cabins for the crew. Nick counted ten doors in the submerged corridor. He pulled out his small underwater laser cutter and prepared to open each one. Johnson had developed the cutter with one of his old pals from DARPA. It could cut through many types of steel like a knife through warm butter and fit neatly inside a pencil case.

Nick cut through all the locks and started opening each door. He started from the one farthest away from the stairs and methodically worked his way back towards them. After checking six cabins, his hopes of finding the missing crew member dwindled.

Perhaps it had been an unfortunate case of a crew member falling overboard. Every two weeks, a passenger or crew member was lost at sea, falling overboard from cruise ships. It is one of the grim realities of cruise shipping that is rarely discussed. However, Nick felt compelled to see it through, as only three cabins were left now. He grabbed the handle of the next door with his left hand, but it wouldn't budge. He placed the laser cutter back in his pouch and used both hands to rip the door open.

16

A PULSATING STREAM of bubbles burst in front of Nick's face as he opened the cabin door, blurring his view momentarily. He squinted, trying to see if there was anything inside the cabin. When the bubbles dissipated, Nick spotted him. Luke Manik was floating, face-down, in the single bedroom.

Nick began taking photos of the stiff and lifeless body dressed in a white t-shirt and grey sweatpants. As he slowly made his way into the cabin, Nick gently turned the body around to take photos of his face.

His eyes were wide open, which gave Nick the chills. Was it the look of a drowning man with no air to breathe or the look of a man staring into his killer's eyes? Both were grim fates, and Nick felt sorry for the man.

He made a mental note of the cabin number he had found the body in and prepared to exit the ship. They needed a proper bag to store his body since retrieving him without one could potentially attract scavengers like sharks or saltwater crocodiles. It was a risk they could not afford so early in the investigation. He then swam near the porthole and toggled his light on and off a few times, a signal to Jason that he was on his way back.

Nick was finally done exploring and was on his way back to the open waters again. He continued his swim through the corridor of the storage room and saw Jason's flashlight shining at the end. It wouldn't take him long now to exit the confined spaces of the World Discoverer. He followed the same procedure as before and carefully exited the ship, ensuring he did not touch any of the sharp edges of the gash.

He gave Jason a thumbs up and pointed upwards. Jason acknowledged, and they both began their ascent towards the surface. On their way up, they had a designated decompression stop to equalise the pressure in their eardrums. The heads-up display on their dive watches vibrated to remind them of that. They broke the surface a couple of metres away from their RIB. Santini reached out, grabbed their arms and helped them both onboard.

'I don't know where to start, Nick,' Santini began, pausing momentarily. 'What you saw can have a really simple explanation or a very complex one. And right now, I'm not sure which one I prefer.'

'Okay, now I am intrigued,' said Jason, taking off his mask and rebreather.

'I bet you all are. Let's start from the beginning,' Nick responded, placing the rebreather back in its case. He began retelling his dive as Santini, Jason and the rest of the crew in the op centre listened intently. 'First off, the ship clearly sank, or should I say, partially sank, because of the gash on its side. There's no doubt about that.

'The thing is, though, that the gash is right on the waterline. I've never seen a reef do such damage so high up the hull. Usually, it's much lower. It's just like your initial take, Boss.' Nick gestured towards Santini, who nodded back in agreement. 'I think the ship must have hit something that was right on the surface or just under it.'

'The weather was superb as well when they were sailing here,' Jason commented. 'The crew described it as akin to sailing in a pool. It should've been easy to spot if anything unfamiliar protruded from the sea.'

'Plus, the metal in the opening pointed inwards,' Nick added.

'Yeah, I noticed that on the footage. I'm leaning towards your theory as well, boys. We will need Bakke and Johnson to do some simulation and calculations to determine the external force required to do such damage,' Santini said.

'We should also send our remote ROV to do some photogrammetry of the entire ship,' Jason suggested.

'That's a good idea. Then, our computers can show a 3D model of the ship to reveal any hidden damage we could not spot on our dive,' said Nick.

OMIA's remote ROV was equipped with a high-resolution camera and a powerful strobe light that could capture still images of shipwrecks. From their base onboard the RV Solander, they could program the ROV to take a specific route and capture footage from all angles of the shipwreck. Since the World Discoverer was partially submerged, they could not scan the entire ship. However, a 3D model of the submerged part of the ship would be more than enough to rule out the possibility of further hull damage.

The ROV would instantly upload all the gathered data and images to OMIA's in-house software. The software would use that data to produce a highly detailed 3D model that could be zoomed in and out as much as required. This software was a game changer since one of the biggest limitations when investigating shipwrecks was that the ship was constantly being viewed close up – either by a diver or a camera with a narrow field of view, usually mounted on an ROV. A 3D model helps to view the ship on a macro level, allowing the bigger picture of an accident to be assessed.

'I agree, boys. We'll have the guys in the op centre scan the ship after sunset. Right now, though, I want to hear about what you found inside the ship,' said Santini.

'So, at the lowest deck, I spotted nothing of significance until I swam over to the engine room. There, I found a device of some sort mounted in a sketchy place behind an engine. It reminded me of the alarm box back in our office. Other than that, I found no specific clues even after swimming two rounds through the room.'

'Hmm...alright, I'll contact the engineer and show him your photos from the engine room. He'll surely know if whatever was mounted there was a part of the engine room or not. For now, we have bigger matters at hand,' Santini said.

'You're right. I searched the submerged section of Deck 1 as well. Jason, you caught a glimpse of me there as well when I signalled with my light.'

Jason agreed with a nod.

'There, in Cabin 103, I found the dead body of the missing waiter, Luke Manik.'

Jason's jaw dropped to the floor. 'So, you mean to tell me that not everyone was evacuated from the ship? I knew from the get-go that these police officers were doing a subpar job,' Jason exclaimed, looking furious.

'On that, we can all agree. Go on, Nick,' Santini urged.

Nick then told Jason about the intel they had received from police officer Ramo the previous night. When he got to the witness report from the passenger, Jason interrupted him.

'Wait a minute. The chief commissioner knew about this and did not inform BEWA, us or the rest of the RSIPF?'

'Yes, you're right.'

'Either they're too corrupt to do their jobs properly or they want to cover something up.'

'No need to jump to conclusions just yet. For all we know, Luke could've been sleeping and gotten trapped in his cabin before he could react,' Santini said.

'Why would the police choose not to inform anyone about that? It doesn't make any sense,' said Jason, scratching his head.

'What we need to do now is dive after the ROV has finished with the photogrammetry process and recover Luke's body. Maybe the doctor onboard can help us identify the cause and time of death,' Nick suggested, crossing his arms.

'Sounds like a plan. We've got our work cut out for us now. You guys get some rest, while I contact the ship's engineer. Let's meet up with the admiral and the agent in one hour at the top deck of the ship to discuss what we've found so far.'

Santini turned the RIB around and gunned for the RV Solander, pushing the throttle forward.

'This is much faster than your RIVA back home, old man,' Nick remarked, causing them all to laugh.

'If you behave on this trip, maybe I'll lend it to you,' Santini offered with an outstretched arm.

'You've got yourself a deal, Boss. Or else?'

'The deal is on. If not, you owe me, Jason and the other guys a dinner at Athénée in Athens,' said Santini, grinning.

'That's all Greek to me, but if Nick is laying out, I'm down.' Jason said.

'The stakes are high, but it's on like Donkey Kong. Believe me, Jason, you'd pray for my downfall if you knew what kind of food they served there.'

Jason rubbed his hands with excitement, while Santini dreamed

about Mediterranean food. Nick estimated the cost of six people dining at Athénée and silently vowed to solve this case. He hadn't come
this far to fail now.

17

BACK ON THE RV Solander, Nick took a moment to clean and prep his equipment for the upcoming night dive. After a quick shower to rinse off the salt from his hair and body, he changed into comfortable navy blue swim shorts and an azzuro blue terry cotton polo shirt and was on his way up to meet with the Australians.

He grabbed an ice-cold bottle of water from the crew mess so he would not be parched from all the talking in the upcoming meeting. The sun was burning orange and on its way down, painting the sky crimson. A southern briny breeze had picked up, hitting Nick straight in his face as he stepped out on the deck. Helen arrived late and was the last one to take a seat around the table. Santini cast a look towards Nick and winked, signalling him to start the meeting.

For the second time that day, he recounted his dive and everything he had found along the way. There was complete silence from his listeners as he continued his monologue. When he finished, Santini took over to discuss the results of their post-dive tasks.

'As you're all aware, Nick came across many interesting things during his dive inside the World Discoverer,' Santini began. 'Our first goal was to get in touch with the ship's engineer to learn more about the device in the engine room.'

'Was it a device monitoring the fuel supply to the engines, by any chance?' Admiral Anderson asked.

'I was thinking along those lines as well, Admiral, but the engineer clarified that he had never seen this device before in his life. When he had inspected the engine room in Honolulu harbour, no such device was mounted behind the engines.'

'Hmm...interesting,' said the admiral, stroking his chin. 'Any ideas about what this device could be?'

'It's difficult to tell. I plan to retrieve it during our night dive. I think our guys in the op centre can provide us with more information on the device,' Nick responded.

'Do that. We can take it apart piece by piece and see what's on the inside. Hopefully, Bakke and I can decipher what kind of device it is. Well, with that out of the way, let's move on to the photogrammetry results. Did anything interesting pop up during the scanning?' asked Santini.

'Nope, Boss, the rest of the hull appears completely intact. The World Discoverer did not pick up any damage except the gash on its starboard side,' Nick replied.

'So, theoretically, the ship can be salvaged if we patch up its gash?' Santini asked.

'I believe so, yes. We just need a magnetic Miko Plaster tarpaulin to cover the opening, ample water pumps to remove the water that has seeped inside the ship and a few tug boats to pull the ship to deeper waters when high tide kicks in.'

Miko Plaster was a magnetic tarpaulin produced in Norway, used to seal off hull breaches under or over the waterline. The seal was made through magnetic adhesion between the patch and the steel surface of the hull. Water pressure helped reinforce the seal in its place. It was arguably the most cost-effective and secure way to keep water out of a damaged ship. OMIA was a frequent customer of theirs, so it would be easy to customise a part for the World Discoverer. All they had to do was send over the 3D scan of the ship's damaged hull and let the engineering department over at Miko Marine handle the rest.

'I believe BEWA and Breland will be delighted to hear that,' remarked Admiral Anderson.

'I like the sound of that as well. Johnson and Bakke, please send the data over to Miko Marine. I'll personally contact their CEO and handle the logistics once we conclude this meeting. Hopefully, we can have a tarpaulin delivered to us promptly,' said Santini.

'I'll make some calls as well to get hold of some tug boats for moving the ship. They'll also transport the water pumps we need for this operation; that way, we can hit two birds with one stone,' said Admiral Henderson, jotting down the names of the contacts.

'Excellent, Admiral! We appreciate your help,' said Santini, giving him a firm handshake. 'Now, moving on to the most shocking revelation from Nick's dive: our dead crew member.'

'Sorry for interrupting, but what's your plan with him?' Helen asked.

'I'll let Nick answer that for you.'

'We plan to retrieve him with Jason and have our onboard doctor do a post-mortem examination to determine the time and cause of death.'

Helen nodded, satisfied with Nick's answer. 'I assume we're dealing with the dead body ourselves and leaving the RSIPF out of it?'

'If the admiral agrees, I think that's the best way to deal with the situation for now. To be honest, the RSIPF does not inspire confidence for this operation, except for John Ramo, the police officer who got in touch with us.'

'I share the same sentiment. We'll handle it and discreetly inform those who need to know about it. We'll keep it low-key, raising no suspicions from the RSIPF. It's clear by now that they want us out of here as soon as we're done with our operation.'

'Alright, I believe we have discussed everything that needs immediate attention. I suggest we all get going with our tasks and let our divers do their final checkups before their night dive,' Santini proposed.

Everyone stood up, stretched their bodies and went along to fulfil their duties on the ship. Nick waited for the others to leave before approaching Santini, who was working on his laptop.

'Boss, you got a minute to spare?' Nick asked in a hushed tone, almost whispering.

'Sure, Nick. What's with the sudden secrecy?'

'Why didn't you tell them anything about our Chinese intruder on the ship?'

'Listen, I want to wait for the doctor to come up with the crew member's cause of death. If it's a case of regular drowning, then we don't have solid grounds to go after that passenger.'

'Yes, we do. We have Officer Ramo's written statement from a fellow passenger and the passenger list. Mind you, on the list, there were no Chinese crew members.'

'I know, but they've probably booked him with a fake name and ID card. Looking up every passenger by name will be time-consuming. Don't forget what our main aim is down here.'

Nick sighed as he adjusted his perspective. 'You're right, Boss. We have to find the cause of the accident and, if possible, salvage the ship.'

'Bingo, That's what we do in OMIA, and that's why they pay us the big bucks,' said Santini, making the money gesture with his fingers.

'Boss, thanks again. I need to go down and get changed. See ya later, ciao!'

Nick went back inside the ship to change into his drysuit. He was ready to enjoy the absolute silence of the underwater world once again, his favourite part of the mission. They had made decent progress on their first day, and he felt proud of how their team was working together. If they could salvage the ship, it would be the icing on the cake.

He imagined the aftereffects of such an achievement and visualised the media's reaction if pulled off on such short notice. Not only would the company benefit from all the positive exposure but it would also show their competitors that OMIA was the premier marine investigation company in the world. Rousseau would definitely be proud of them and reward them accordingly when they returned to Oslo.

But as his thoughts focused on the monetary bonuses and potential media frenzy back in Oslo, he reminded himself of his father's wise words to eradicate these thoughts: 'When things go well, son, do not rest on your laurels. That is when you have to be the most alert. Everything can turn in an instant, but being ready for anything helps us to avoid being overwhelmed and to enjoy peace of mind.'

His father, Giorgos, was a sharp-witted and loud-mouthed businessman from Piraeus, the port city of Athens, who made a name for himself as a shipbroker in Geneva. He could offer the best advice without being patronising. As a man with a fiery personality and a matching short temper, he could control a room as soon as he set foot in it.

Without his parents' guidance and bilingual background, Nick was sure that he would've never ended up being a marine investigator. He always liked to joke about that when the three of them hung out. Although Nick knew his parents and their small social circle would always be proud of him, he knew this case was a big one, and he did not want to fail. He believed the Diamantis family name could not be associated with failure after all of their impressive accomplishments in life.

As he reflected on this last thought, he felt a tightening in his chest from the pressure. To counter that, he put on his airpods and played some upbeat hip-hop music to relax and release dopamine to his brain. When he felt ready, he stood up and began heading towards the bathroom to change when an alarm sounded through the ship's speakers.

'Attention, all OMIA personnel, please assemble by the RIB ASAP. I repeat, please assemble by the RIB.'

It was Captain Spencer Clark's raspy voice relaying the message from the bridge. Nick grabbed his drysuit and rushed out to the deck and towards their RIB. Jason was already there, standing in his drysuit. Santini burst through the door and joined them.

'Where are Johnson and Bakke, Boss?' Jason asked.

'They won't be joining us. I only need the two of you.'

'What's the matter?' Nick asked.

'A nearby vessel issued a Mayday call, two nautical miles northeast of our position. We need to take the RIB and get to them ASAP. They fear the ship may go down soon.'

Realising the gravity of the situation, both Nick and Jason rushed aboard the RIB and helped Santini with lowering it into the sea.

'Hold on to your hats, boys. It's gonna get bumpy,' Santini cautioned as he powered up the RIB to full throttle.

18

Santini pushed the RIB to its absolute limits on a northwestern course out of Roderick Bay. The digital speedometer was displaying speeds of up to seventy knots. The man was locked in and focused, constantly shifting his gaze between the GPS display and the sea ahead.

When responding to such calls, time is of the essence and can determine whether the victims make it out alive or meet a tragic fate. An unwritten law dictated that they must help any vessel issuing a mayday call.

Nick barely had time to change into his drysuit while they were lowering the RIB into the sea. They were moving at such high speeds now that attempting to speak to Jason or Santini was pointless because of the noise from the wind.

The sun had completely set by now, leaving the moon and stars as their sole sources of light. It was a cloudless night with the moon shining like a silvery claw in the night sky. Nick looked up at the blanket of stars that stretched to infinity and beyond, the same stars the Spanish explorer Álvaro de Mendaña y Neira had used in 1568 to navigate his flagship Los Reyes when he discovered the Solomon Islands. Nick wondered about the thoughts and emotions that had been going through his mind. He was just a man on a mission, unknowingly on the brink of such an important discovery. In moments like this, the universe reminded him of how small he was. Humans are not as indispensable as our egos make us out to be.

On the horizon, Nick could discern faint lights from a ship. As they drew closer, the ship's lights got bigger and brighter. Nick could now make out its shape in the dark, and he realised it was a really old and banged-up fishing trawler. Santini eased off the throttle, making it possible to speak again, and switched on a strobe light. Jason directed the light along the hull of the vessel.

'You sure that's our ship?' Nick asked, confused. 'I thought they were sinking.'

'That's our ship based on the coordinates we got. The Bonheur, a Liberian-flagged fishing trawler,' Santini replied, scratching his head. 'And yes, you're right; it's not sinking.'

The ship had seen better days. A layer of rust enveloped the ship's superstructure and hull, and the paint coating could be peeled off if someone were to scratch it. Santini circled the ship to check for any signs of life aboard. As they circled the stern, Nick spotted the waving Liberian flag and the text underneath it: BONHEUR, MONROVIA.

Yet another ship registered under a so-called flag of convenience, Nick thought as he perused the ship. It was a regular practice among shipowners to cut down on labour expenses, registration costs and taxes, by choosing to register their vessels in countries with more lenient restrictive regulations. This method was so popular that in 1969, Liberia momentarily surpassed the United Kingdom as the world's largest shipping registry.

However, the eerie silence from the Bonheur put Nick on edge. He felt like they were watching a ghost ship.

'Jason, pass me the ladder. I'll look around the ship to see what's up,' said Nick.

'Here you go, partner. But are you sure that's a good idea?'

'Jason's right. This doesn't feel right. I know it's kind of cliché, but it's too quiet out here,' Santini cautioned, looking worried.

He had a valid point but Nick's curiosity always got the best of him.

'Don't worry about me, guys. Keep the engine running, and I'll return as soon as possible. The ship looks to be about thirty to thirty-two metres long. It shouldn't take long to investigate it.'

He picked up the ladder, which had a grappling hook attached to it, aimed just above the railing of the ship and fired. The hook secured itself to the railing, allowing for the ladder to hang right above the waterline.

'Bring her closer, Boss,' said Nick, placing his right foot on the RIB's gunwale, preparing to grab the ladder. When the RIB was parallel to the ladder, Nick grabbed it and jumped towards the Bonheur. He quickly climbed up the ladder and pushed himself over the railing.

His first stop was the bridge, where he hoped to find signs of the crew. The deck was messy, with fishing nets strewn around. The whole place reeked of fish, fuel oil and salt. It was almost impossible to keep a straight face when the overwhelming smell hit him. A few metres down the deck, Nick reached a staircase on the port side of the ship. He set off at a fast pace up the stairs, stopping himself when he reached the entrance to the bridge.

He tried to listen for any sounds before slowly grabbing the door handle. The door squeaked open, revealing the old and crummy interior of the bridge. The lights were turned off, and the room was empty, so he pulled out his flashlight and turned it on. Nick rummaged through some papers and various folders that were strewn around the room. Nothing of importance showed up, so Nick explored the rest of the ship.

The crew's cabins looked empty, with no signs of occupancy. The bunk beds were the only furniture in the cabins, and even those were missing mattresses. Further back, in the crew mess, Nick looked for any clues that the crew had left behind.

On the table, he found some banana peelings, watermelon rinds and an ashtray filled with cigarette butts. The leftover fruit appeared to have been eaten recently since no flies had gathered around them. Someone had clearly been aboard this ship, and Nick wondered where they were hiding now. After Nick had completely fine-combed the crew area down to the last square metre, he followed the narrow corridors down to the storage room to check if the trawler was carrying any fish.

Much to his surprise, the storage room was empty. What kind of fishing trawler carried no fish? What a strange ship, Nick thought and moved over to the last unexplored area above the Bonheur – the engine room.

Guided by his flashlight, he tried to look for anything that could give him an idea of what was going on on this ship. Suddenly, he froze when he heard a faint beeping sound coming from the depths of the engine room.

With each step, he tried to be as quiet as possible to zero in on the sound. As Nick slithered his way through the room, like a cheetah hunting in the savanna, he felt the sound grow slightly stronger. It did not take him long to find the origin of the noise.

He was staring into a plastic explosive C4 charge mounted on one fuel barrel with gorilla tape. A small burner phone, rigged with coloured cables, had a timer set on its small screen. Nick squinted and figured out he had forty seconds to abandon the ship.

His pulse quickened as he swiftly retraced his steps back to the deck. He sprinted in the dark, trying not to trip himself over any hidden objects. The wooden door leading to the deck burst into pieces as he kicked himself out and continued with his sprint towards the portside railing.

'She's about to blow up, guys. Move away from her as fast as you can,' Nick yelled at the top of his lungs.

Both Jason and Santini looked at each other in shock and instinctively reacted to Nick's order. Nick took a few steps back to gain some momentum before his leap of faith. He timed his steps and launched himself into a swan dive over the ship's railing. The moment he was airborne, he heard the thundering roar of the explosive charge detonating. Shock waves from the explosion shook his body and eardrums before he landed in the sea. He persevered and kicked himself upwards to the surface. Then, Nick began swimming away from the ship as fast as he could to avoid being dragged down by its wake.

Santini shouted to Nick and ordered Jason to pull him out of the water. When he was finally onboard the RIB, Nick was furious. Everybody in OMIA knew that if Nick was cursing in Greek, it was best to let him blow off some steam before engaging in any form of communication. Nick tried to catch his breath as he looked back at the Bonheur, now fully ablaze and sinking. The trawler's stern dipped below the surface as its machinery tore free at sharp angles, making loud, ominous noises as it sank.

'Someone out there is trying to get us killed. They don't know they're messing with the wrong guy,' Nick growled through clenched teeth.

19

BAKKE, JOHNSON, THE Admiral, Helen and the rest of the crew were preparing the deck to welcome the survivors of the Bonheur. They had gathered some towels, clothes and medical equipment, just in case anyone had sustained injuries while escaping the sinking ship. Now, they anxiously awaited the arrival of Santini and the guys with the RIB. Almost an hour had passed since they had left the RV Solander.

'They should arrive any minute now; they can't be that far away,' Bakke said to Johnson as they stood by the railing, overlooking the sea.

'Hmm...I can't just sit here and overthink. I'll go inside to check.'

Johnson went inside for a moment to check on the GPS signal from the RIB. He pulled up the round reading glasses hanging from his neck and looked at the monitor. The green blip representing the RIB on the map was steadily approaching the RV Solander.

'Give them three minutes tops, and they should be here. Let's go down and help them with the rescued crew members,' said Johnson, pointing towards the aft part of the deck.

'For sure, I'm right behind you,' said Bakke, finishing the last sip of black filter coffee in his paper cup. It was his third cup of the day, his go-to placebo to endure the upcoming night dive.

When the RIB was within range of the RV Solander's deck lights, everyone was surprised to see only the three of them. They secured the RIB and raised it up to the deck.

'What happened? Didn't you find the ship, or did nobody make it out alive?' Johnson asked.

'The ship was a trap. Someone had booby-trapped it. Nick barely made it out. He got out just in the nick of time before it blew up into smithereens,' Santini explained as he climbed out of the RIB.

'They were more than one person; I'm a hundred percent sure of it.

I found some traces of cigarettes and food inside the crew mess of the ship. It had to be planned.'

'Johnson, will you please look up the Bonheur and see what comes up in our system?'

'Yes, sir, consider it done.'

Nick and Jason joined the crew inside the op centre to access the database. Johnson was clicking and typing rapidly as if his life depended on it.

'Aha, there she is – the Bonheur, a Liberian-registered vessel.'

'Can you find the owners of this ship?' Nick asked.

'Of course.' Johnson scrolled through the page, clicked on a document and waited for the page to load, nervously clicking his pen as he waited. 'Bingo, let's see. It's owned by a company called Shellshock LLC and has a registered address in Waterloo, Belgium.'

'You can't be serious now. Does it really say that?'

'I'm not joking; look for yourself.'

Nick leaned over, resting his hands against the desk to get a better look at Johnson's monitor. It was indeed the correct information. 'Man, they're playing games with us. Please tell me I'm not the only one seeing this right now.'

'Seeing what, Nick? Please elaborate,' said Santini.

'In Waterloo, Napoleon's imperial power was crushed forever. That's what their plans are for our investigation. And 'shell shock' is a type of PTSD you experience if you have faced heavy bombardment. I'm telling you, whoever is behind this is rubbing it in our faces right now.'

'It could also be a pun for the term 'shell company,' remarked Jason, but he was immediately stared down by everyone in the room. 'Hey, guys, it was just a thought. Don't sue me.'

'Alright, let's not lose ourselves in frivolous mind games,' Santini said, taking command of the situation. 'I'll get the Australians to do some digging for us. Meanwhile, you two should focus on our night dive. I promise you that whoever is behind this will get what's coming for them. Capiche?'

Everyone in the room agreed and tried to move past this shocking turn of events. Clearly, it was in the back of their minds, but as professionals, they had to push on with the operation.

'You heard the boss, people. Let's get busy. We start our dive in forty minutes,' said Bakke, addressing the whole crew.

Nick still couldn't fathom the fact that somebody out there had intentionally planned to sabotage all of their work. They did not have any qualms about killing people in the process either. And the silly mind games with the ship's registry were something only an educated person with a dark sense of humour could come up with.

'Hey, snap out of it. I don't want your mind to be anywhere else but on the World Discoverer. You hear me?' said Jason.

'Damn, kid, will the real Jason please stand up? This is not the field partner I know, but I really like this new Jason. I won't lie,' Nick said with a chuckle.

'It's just that we need to dive together in closed spaces within a cruise ship that might slide to the side without warning and block our exit route. Ah, and let's not forget that a bunch of lunatics are out there and getting a kick out of blowing up derelict ships.'

Nick laughed, but Jason was right. He had to snap out of it and get in the zone again, more focused and motivated than ever before. There was no point in wasting his energy on things that were out of his control.

'All right, partner. Ready to do it?'

'Hell yeah! Don't forget, I'm the Dumas to your Cousteau. Let's do this.'

20

When Nick's squale indicated it was midnight, both he and Jason leapt from the RIB and plunged into the pitch-black water. The conditions had completely changed since their first dive earlier that day. The underwater colours looked far brighter at night when illuminated by their flashlights. Sea creatures that typically spent their daytime hiding and sleeping inside reefs would also show up, prowling the ocean.

What Nick liked the most about nighttime was that his senses felt more acute, and he consequently became more aware of his surroundings. Since he could only see whatever the beam of his flashlight allowed him to, he was able to better appreciate what surrounded him. Night dives excited and relaxed him at the same time. By night, shipwrecks turned eerie and rock walls that seemed lifeless during the day awoke with different hidden species. Also, the chances of crossing paths with an opportunistic scavenger were heightened, making him more on edge than earlier in the day.

The plan Nick and Jason had devised with Santini was simple. Their first objective was to dive with an underwater body recovery bag and place it outside the gash of the ship. They would then head straight to Luke Manik's cabin and remove him from the ship. On the way out, Nick would take a quick detour through the engine room to remove the mysterious device, while Jason continued towards the ship's opening. They would then regroup outside the ship and move towards the surface together.

What should have been a routine dive was now clouded by the added uncertainty of the fake distress signal and explosion at the Bonheur. Nick and Jason tried to downplay these worries in their minds during the dive. One thing was for certain, though: the rest of the supporting crew around them would have a nail-biting experience throughout the tropical night ahead.

Nick pointed his body downwards and propelled himself deeper into the sea. Jason followed closely behind, the body bag slowing him down slightly. Visibility was good and unhampered by sediment particles. It seemed that some much-needed luck was back to boost their morale, which had abandoned them during the evening.

When they finally reached the opening, Jason securely positioned the bag. He pulled on the line to double-check that it was tightly locked in position. Nick grabbed his laser cutter and cut off the sharp edges of the ship's gash to make the opening bigger and remove potential spots where they might damage their diving equipment.

In a couple of minutes, he was done and placed the cutter inside his pouch. After supervising the results of his work, he signalled Jason to move inwards. Since Nick knew the way to the cabin, Jason followed his lead inside the underwater maze of the World Discoverer. They slowly and meticulously navigated their way through the corridors of the ship until they reached the stairs leading to Deck 1, where the cabin was located. Swimming inside the ship at night sent chills down their spines.

Thankfully, they would not spot a dead passenger around every corner like in other shipwrecks. One particular incident would forever be etched in Nick's mind. Back in his days as a diving instructor in Zakynthos, he had assisted in the removal of dead bodies from a shipwrecked vessel full of migrants. The captain had issued a distress call forty nautical miles southwest of Zakynthos after the ship lost power. It was around midnight, and by the time Nick, some local fishermen and the Greek coastguard had scurried to the scene, the yacht had already disappeared beneath the dark waves of the Ionian Sea. One hundred and seventeen. That was the final number of bodies Nick and the coastguard managed to pull out from the mangled vessel. All of them blankly stared back at him, their eyes open as if they were just lying awake at the bottom of the sea, still waiting for the captain to take them to their promised destination.

Nick shook off the haunting visions and thoughts of this harrowing experience and turned around to see if Jason was keeping up with him. Nick gestured towards the stairs, did a 180-degree turn and continued up to the crew's living quarters.

When both of them reached cabin 103, Nick ordered Jason to wait outside. The cabin was too cramped for two people with diving equipment on their backs, especially if they intended to move a dead body out of the room. However, when Nick pulled the door open, he froze. The cabin was empty. He had purposely closed the door during the first dive to protect the dead body from predators. Suddenly, he realised that somebody must have used the explosion on the Bonheur to dive undetected and remove vital evidence from the wreck.

The first suspect that crossed Nick's mind was the RSIPF. Nick believed that if the RSIPF had been involved, they would have left the engine room untouched since they only had intel about the dead crew member and were unaware of a malpositioned device there.

Jason was really confused and could not believe his eyes when he looked inside the cabin. All he could do was shake his head in disbelief. Nick took the lead again and began swimming towards the engine room with Jason right behind him.

Inside the room, Nick quickly swam to the spot behind one of the engines. This was the last straw for him; his annoyance was slowly turning into anger. All he could see was a scorched area on the wall where the device should have been. The same people who had removed the body had also taken away the device that was attached there.

Once again, his suspicions about the RSIPF had to be thrown out of the window. They were up against people who knew way more than what Officer Ramo had revealed to them. However, at this moment, his mind was clouded by anger and exhaustion. They had to resurface and talk it over with Santini. It had been a really long day, and it was taking a toll on his body.

He signalled to a discouraged Jason that they needed to abort the mission and resurface. After making it safely out of the ship, they had a quick decompression stop on their way up. They were just floating in the dark, gazing into the nothingness, both of them looking heavy-hearted behind their masks. All of their hard work had been undone, and there was nothing they could do about it at the moment. When their heads-up display vibrated, they continued swimming the last metres up to the surface.

Santini helped them up onto the RIB without a word. He had watched the entire sequence of events on his laptop, and he was also disturbed by the revelations from this second dive, so he preferred not to say a word. No one spoke as they made their way back to the RV Solander.

Suddenly, Nick heard a rumbling sound coming from under the water.

'Did any of you hear that?'

Santini switched off the engine so they could hear better, and the RIB stopped after a few metres.

'Yeah, it felt like the earth moved underwater,' Jason confirmed.

At that moment, water surged like a geyser from the starboard side of the World Discoverer, precisely at the point where it was connected with the underwater rock shelf.

Nick shouted in disbelief and frustration as he knew what would happen next. The World Discoverer immediately began listing to its starboard size until it was totally capsized and lying flat on its side.

'These bastards blew up parts of the rock shelf to submerge the ship. Boss, we're up against something really sinister and serious,' Nick seethed, his anger bubbling like a volcano ready to erupt.

Santini and Jason were frozen in place with their eyes widened as they tried to process what just happened in front of them. Nick continued talking until one of them replied.

'Nick, we're just as upset as you are. Can't you see? We just don't resort to cursing and screaming the minute things go sideways,' Santini said to calm him down. 'Listen, I know both of you feel like shit right now, but here's what we're gonna do. I'll check up on Agent Chapman and see if she found anything from the shell company connected to Bonheur. Then, I'll call Breland himself to inquire about any potential threats he may have received recently or if he knows of any business adversaries who are out to get him.'

Calmness prevailed again on the RIB, and everybody agreed it was the best way to handle things for now.

'I need you guys to lay low, eat something and try to get some sleep. In the morning, we'll turn over to a new page and see where all of this takes us.'

'Appreciate it, Boss. Let's return to the RV Solander.'

After thirty minutes had passed, Nick was lying in his bed and staring at the ceiling. He tossed a small stress relief ball into the air, like shooting free throws in basketball until he misfired it and it landed on the floor. He was totally drained, so he did not even try picking the ball up. He sighed and just continued to lie there. At the moment, nothing could make him feel better, but he was thankful their boss was pulling a long all-nighter to dig up any useful information. He turned to his left, switched off the bedside light and tried to fall asleep, hoping to wake up to some good news from Santini.

21

GUSTAV BRELAND, THE multimillionaire owner of BEWA Cruises, had just finished a late-night tour of his geothermal energy plant on Savo Island. The island itself was small, circular and thirty-five kilometres off the coast of Honiara. A stratovolcano with a height of four hundred and eighty-five metres was the highest point on the island. Most of the villages and settlements were situated along the coast. Dotted around the island were hot springs, geysers and hot mud lakes with healing properties. The coast encircling the island had played a major role during World War II, witnessing seven major naval battles during the Pacific War. As a result, the island attracts many recreational divers from all around the world who explore the many shipwrecks surrounding it.

This was the second plant Gustav owned with GEOrganic, the first one being in Iceland. Both islands had been specifically chosen because of their proximity to major tectonic plate boundaries, where geothermal energy could be located and harvested for human use. According to his chief scientist, the source of geothermal energy was practically unlimited, at least for the next seventeen billion years. Thus, this form of energy, which is essentially heat generated by the Earth's core, is completely renewable and an extremely lucrative business venture for him.

Gustav's role at his plants comprised converting this energy into electricity and storing it in zinc-manganese oxide batteries. These batteries were only engineered by him and his elite team of scientists and were much more cost-effective and had a higher energy density than any other battery on the market, thus storing more energy and lasting way longer than their competitor brands.

Zinc-manganese batteries also presented an environment-friendly alternative to storing renewable energy, with the ability to support an entire nation's power grid. Gustav had started testing in smaller countries like Iceland and the Solomon Islands to assess if the batteries could support the power grid of the two nations. After implementing this solution, both countries suddenly did not have any use for their conventional electricity plants reliant on coal or oil. The rest of the European countries soon caught on to this development and started using these batteries on their own power grids. Thus, more countries were knocking on his door, and GEOrganic's stock and revenue shot up to the stratosphere. Gustav estimated he could support the power grids of Europe and Oceania with these two power plants alone, which was his primary goal at the moment.

His ultimate ambition, however, was to expand further and set up power plants along the East African rift, in Chile and Indonesia. By doing so, he could provide energy for three more continents – Africa, South America and Asia. This would be a total game changer for a world that desperately needs to combat the climate crisis and replace its outdated ways of generating power.

Gustav's passion for environmental conservation had been planted by his father's confidante, Einar Iversen. From a young age, Gustav would join the two of them on cruise trips through the Norwegian Sea, exploring the magnificent natural beauty of the country with its enchanting fjords, huge snow-covered Alps and beautiful coastline stretching from south to north. As he grew older, he joined them to far-off destinations like the Galapagos, exposing him to more exotic locations.

In his teenage years, when he could better grasp the impact of humanity on the climate over the last two hundred years and the grim predictions for the future, he promised himself he would turn the world into a greener place for the coming generations and devote his life to the cause.

To pursue that dream, he moved to Switzerland to pursue a master's degree in sustainable management and technology at the University of Lausanne. He spent the next years hopping among countries and working for various big energy companies until he gathered the funds and network required to start GEOrganic. Nothing had been handed to him by his father, contrary to popular belief. They hadn't even shared a close connection, much to his disappointment. His father had been so caught up with running his shipping company that he always ended up sending Iversen to watch over him. It was no wonder all his family members gradually estranged themselves from his father. Perhaps his father's burdens were too heavy for his heart to carry, which may be why he passed away from heart complications two years ago. After all, nobody wants to be seventy and alone. Sadly, Gustav didn't even feel like he had lost somebody close to him. Nevertheless, he felt responsible for carrying the family's legacy into the future, so he decided to continue running BEWA Cruises as a family-owned company.

Gustav split his time between his three private villas in Oslo, Reykjavik and Savo Island, living the life of the most hardworking and sought-after bachelor in Norway. Forbes had estimated his net worth at ninety billion dollars the previous year, adding more incentive to any potential female suitor.

His villa on Savo Island was in a secluded bay with his own private beach and dock where he anchored his sailing yacht, Spirit 111 by Spirit Yachts. The villa was inspired by the British colonial mansions in the Caribbean during the late 1650s. It had two floors and a huge balcony that overlooked the bay. The interior was sleek, modern and furnished with imported Boca Do Lobo furniture from Porto, Portugal.

Despite having a long day of helping the passengers in Honiara and handling the press from all over the world, Gustav had visited his office at the energy plant to oversee their day-to-day operations. After wrapping up some late meetings with people back in Europe, he returned to his villa.

Fortunately, his personal assistant and quasi-father figure, Einar Iversen, had instructed the chef to have supper prepared for him when he returned home. Since it was midnight, the chef had prepared two avocado toasts and a smoothie with locally sourced fruits from the garden.

As he sat there in front of his empty plate and glass, he felt like taking a drink to ensure a good night's sleep. He went to his liquor cabinet, pulled out an old-fashioned glass and started mixing up a French Connection cocktail. Gustav combined Hennessy XO and Disaronno

Originale and stirred before adding a big ice cube to the glass. He then walked towards the balcony with his concoction in hand.

Gustav was wearing a black cashmere and silk blended robe by Loro Piana, his blonde hair still damp from his shower earlier that night. He sipped his drink slowly, taking his time to unwind and enjoy the flavours.

He turned around at the faint sound of footsteps and noticed Iversen holding his phone. While at home, he preferred to distance himself from work and passed on secretarial duties to Iversen. Only for important matters would Iversen ask Gustav to answer a call.

'Sorry to interrupt you, Gustav, but Mr Santini from OMIA is on the phone, and he desperately needs to talk to you.'

'It's probably something about the World Discoverer,' Gustav replied with a smile. 'No worries, I can take the call. Have a good night's sleep, and see you tomorrow.'

Iversen thanked him, passed the phone over to him and retreated to his room.

'Mr Santini, to what do I owe the pleasure of this late-night call? I hope you have some good news about my ship.'

'I'm afraid not at the moment, sir. Before we delve into that, though, I wanted to ask if you know of anyone who might want to sabotage your businesses. It could be a single person or a competitor in your industry. Either works for me.'

'In my line of work, there are many people and companies who want to see me fall. I have one of the most recognised brands at the moment, and every day, articles about me or my companies generate thousands of views.'

'I understand that, but has anyone attempted to spread bad press about any of your businesses, for example?'

'The only ones I can think of, off the top of my head, are the initial sceptics in the press who accused us of setting unattainable goals and greenwashing.'

'Many years have passed since then, so I wouldn't list them as potential suspects.'

'Suspects?'

'Suspects, yes. You see, someone has gone on a rampage since earlier this evening, trying to jeopardise our whole operation.'

'What do you mean by that, Mr Santini? Be more precise.'

'Let me start from the beginning. Initially, we were on track to finding the actual cause of your ship's sinking and had a realistic plan to salvage it. All that after just our first day working this case.'

'Then what went wrong along the way?'

'Then, someone lured us away with a false Mayday call, diverting us to a fishing trawler far from the World Discoverer. We thought it was a rescue mission to save passengers, but the trawler was rigged with explosives and had no one onboard. During the explosion, I nearly lost my lead investigator on the case.'

'That's horrible! Who would do something like that?'

'That's what I'm trying to figure out myself. Unfortunately, the bad news doesn't stop there.'

'Oh my God, what next?'

'Let's just say that those same people removed all our leads and evidence from inside the wreck while we were busy escaping from the exploding ship.'

'So you're essentially back at the drawing board?'

'Correct. However, these individuals went a step further by setting off explosives to dislodge parts of the underwater rock shelf that were preventing your ship from being submerged. Those explosions have caused the ship to capsize and lie flat on its starboard side in Roderick Bay, further complicating this salvage mission.'

The news completely shook Gustav, leaving him speechless.

'Mr Breland, are you still there?'

'Yes, I just needed a moment to grasp what happened. Does the ship have any hope left?'

'I'll let our investigators and engineers assess if it is doable and worth the extra money at this point.'

'Sure, I understand. Money is not the issue, by the way. I just won't have one of my ships polluting one of the finest underwater habitats in this part of the world.'

'I'm totally with you on that one. In the worst-case scenario, if the ship is deemed unsalvageable, we will have to dive and drain the engines of fuel oil.'

'So, what's next for your crew tomorrow? Any hope of finding the people behind this sabotage?'

'Right after our call, I have a meeting with an Australian agent from ASIS. I've requested them to look into some clues we have, so we're hoping to track down the perpetrators.'

'Good. I hope they will have good news for us.'

'Me too, Mr Breland. Thanks for your time, and hopefully, the next time we speak, I'll have some positive news for you.'

'I really appreciate you and your crew's efforts. Good luck for tomorrow; we'll be in touch soon.'

Santini ended the call and placed his phone on the table. He stood up and opened the door.

'Please, Agent Chapman, come in,' Santini said with a smile as he welcomed her into the op centre. 'Any news from your side?'

'I had contacted some key people from our agency's HQ in Canberra to look into our information. Sadly, though, they've found nothing that can help us at the moment. It's been a dead end.'

'Damn it, then it seems we're back to square one. Breland didn't have any leads either.'

'That's a shame.'

'Well, it is what it is. I think it's time for us to get some shuteye as well. We've been working on overdrive since we arrived at the shipwreck.'

'You're definitely right. It's a new day tomorrow. Good night, then.' Helen stood up and closed the door on her way out.

As she walked through the corridors, she tried to not make any noise, knowing that everyone else on the ship was asleep. She carefully closed her cabin door and changed into her pyjamas. While brushing her teeth, she thought about her previous interactions with Nick.

That man had something in his eye and a distinct energy that set him apart from all the other men she had previously met in her life. Helen was curious to uncover what was hiding beneath his hard exterior and learn more about him.

22

A SATELLITE PHONE strapped on a military backpack began buzz-ing in the dense tropical forest of Ngella Sule, one of four islands in the so-called Florida archipelago. Perched high above the bay, this vantage point offered a complete panoramic view of the World Discoverer and the surrounding area.

Lei Cheng, who had been busy scouting the shipwreck and the pair of OMIA divers, switched off the night vision mode of his Trionyx T3 multispectral binoculars and reached for his satellite phone.

'Come in, Cobra; this is Voodoo. Do you copy?'

'Copy that, Voodoo. Cobra here, reading you loud and clear,' Lei responded.

'Is it done?'

'The bombs went off as planned, and the ship has completely sunk.'

'Splendid. Did the dive crew remove the body and the remote con-trol device?'

'Affirmative. The ship's been stripped clean.'

'Good. Are we ready to move on to the last phase of our plan as dis-cussed earlier?'

'Roger. I'll have the malware ready ASAP. In a few minutes, while everyone is asleep, the malware will corrupt all the data they've gath-ered in the last twenty-four hours. I just have to bypass their firewall and upload the malware into their system. They won't know what hit them,' said Lei, working on the malware code as he was speaking.

'Excellent. I trust you will deal with this matter swiftly.'

'Of course, Voodoo. Working on it as we speak. By the way, did B Squad recover the payload?'

'Affirmative, Cobra. B Squad located the payload and is returning to our base with it.'

'Perfect.' Lei pressed the enter button on his laptop. 'The malware has been uploaded and is ready to hack into OMIA's system in about twenty seconds.'

'Can't wait for their reaction tomorrow when they find out that none of their video footage can be used as evidence. Our boss will be really pleased, Cobra.'

'Me too, Voodoo. Send him my regards the next time you two speak. Cobra over and out.'

'Will do, Cobra. Good luck with the exfiltration. Voodoo over and out.'

When the laptop notified that the malware had been successfully uploaded, Lei immediately switched it off and stowed it in his bag. He checked around to ensure he had not left any traces or rubbish behind him. Pleased with the removal of his makeshift camp, he began the three-kilometre trek down to the coast, where he had hidden his Zodiac.

If all went to plan, a six-digit amount would be wired to his money laundering bank account in the Cayman Islands tomorrow for a job well done. He had already arranged a luxury suite at the 55-storey tower of Marina Bay Sands in Singapore. The finest escorts in all of Asia were booked and would join him for a three-day debauchery fest in his suite. The tantalising mix of sex, drugs and alcohol was just what he needed to unwind after a long period of working on this assignment. He knew the pleasure would be short-lived, though, and a new assignment would be added to his schedule soon after.

23

NICK'S ALARM RUDELY woke him up at precisely 7:00 a.m. He never hesitated to switch off the alarm and promptly get out of bed. Snoozing was not an option for him since he always picked the most annoying alarm tone. Waking up was the best choice since no sane human would want to endure that horrendous sound twice.

The outfit for the day was always selected the previous night so that he would not have to exert his mind over insignificant choices in the morning. For him, the Latin phrase 'carpe diem', seize the day, was of great importance, and he lived by it.

When on investigations out in the open sea, he preferred to wake up one hour earlier than the scheduled start of the day. Nick enjoyed calibrating and stress-testing all of his tech devices before the rest of the crew woke up and went about their usual business.

He enjoyed having the first hour to himself, working with no interruptions and total silence. This allowed him to address any bugs or issues that might appear before the others started their work. It was a win-win situation for everyone: his fellow crew members benefited from it by getting a flying start to their day, while he could retreat to the op centre without having to worry about anything until some underwater activity began.

This morning was no different from any other. After changing into his freshly ironed clothes and ensuring his breath was fresh, Nick went to the crew mess for a quick bite. When breakfast was over, he made a beeline for the op centre. He switched on the lights in the room and began waking up the systems from their slumber. A password request was the only thing separating him from his computer's start screen. He typed without looking at the keyboard and was greeted by OMIA's home screen.

An idea that had planted itself in Nick's mind since the previous night came back. He wanted to go over the footage from the second dive and compare it with the first one. He hoped to spot anything out of the ordinary that may have been overlooked since their focus was targeted on the dead crew member and the strange device in the engine room. It's easy to hit a wall in an investigation when you can't see the forest for the trees.

If his plan failed, he would email a screen grab of the device and check if any of his old diving pals had ever seen a similar device. He navigated through the main menu and selected the date he wanted to watch the footage from. Much to his surprise, the file from the previous day was completely empty.

That can't be right, he thought, furrowing his eyebrows. The system had stored almost eight hours of underwater footage from the remote-controlled ROV and the diver's cameras. Nick tried to see if the system could access the files from other dates. Much to his relief, the videos from other dates were still accessible, which meant something recent had caused the footage to go missing.

Nick checked the system log for any activity from the IT department in their Oslo office while he was asleep. Nothing came up except for a notification about an error message at around three in the morning. Nick clicked on it to view the written report the system usually creates about the issue and the countermeasures it uses to recover from it. But this report contained only four words:

'Shellshock LLC was here.'

Utterly dumbfounded by the message, cold sweat trickled down from Nick's armpit. This message could only mean one thing. The same guys who had waged a crusade of sabotage against them had struck again. This time, they attacked the heart of their operation, removing any trace of work they had done up to that point.

But Nick could not give up without a fight, so he began typing and clicking away to see if there was anything he could do to recover the lost footage. Sadly, all his actions were met with the same pop-up message:

'Shellshock LLC was here.'

Then, he remembered the photos he had taken during the dives. Maybe they had escaped the hacker's clutches and were still online. Nick exited the program and searched for the photos in their database.

However, just like the videos, the photos from the last twenty-four hours were long gone. If the folder had a sound effect, he would be able to hear crickets at that moment.

Nick scratched his head and sank deep in his chair, a lump forming in his throat. Santini and Johnson would not be happy at all. But since there was no point in feeling sorry for himself, he picked up his phone to call Santini. It rang twice before Santini answered the phone.

'Boss, they've hit us again. Someone has hacked us.'

Santini took a moment to reply, still groggy from his sleep. 'They did what now?'

'They've deleted all our video footage from the last twenty-four hours. We're screwed, Boss.'

Nick heard a 'click' as if he had been put on speaker.

'Hold up,' said Santini, 'so you mean to tell me there's no way to fix it?' His voice came from a distance, so Nick assumed he was quickly getting dressed in the background.

'No, sir. I gave it my best, but nothing worked.'

Santini was quiet for a moment. Nick could imagine him pacing back and forth in the cabin.

'You know what? Let's rally up the rest of the crew. I am completely out of ideas and in need of coffee. I'll get Jason and Johnson. You get Bakke, and we'll all meet at the op centre.'

'Copy that. See you in a bit, Boss,' Nick said and hung up the phone.

It took them two minutes to knock on the cabin doors and get everyone out of bed. This rude awakening had everyone looking moody and irritable. Santini closed the op centre's door and served everyone a cup of coffee.

'Buongiorno signori,' Santini addressed the room, while the crew nodded in response. 'Our greatest nightmare, I'm afraid, has come true overnight.' Santini paused dramatically as he took a sip of his coffee. 'We have been victims of a cyberattack that has cost us all of our video footage and photos from both dives at the wreck. This means that we don't have any proof to back our findings from yesterday. Now, we're faced with two choices: we either come up with a great idea to continue our search for clues or throw in the towel and brand this operation as a missed opportunity.'

Suddenly, the room was filled with murmurs as the OMIA crew discussed the two choices they had. Santini took a step back and tried to listen to their conversations. Several interesting ideas were proposed, but no one could pinpoint one that could reinvigorate this investigation.

Nick, swivelling in his rotating chair, was playing nervously with a pen. His mind was working twice as fast as normal, hoping to come up with a breakthrough. When his coffee cup was one sip away from being empty, something sprang into his mind. Amidst all the chaos, he had forgotten about the observation he had made during the first dive – the sharp metal edges of the gash, pointing inwards to the ship. Maybe they could dive around the area where the ship had first contacted the reef. If the ship had contacted anything other than a reef, there would surely be some debris on the seafloor. The idea sounded too simple to be taken seriously, but he needed to muster the courage to just say what he had to.

'Guys, I think I've got it. Hear me out,' said Nick, and the room went quiet. 'You remember what I said about the gash being on the same level as the ship's waterline?'

Santini's eyes lit up, and he stared googly-eyed at Nick.

'Yeah, I remember it now. You mentioned it to me right after the first dive, when you boarded the RIB. How did I forget that?'

'Boss, I can't fault you. So much has transpired since... it's crazy. No wonder our minds are playing tricks on us.'

'You're right, but go on; I don't want to interrupt you.'

'So, here are my thoughts, guys. I suggest we investigate the area where the ship made contact with the supposed reef. If the ship actually hit a reef, we'll have to toss out my idea as well. But if it contacted something else, we should be able to find debris around that area.'

'What are you suggesting? We need more information to go on,' Johnson interjected.

'Here's what needs to be done. We need to gather the GPS data from the Automatic Identification System transponder to pinpoint when and where they hit the reef. Next, we set up a search area around those coordinates and use our submersible to sweep the seafloor. If we pick up on any irregularities from the readings, we should dive immediately. Worst-case scenario, Jason and I can take the Viperfish II for a spin in the search area.'

'Alright, we don't need to discuss this one any further, I think. What do you think, boys? Let's keep it democratic in here,' Santini said.

Jason looked at his silent colleagues and addressed the room.

'I think we should go with Nick's idea. It will keep our wheels moving for the next couple of days, buying us valuable time. Hopefully, we can get closer to solving the case than we were yesterday.'

'I totally agree with you. Let's try it,' said Santini before switching his focus to Bakke and Johnson. 'Has BEWA sent us the AIS transponder data?'

'I think it's in the files we received on our first day here in the Solomon Islands. Let me double-check, Boss.' Johnson quickly searched through the system. Yup, I've got them here.'

'Excellent. Could you pinpoint the coordinates of the crash and help us set up a search area for our submersible?'

'Just give me a second... Aha, here they are.' Johnson pressed a button and projected the map on the big screen inside the op centre. 'Here are the coordinates as well.'

Looking satisfied, Santini pulled out his sat phone and called up Captain Clark. 'Change of plans, Captain, I want you to set a course for the coordinates I've just transmitted to you.'

'Aye, Santini. I'm cross-checking it now,' responded Captain Clark, like a true pirate captain.

Soon, the RV Solander was pushing ahead in full steam towards the World Discoverer's crash site.

24

THE AREA NICK and Jason needed to explore with the Viperfish II was between the Hanipana and Kipua points in the Sandfly Passage. It was a stretch of water where lots of locals liked to fish because the currents brought in a lot of different fish every day. The coral reef, called Mid Reef, was brimming with marine life and was split into two separate sections, creating an underwater canyon. Smaller cruise ships, like the World Discoverer, and local ferries used this passage to ferry passengers and transport goods to the various islands in the Solomon archipelago.

For the second day in a row, the weather was absolutely spectacular, with the sea glistening like Cartier diamonds under the bright sun. Nick was on the top deck, looking out over the sea. He was trying to get as much fresh air as possible until it was time for him to lock himself inside their manned submersible and dive into the dimly lit waters of the Sandfly Passage.

Captain Clark had steered the ship within range of the search area marked by OMIA. At the moment, Bakke and Johnson were working on monitoring the LiDAR scans coming from their airborne UAV drone. They tasked Jason with piloting the drone from the bow of the ship. It was a tedious, time-consuming task but was a necessary step in the investigation.

Bakke had mounted a Leica HawkEye 4X deep bathymetric LiDAR sensor on a custom-built UAV drone, allowing them to generate an accurate picture of the sea floor by combining 3D and laser scanning. Research ships like the RV Solander used this method for environmental monitoring and habitat mapping. OMIA used it to create an underwater map for their divers to use as a reference when diving with their manned submersibles or remote-controlled ROVs. Objects of interest could also be added to the map, as the LiDAR sensor could showcase things that OMIA eagerly sought, especially debris and shipwrecks.

After an hour of flying, Jason safely landed the UAV drone a few metres beside him. Nick applauded his partner for the clean landing.

'How does it look on your end? Did we cover everything?' Jason asked the guys in the op centre through his bluetooth earpiece.

Bakke and Johnson were waiting for the software to process the collected data. When the message indicated they had decent scanning results, they turned on their microphones.

'Seems like it, Jason. We'll double-check to see if anything stands out,' Bakke replied.

'Alright, shall we prepare the Viperfish II while you wait?'

'Yes, you two can start prepping it for the dive. We can start the dive in about ten minutes.'

'Perfect. Any area in particular you'd like us to focus on?'

'Just start at the spot Nick mentioned earlier. Focus on the two reefs and the underwater canyon, especially around the shallowest parts that are closer to the surface.'

'Roger that. I'll get Nick to join me so that we can board the Viperfish II.'

Jason switched off the transmission and removed his earpiece. He then raised his right hand to signal Nick.

'Ay, Nick! Join me back at the stern. We've been cleared to go.'

Nick nodded and began walking towards the stern, where the Viperfish II awaited them. Three crew members helped them enter it and wished them luck as they closed the hatch behind them.

Nick strapped himself to the seatbelt and turned on the overhead touch screen inside the cabin. He booted up the submersible and began meticulously going through the checklist, one point at a time, with Jason confirming each point.

'The telemetry looks swell. We're good to go,' said Nick, switching on the onboard communication with the op centre.

'Mic check one, two, one, two. Do you guys hear us loud and clear?'

'You sound crystal clear, Nick. The boss has joined us as well and will follow your dive alongside us.'

'Good luck, and stay safe,' Santini said on Bakke's mic.

'Thanks, Boss. Alright then, time to lower us into the sea.' Nick gestured downwards to the ship's crew members.

One of them replied affirmatively and began steering the crane. He positioned the Viperfish II to safely hang above the open sea. Then, he pushed another button that began lowering it. As soon as it touched the surface, he pulled a lever to free the submersible from the clutches of the crane. The submersible gracefully splashed in the sea.

'Ok, let's begin our descent, Nick.'

'Sure. I'll take us a couple of metres underwater first and steer us towards the reef closest to us.'

'Sounds like a plan.'

Nick took control of the submersible and began its descent into the sea. Suddenly, the submersible was completely submerged, and they had an unobstructed view of the underwater world through their fully acrylic pressure hull in the front. Unlike other submersibles, their view was not obstructed by ballast tanks, batteries or other components. They truly felt like they were one with the sea inside the Viperfish II.

'The first reef should be dead ahead of us.'

Nick acknowledged Jason's message and began speeding up the Viperfish towards the reef using the MANTA controller in front of him. The Viperfish had a maximum speed of three knots, and Nick maintained a steady pace.

Their search area was forty metres at its deepest and a mere 8.8 metres at its shallowest. With the depth fluctuating at so many points, the passage could be tricky for ships if they were not careful.

'I'm going for the shallowest part of the first reef, which is listed at a depth of almost nine metres. Wasn't the depth of the World Discoverer 8.7 meters?'

'Yes, Nick. It was 8.8 metres, to be exact. If it made contact with a reef, it should have happened around that area. It could not be anywhere else,' said Jason as he was going over the sea floor scan from their UAV drone on his device.

'We're just a hundred metres away from it right now. Shouldn't take long to reach the spot.'

The submersible gracefully made its way underwater like a manta ray. Visibility was still good but a little murkier than the previous day. They were in much deeper waters now than in Roderick Bay, and the currents were stronger, contributing to the reduced visibility.

'There it is, my friend, look,' said Nick, pointing forward.

They were approaching the reef, which was in clear view now. It protruded from the bottom with a steep incline. Nick adjusted the position of the submersible to levitate a few metres over the top part of the reef. Small fish were going about their everyday lives on the colourful reef, swimming around and inside it.

'You see those parts slightly protruding from the reef?' Nick asked.

'Yes, I do. They look so sharp, damn. Oh shit, look at this one! It must be about five metres above the rest of the reef.'

'It looks capable of delivering a fatal blow to a ship, don't you think?' Nick asked as he circled around it with the Viperfish II.

'Oh yeah, for sure. I mean, theoretically, it could slice a hull open.'

'Even a reinforced one?'

'Hmm...that, I highly doubt. Only if they were moving at full speed and made contact head-on.'

'I agree. Write down the coordinates of our current position, just in case.'

Jason referred to the monitor and began scribbling on his notepad.

'Let's look around for any debris or parts of the hull.'

Nick engaged the MANTA controller and manoeuvred around the reef, looking for anything that could have dislodged from the World Discoverer. After thirty minutes, it felt like looking for a needle in a haystack, and their motivation dwindled.

'I feel we've looked everywhere we could. Let's try the second reef on the opposite side,' said Nick, pointing to the monitor showing the map.

The second reef was located exactly on the other side of the first one but was much longer and covered a bigger area. Nick turned the Viperfish ninety degrees to the right and moved full throttle towards the second reef. Between the two reefs was a narrow passage with a depth of twenty metres. All they could see down this underwater canyon was a blurry and dark mess.

When they crossed this gap, they were once again floating over the top part of the second reef. This reef, however, seemed to plateau at around eight metres from the surface, with no visible sharp edges sticking out. Nick began moving around to explore every part of the reef. Since it covered a larger area, they took almost double the time they had spent on the first one.

'I don't think it's this one, Nick. There's nothing here that could damage the World Discoverer. Plus, there's not a single item here that we can trace back to the ship.'

'I partially agree with you, Jason. But I want us to descend to the passage between the two reefs. There's a chance something may have fallen down there.'

'That's a possibility because the currents are more lively here. Bring her down.'

Nick rotated the Viperfish and steered towards the passage.

'Shall we start from one end and finish on the other instead of going straight down?' Nick asked once they were levitating over the passage.

'Yeah, doing one sweep like that will be much more effective.'

'Copy. Let's position ourselves over the end that's closer to us.'

After ensuring they were positioned correctly, Nick began to lower the submersible. When they were just above the sea floor, he increased the intensity of the lights and moved at a slow pace, allowing them to look around for any clues. They continued like that for ten minutes until something caught Nick's attention. He increased the speed slightly to get a better look at what was taking shape in the darkness ahead. When he knew what it was, he brought the Viperfish to a complete stop.

'Sweet mother of Jesus. Are you seeing what I'm seeing now?' Nick exclaimed, stunned at the sight.

'No, no, no, you've got to be joking!' Jason replied, his hands on his head in disbelief.

They both turned to each other, wearing expressions of astonishment, wondering what the hell they had just discovered.

25

NICK ENGAGED THE MANTA controller and slowly approached the object that had caught their attention. Jason tinkered with the lights to understand what they were seeing. Right in front of them was a badly damaged submarine lying in an upright position on the seafloor. It was sausage-shaped and not more than twelve metres long. Its nose was completely broken and was lying four metres away from the rest of the submarine. The hull was also badly damaged and had almost broken in half at its midsection. Two hydroplanes were sticking out of either side of the back section like the wings of a firefly. The other two from the nose section in the front had detached themselves from the hull and lay partially submerged in silt.

'It looks like a submarine and then kinda not like one. I know it makes little sense, but do you feel me, Nick?'

'I completely understand you. Judging by its construction, this looks like a Fully Submersible Vessel, similar to the ones South American cartels use, to be honest. I'll take us over its watertight hatch to see if it's square or round shaped.'

'What's the difference between the two?'

'If you want to fully submerge a narco sub like this, you need a good hatch, preferably a round one that offers more security. Cheaper semi-submersibles mostly use square ones.'

'So, what we have here is a narco-sub?'

'It sure looks like one,' said Nick, pointing down to the sub's hatch. 'Look, it has a round hatch, so it's an FSV for sure.'

'But what's it doing down here?' Jason asked.

'It could be an older sub that failed to make it to the drop-off point. Don't forget that the Solomon Islands is a transit point for cocaine and methamphetamine going to Australia and New Zealand.'

'They must have failed to navigate the Sandfly Passage and just sank straight down this underwater canyon. They surely sustained some heavy damage on the way down.'

'I know, but look at how the nose section has been ripped off. Heavy force would be required to do such damage; those don't break off like that. Remember, these narco subs have a maximum speed of six knots.'

'Hmm, you're right,' said Jason, still a little sceptical.

'I know this sounds crazy, but hear me out.' Nick locked the submersible in its position after activating the auto-heading function. 'What if this sub is responsible for the World Discoverer's damage and not a reef?'

'You realise what you're suggesting, right?'

'Yes, but let me explain. The damage on this sub aligns with the damage a Russian sub sustained back in late 2020.'

'I can't recall anything about that; fill me in on this.'

'Alright, back in late 2020, a British Royal Navy type 23 frigate, the HMS Northumberland, was on a mission in the Arctic Circle. It was working on tracking Russian submarine activity. The HMS Northumberland was using a towed array sonar to track the submarines.'

'Towed array sonar?' Jason asked.

'Yes, it's a system of hydrophones that is lowered into the sea from the stern and towed by the ship. They trail the ship and act like an underwater microphone, picking up a multitude of underwater sounds.'

'Gotcha!'

'The media portrayed the news as if the Russians had only hit the sonar being towed behind the ship. What they didn't say was that the Russians had actually made contact with the ship itself.'

'No way! And how did it go?'

'They had to abort the mission, return the frigate for repairs and replace the sonar.'

'And what happened to the sub?'

'Ah, you are gonna love this part. It completely sank. But guess what happened next?'

Jason tried to think of an appropriate answer but could not come up with anything.

'I don't know, Nick. You tell me.'

'Okay, after it sank, the Brits contacted OMIA to investigate the accident and look for any evidence or traces of the sub on the seafloor.'

'Really? Wow! Why didn't they do it themselves?'

'Good question. They didn't want to raise any suspicion with the Russians, so they hired OMIA to investigate, under the guise of oceanographic research from the University of Oslo led by Jacques Rousseau.'

'Smart move. What did they find out on this operation?'

'The Russians miscalculated their speed when making contact with the frigate, and it backfired on them. They located the sub at the bottom of the sea, but the Russians had stripped it clean of anything important. Dead bodies had also been recovered, but our OMIA divers had to investigate the sub further.'

'Shit, all of this sounds like 'Hunt for Red October'. Why did they hit them like that? And how did they bypass the sonar?' asked Jason, frowning as he tried to figure it out.

'I know, right? Santini, who worked with Rousseau, mentioned the possibility of the Russians experimenting with a new type of anechoic tile. They are usually rubber tiles that cover the hull of the sub, absorbing the sound waves of active sonars and reducing the sounds generated by the sub as far as possible for passive sonars.'

'Oh, that's impressive. It could make their subs into silent underwater death machines.'

'That's a bit of a stretch. The Royal Navy probably has its own countermeasures. Sorry for the digression, but here's the main takeaway from this story: the Russian sub had also lost its nose section.'

'Exactly the same as this sub right here...interesting. Did the frigate make it?'

'Yeah, the Brits nursed it back to the nearest drydock for repairs.'

'I'm impressed. How do you know all this stuff?'

'Hold on to your horses, partner. A gentleman like me doesn't kiss and tell.'

'Okay, so now that we have the sub right here, what do you suggest we do?'

'If this sub was involved in a collision with the World Discoverer, I assume there will be dead bodies inside.'

'I see. Let's return to the surface and get you ready for a dive then. There's no need for the both of us to squeeze into that sub; it's probably cramped as hell in there.'

'Perfect. Let's head to the surface then,' said Nick, activating the controls of the Viperfish II.

The submersible began its steady ascent to the surface. When they broke through the surface, they had to shield their eyes from the bright sun reflecting off the sea. Nick then began steering the Viperfish towards the RV Solander. It took them roughly a minute to return to the ship.

The ever-so-helpful crew members of the RV Solander assisted with raising the Viperfish II back onto the deck again. As soon as the hatch opened, they were greeted by Santini, who helped them jump down from the submersible.

'I'm thoroughly impressed with you two. You didn't give up and ended up finding something huge in the end. So, what's next?'

'Boss, I'm gonna dive into the sub to see if it sank recently. Hopefully, this next dive can answer some of the questions we've had since yesterday.'

'I like the sound of that. Okay, I'll get out of your way and let you prepare for the dive. Jason, please grab something to eat and drink and then join us in the op centre,' said Santini before patting them both on their backs.

Jason gave Nick a high-five and retreated into the cool, air-conditioned interior of the RV Solander. Nick entered his cabin to change into his wetsuit. In the meantime, Captain Clark repositioned his ship and brought it closer to Nick's diving location.

Bakke helped Nick prepare his diving equipment out on the deck. It was way faster that way, and Nick saved some of the time required for the tedious prep work. When everything was ready, they both boarded the RIB and put some distance between them and the RV Solander.

'X marks the spot,' said Bakke, easing off the throttle.

Nick nodded, adjusted the aluminium bezel of his Squale and bit his mouthpiece. He was ready for a new dive that could potentially provide crucial answers for their investigation. His mind was consumed by the two outcomes this dive could have: he would either find out if the sub had hit the World Discoverer or if something else had slashed open its hull. The option that intrigued him the most was, of course, the first one.

26

NICK SALUTED BAKKE and prepared to jump into the sea. He quickly surveyed his surroundings, took a deep breath and jumped into the sea, creating a big splash. As soon as the water enveloped him, Nick began his descent towards the sub. He switched on his light when the darkness grew as he went further down.

He maintained a steady pace without overexerting himself, constantly equalising the pressure in his ears. The deeper he descended, the more he felt the power of the underwater currents in the area. Though it could not push him far away, he had to be extra alert when positioning his body.

After swimming for around three minutes, Nick made contact with the sub. He studied it carefully, wondering which way to enter it. It had a huge opening in the front since the round bow was missing, but it also had an opening on its starboard side, where it had almost broken in two.

He ultimately entered from the front since the opening on the side was pretty small. The light illuminated the front of the submarine, revealing an internal bulkhead with a damaged door. Nick propelled himself closer to the door and applied some pressure to open it. After a gentle push, the door detached itself from the hinges, allowing him to swim further into the sub. This was good, as it ensured nothing was blocking his way out when he had to leave. As he swam through the door, he entered a room that looked like the crew's living quarters. On either side of the room were two sleeping bunks on top of each other. Bags of food, clothes and rubbish were floating inside the room.

Right above him was the submarine's cockpit, where an elevated platform had a basic chair mounted on it. A rudimentary steering wheel with some basic devices was attached to the metal wall. The cables were all visible and tangled up, revealing the do-it-yourself philosophy they had followed to construct the vessel. The cockpit allowed the one commanding the submarine to look outside when steering the vessel.

Nick saw no sign of the crew, so he swam deeper into the submarine. As he moved into the next bulkhead compartment, he encountered the four unfortunate souls that had once sailed on this sub. They were afloat, their bodies contorted into awkward positions. He swam closer to them, checking them one by one. Inside this compartment was a ladder leading up to the watertight hatch. The heavy-duty batteries powering the sub were lined up on either side of the walls.

It looked like they had tried to hastily escape out of the hatch when the submarine was sinking. Nick was no coroner, but these bodies looked recent. Dead bodies inside wrecks typically took an entire week to decompose, and these looked eerily alive, with all of their eyes open. The same petrifying feeling Nick had experienced the previous year in Zakynthos when diving into the sunken migrant ship spread across every inch of his body.

There was no doubt in his mind that these guys had crashed into the World Discoverer. The big question was why this narco-sub had crashed into the cruise ship at all. Was it a matter of being at the wrong place at the wrong time or did this incident have a more sinister motive?

Typically, narco subs stored their illicit cargo in the front section, which, in this case, had completely broken off the hull. Nick had not seen any bales with drugs when they swept through with the submersible earlier that day, and the sub looked pretty empty as well.

The sub had one last bulkhead compartment, which Nick ventured into. Here, he found the engine room, where a set of twin electric motors were installed. They powered the propellers on the aft part of the sub.

With no toilet and ventilation, this vessel was surely a nightmare of claustrophobia, stale air and constant danger. Since all drug smugglers are expendable to the cartel, these crew members were just another necessary loss to maintain the cartel's revenue streams.

Nick was puzzled at how empty the sub was. They couldn't have just taken the sub to test it out and roleplay Captain Nemo. These subs were made to fulfil big shipments before being scuttled to hide any evidence. Minimum costs, maximum revenue – that's the mentality of drug smugglers.

He wanted to swim outside and check the round bow that had detached itself from the ship. Maybe it contained clues regarding this vessel's purpose. Nick backtracked his way out of the sub, gently pushing the dead bodies away from his path. He had seen everything that needed to be seen inside the vessel.

When he got out, he made his way towards the round bow lying on the seafloor. Nothing stood out until he saw the tip of the bow. The smugglers who had constructed this sub had set up a towing hook mechanism. The hook fascinated Nick because it had two functions: it could tow the sub to port and be used to grab and tow objects underwater. Despite their criminal use, Nick had to applaud the human ingenuity involved in designing and manufacturing these submarines.

Nick felt satisfied with his exploration of the sub and was ready to ascent to the surface. But when he lifted his head and saw what was coming his way, his heart rate skyrocketed, goosebumps covered his body and he had trouble concentrating. All his muscles tensed up as a six-metre-long saltwater crocodile prowled the seafloor, looking for anything to prey upon.

For thirty millennia, humans and saltwater crocodiles shared the Solomon Islands, each playing a supporting role in the other's existence. Even the country's coat of arms depicted two of the most fearsome predators known to man, a crocodile and a shark, which came as no surprise to Nick. These two creatures were the undisputed kings of the seas in the Solomon archipelago, and their power and ferocity were known to all who lived there. Now, it was his turn to experience the same.

Nick had to think and react swiftly to have any chance of getting out of this sticky situation. He had better odds of fighting the crocodile in close quarters than in the open, so he quickly swam back to the submarine. When he looked back, he saw the crocodile zeroing in on him, increasing its pace.

Nick grabbed a handle and propelled himself forward to boost his speed. He frantically looked around the living quarters for anything he could use to defend himself. Nothing looked remotely sharp or capable of fending off the crocodile, so he swam to the next room with the bodies.

It was pretty macabre, but he began pushing the dead bodies to create a human barricade. If the crocodile was hungry, it could feast on them and buy him some time. As soon as he had pushed the fourth body inside the room, the crocodile's head peeked into the sub and began chomping on one of the dead bodies, frantically turning and twisting around, tearing off huge chunks of meat from the body.

Nick had already turned around and was busy opening the watertight hatch. After twisting it four times counterclockwise, the hatch burst open. He did not waste any time and swam through the opening. The second he was out, he pressed the hatch, sealing it down. A metallic thud caused the hatch to vibrate as the crocodile hit its head against it.

Nick positioned his feet against the sub's hull and pushed himself upwards, swimming as fast as he could, moving his arms and legs in perfect synchronisation. The only thing he could do now was swim up the canyon and hide in the reef, where he also had to complete his decompression stop.

Meanwhile, the crocodile struggled to turn its six-metre-long body inside the sub and cut its right front leg on a sharp metal edge as it swam back out again. Fresh blood coloured the surrounding water as its body left a red trail behind.

Nick was almost at the top of the reef now, only ten metres away from the surface. He could see the sun's rays penetrating the sea and lighting up the reef beneath. Finding the right spot in the reef was of the essence now. He concealed himself inside a hole within the reef, overgrown with seagrass, doing his best to remain motionless.

The perks of using a rebreather were evident now as he was not generating any bubbles that could alert the crocodile. Trapped in his hiding spot, he watched his watch's minute and second hands move painstakingly slowly.

When enough time had passed and he was ready to resurface, Nick slowly raised his head to check if the coast was clear. He counted the seconds down in his head and began swimming as fast as he could up to the surface. After only two strokes, the silhouette of the crocodile became visible again. He noticed it swimming straight towards him, going for the death roll.

This move could be the end of me, thought Nick as he prepared to hit the crocodile on its sensitive snout as hard as possible. Gouging its eyes was also a possibility, but it was much more difficult. Either way, his chances of survival were pretty low.

While Nick was busy calculating when to hit the crocodile, five enormous creatures suddenly appeared from behind and swam beside him at super-fast speeds, their wakes pushing him sideways. His eyes widened in amazement as he witnessed a group of two-metre-long grey reef sharks circling the bleeding crocodile, halting its progress.

Although Nick wanted to savour this marvellous underwater stand-off, he used the opportunity to swim up and break the surface. He waved his arms around until Jason and Helen, who were in the RIB, made eye contact with him. The RIB was about thirty metres away.

27

JASON DROVE THE RIB like a maniac until Helen pulled Nick on-board before any of the sharks could turn their attention to him. He frantically took off his mask, spit out his BOV valve and removed the rebreather to catch his breath. He lay flat on his back for ten seconds, attempting to shake off the near-death experience he had just experienced.

'Look!' Helen pointed to the shark fins slicing through the surface around the RIB.

Nick stood up and watched as the sharks began moving, each in its own direction, and the fins disappeared into the sea.

'I can't believe what you just witnessed. Nick Diamantis, you are one sick person to keep your head cool down there. I was screaming like crazy just watching your live camera feed,' Jason exclaimed.

Nick shrugged and played it cool by smiling.

'Are you alright? You didn't pick up any injuries on the way, did you?' Helen asked, placing her arm on his back.

'No, miraculously, I'm all good. Thanks for asking. It's insane that I walked out of a situation like that.'

'That is the understatement of the year, my friend. Alright, let's return to the ship. The rest of the crew will be so relieved to see you alive and well after this dive.'

Humbled by the response, Nick took a moment to thank Helen and Jason for their thoughtfulness. Santini, who was waiting on the deck, grabbed him and gave him a fatherly hug.

'I have no doubt you are as ingenious as Ulysses. I know you will enjoy telling this story to your grandchildren, but please don't ever do that again. That was too much for my heart to handle,' Santini gushed.

'Boss, you just need to steer clear of salt and those Toscano cigars of yours. Your heart will thank you later.'

'I guess it's too late for that now. Back on to the serious stuff, though, what's your plan with the submarine?'

'I think I'll look into it further. I'm not satisfied with just concluding that the sub had crashed into the World Discoverer. I want to know what it was doing there and why the two vessels had come in contact with each other.'

'I was afraid you'd tell me that. From my end, you're free to pursue any leads or hunches you have.'

'Thanks for that, Boss. I really appreciate it.'

'Go on now and do your thing. Let me know if you make any progress along the way. Just so you know, the Australians have been on my back lately and want to see us wrap this case up real soon. Capiche?' said Santini with a wink.

Nick nodded in agreement and went inside to change into some regular clothes. He was thinking about the best approach to this situation now. On one side, there was the narco sub and on the other side, the reef. He could easily blame the uncharted reef and close the case then and there. However, Nick wanted to pursue the narco angle to see what was hidden there.

Since he knew nothing about the local drug kingpins and cartels, he had to talk to the only person in the Solomon archipelago he trusted, Officer John Ramo. He walked to a secluded spot on the ship's deck and dialled Ramo's number on the satellite phone, hoping the unknown number would not prevent him from answering the call.

'John Ramo speaking. Who am I talking to?'

'It's Nick Diamantis from OMIA.'

'Oh, Nick, it's you. I wasn't expecting you to call back so soon.'

'Why not? I'm a man of my word.'

'Clearly! So, what gives? How's it going out there in the field?'

'First, let me just say that you were spot on with your intel regarding the dead crew member. I located him, dead in his cabin.'

'Damn, you're positive it was Luke Manik?'

'Super positive! He looked exactly like the photo from your mail, only less alive. Well, that sounded harsh.'

'Ah, don't worry about that. In my line of work, we speak bluntly as well. So, what about the suspicious Chinese passenger?'

'To be honest, I've found nothing to connect him to the World Discoverer. The reason I called you, John, is to learn more about the major players in the Honiara crime scene.'

'Of course, I can help. But how exactly?'

'You see, I came across a sunken narco sub in the Sandfly Passage and was wondering who would have the balls and budget to pull something like this?'

'A narco sub in the Solomon Islands? That's unheard of. Smugglers and pirates usually transport most of their drug deliveries on small vessels.'

'So, this suggests we're dealing with someone outside the Solomon Islands who may not have direct ties to the country?'

'Or someone just passing through our islands to get somewhere else. A narco sub is way too advanced for the criminals steering the underworld here in Honiara.'

'You're thinking of Australia and New Zealand, right?'

'Exactly. That's where most of the drugs from our islands end up.'

'Hmm, interesting. Let me ask you something then. If the narco sub were to offload something in the Sandfly Passage, where would you turn your focus on?'

'I'm not so familiar with the islands there, but I believe I've heard some local tales from my uncles back in the day. The people there are very spiritual and have many local legends and superstitions. As a criminal, I would use some of these superstitions to find a place where nobody would dare to set foot.'

'That's a brilliant perspective. You've opened my eyes yet again. I'll try to mingle with the people in the village of Roderick Bay and see if anyone can point me in the right direction.'

'Do that, Nick. And if you ever get stuck, don't hesitate to reach out. I'll help in any way I can.'

'I appreciate it, John. Stay safe, and we'll keep in touch.'

Nick hung up the phone and thought about what he needed to do next. He would ask Santini for the RIB for an evening trip around the village.

Captain Clark, Santini, Helen and the Admiral were engaged in a serious discussion in the crew mess, their body language tense. Nick peeped inside and figured he would be stuck in an endless conversation for the whole day if he entered the room at that moment. Instead, he went out to look for Jason, who was back at the stern, controlling their diving equipment.

'Yo, what are you up to, partner?' Jason asked.

'I was thinking of taking the RIB and paying a visit to the local village,' Nick replied, pointing towards the shore.

'The RIB is refuelled and ready to go. What's happening in the village tonight?'

'Nothing in particular. I want to learn more about the local culture and see if it can help us find any drug smuggling hotspots in the area.'

'I see. Well, I hope you find what you need. I'll let the others know about your whereabouts. Just take the RIB in the meantime; I don't think any of us will need it tonight.'

Nick bid Jason farewell. It took him just a few seconds to figure out how to start the RIB. In less than two minutes, he was out in the open sea, cruising at a speed of seventy knots over the waves. He had forgotten how fun it was to commandeer the RIB. When Nick turned back to look over his shoulder, the RV Solander was just a small dot on the horizon.

<h1 style="text-align:center">28</h1>

THE WOODEN WHARF of the village was getting closer by the second, and Nick babied the throttle when he entered the shallow waters of the bay. He waved and smiled at the kids who were out playing with their parents' wooden canoes. They paddled closer to Nick to get a close-up view of the Goldfish RIB.

A grown man sitting in a plastic chair and fishing from the wharf offered to help tie the boat. Nick thanked him for his help and asked what the village was called.

'Our village is called Hideaway,' the man replied proudly.

It was a fitting name indeed. As Nick walked towards the beach, he noticed many rope hammocks tied to low-hanging tree branches. All trees were a stone's throw away from the sea. He could envision people taking refuge under the shade after a plunge in the crystal clear waters.

The village itself was a combination of elevated wooden houses, a Christian church deeper into the forest and a two-storey school building. Given the unpredictable weather of the Sandfly Passage, the school walls were reinforced with metal plates. It was the only building in the village that could offer shelter during big storms.

When Nick stood outside the school's main entrance, he could hear the muffled voices of kids from within. He followed the sound and found the source of this commotion: an 11-a-side gravel pitch hidden behind the school. Two teams, one in red and the other in blue jerseys, were going at it in a football match.

Nick walked to the sideline and watched the match for a couple of minutes, reminiscing about his school days when he did the same. A group of dads were cheering on both teams, encouraging the kids to go for a goal. When they caught sight of him, they suddenly became slightly apprehensive. After conferring with the rest of the group, one of the dads walked up to him.

'What brings you here to our village, stranger?'

'I'm Nick Diamantis, and I'm investigating the World Discoverer shipwreck. I came here to your village to learn a few things.'

'Like what? That metal beast is going to pollute our bay for the next two hundred years.'

'And make it impossible for us to fish anything. Do you know how important fishing is to us?' added another from the entourage as they closed in on him from every angle.

Nick sensed the tension among the locals and sought a way to calm them down.

'I completely feel your agony. Let me promise you this, though. We will extract all of its remaining fuel so that the ship can, in the worst case, turn into a viable habitat for marine plants and animals.'

They stared at him, unimpressed, until one of them broke the silence.

'Cut him some slack, guys; it's not his fault. What are you looking for in our village, Nick? Are you sure you're not some scout trying to take our kids to Central Coast FC in Honiara? I heard they brought in a new European coach,' he said, hoping to lighten the mood.

'I'm afraid not, but I hope your kids can make it as professionals,' Nick replied with a warm smile.

As a kid, he had also dreamt of being a professional and playing in a World Cup for Greece. That was until his father had sent him to summer camp for the most promising prospects in Norway, and it really hit him how unrealistic his dream was.

'What I'm really looking for is someone in this village who is an expert on the local culture, its legends and mythology.'

The group of dads huddled together and began discussing who would be the most appropriate person. When they reached a consensus, they turned to Nick.

'You should go find Eroni Kumana. He's the oldest resident of our village, but his mind is as sharp as a razor. You can find him in the house down by the other end of the beach,' one of the dads said, pointing to a small bungalow by the sea. 'He's an expert in Melanesian mythology and local history.'

Nick thanked them and began walking along the beach. He could still see them suspiciously staring at him when he looked over his shoulder.

Nick marvelled at what a unique place it was to live and grow up in. No distractions and certainly no noise pollution. Of course, there were downsides to living in such a secluded place, but in this village, he couldn't help but notice smiling people all around. Happy kids played in the streets and swam with their older siblings and parents. Elderly people prepared food over fires, cut fresh fruits and engaged in meaningful conversations together. Grown men and women prepared their fishing equipment for the next morning. It was the purest form of down-to-earth everyday life he had ever experienced as an adult. Even though they were surrounded by poverty, they faced life with a smile.

Outside the secluded bungalow by the beach, he noticed an old man in an orange t-shirt, sitting in a rocking chair. He had a short grey afro, and his face radiated positive energy as he rocked back and forth in total bliss.

'Sorry for interrupting. Am I speaking to Eroni Kumana?'

The old man's face lit up as soon as he heard his name. 'Oh, that's me,' he said with a toothless smile. 'Who do I have the pleasure of meeting? You certainly don't look like you're from around here, young man.'

'I'm Nick Diamantis, a marine investigator working for OMIA. I'm on the lookout for the local expert in history, culture and mythology.'

'Ah, you must be working on the shipwreck. Nasty business that one, but you've definitely come to the right place. Come, grab a seat beside me.' Kumana ushered him towards the bungalow's patio. 'Let me get us some coconut water. You look like you haven't had a drink for a while.'

For an old man, he was pretty agile and gracefully retreated inside to grab a pair of tender coconuts and his fine-edged machete. He picked up one coconut and placed the palm of his right hand underneath it. In his left hand, he held the machete, and with a few swift slashes, the coconut had a perfectly round opening, just enough to drink out of. The process fascinated Nick, so he paid close attention to the old man's every move.

'Here you go; one for me and one for you.' He handed the coconut to Nick. 'Bottoms up.'

They both drank until the coconuts were empty. It tasted divine, like nature's gift to humanity.

'Wow, this is amazing,' Nick said, savouring the aftertaste of the coconut.

Kumana smiled, looking pleased. 'Be careful, though; I only drink two cups per day. Anything more will mess up your stomach.'

Nick chuckled and promised to follow his suggestion. 'I was wondering if you could help me with one thing, Mr. Kumana. I'm trying to find out if there are any areas in the Sandfly Passage that people are afraid of. I'm especially interested if the location has a specific reason behind it, tied to a historical event, a local tale or even a curse.'

Kumana went quiet, buried in his thoughts. Nick decided not to interrupt the old man and let him think in peace. Time seemed to stand still until Kumana had his eureka moment and began talking again.

'Very interesting question, Nick. Nobody has asked me that question in my ninety-five years of life. Our islands have a lot of history, but I think this one stands out for me – have you heard of the La Pérouse expedition?'

Nick shook his head and prepared for Kumana's story time.

'I thought so because this is a story that hasn't been particularly talked about. Back in 1785, the French wanted to emulate the discoveries made by Captain James Cook, a British explorer who made a name for himself with his three voyages in the Pacific Ocean. He is mainly remembered here for all the wrong reasons. If you ask me, he was a rotten crook, but anyway, I'll continue with the story.

'The French set up a covert expedition led by an experienced naval officer. And by that, I mean a proper sea dog. Their main objective was to correct and complete maps of the Pacific Ocean, establish trade contacts, open new maritime routes and enrich their scientific collections.

'The magnitude of this expedition was enormous. With him, he had two frigates, the L'Astrolabe and La Boussole, and a crew of two hundred and twenty-five, including officers and scientists. The Frenchmen took this expedition seriously.

'Long story short, these frigates took him to many places around the world, like Chile, Hawaii, Alaska, California, Macau, Japan, Australia and the Solomon Islands, where his expedition met a tragic end. Here's where things get interesting.'

Nick, who had been listening intently since the beginning of Kumana's story, was excited to know where this was going.

'When they left Botany Bay in Sydney and were on their way to the Solomon Islands, the frigates got caught in an insane storm. The storm damaged the ships so greatly that both were wrecked in the reefs off the coast of Vanikoro Island. Stranded on the island, the remaining survivors tried to scavenge resources from the ships to construct a makeshift schooner to continue their journey. They used wood from the nearby forest and salvaged timber from the shipwrecked frigates to complete their two-masted schooner.

In six months, they had completed their project and set sail for Tulagi. Along the way, they had to endure many difficulties and hardships, but fate saved the worst for last. As they sailed northbound in the Indispensable Strait, a new storm forced them off their charted course, and they had to seek shelter in the Sandfly Passage. Their makeshift schooner finally succumbed to its damage close to Mbike Island, the only island inside the passage itself. Though afraid of the locals, they thought they could temporarily find safety by casting their anchor near the island.

The locals, seeing the foreigners setting up a temporary camp on the island, were tempted to raid their supplies. At nighttime, a group went after their supplies but were met with a shocking sight – all the Frenchmen were dead with no logical explanation for it. However, that didn't stop the locals from looting them, but while they were loading the supplies onto the derelict schooner, the ship unexpectedly caught fire, engulfing them all in its flames. The locals saw it as a divine intervention from Agunua, the Melanesian god, punishing them for their inhumanity and greed. Since then, Mbike Island has been referred to as the Island of Death, and no one has dared to set foot on it.'

29

KUMANA'S ENGROSSING RETELLING of the story had Nick hanging onto his every word, leaving no doubt that he'd have to investigate Mbike Island upon returning to the RV Solander. It had everything he was looking for, a dark past, a strategic location, and the most important aspect —no one dared come close to it.

'It's getting late now, Nick. Let me make us some dinner. You're probably famished,' Kumana said as he cleared the empty coconuts off the table.

Nick accepted the invitation and went inside to offer help with dinner. Kumana wanted to show him what a traditional recipe from the village looked like, so he brought out a fresh red mangrove snapper he had caught a few hours earlier.

He showed Nick how to prepare their side dish and went out to light a fire they could grill the fish on. Nick's task was to make Poi, the national side dish of the Solomon Islands. He began by cooking taro, a starchy root vegetable, to remove its acrid flavour. When the taro had finished cooking, he began mashing the cooked starch on a wooden pounding board with a carved pestle. Afterwards, he added it to a bowl, drizzled water over it to adjust its viscosity and continued mashing the poi with the pestle to achieve the desired consistency.

Kumana came back to check on him and was delighted with Nick's progress. 'Look at you; you're a natural! Let me get a taste.' He scooped up a small amount of poi. 'Mmm, nice and sweet. Alright, take the bowl outside. The fish should be ready in a few minutes.'

Outside, the fish was sizzling over the fire, and the smell was enough to make Nick's mouth water. When the fish had finished grilling, they both began the delicate process of removing the bones and eating the fish meat. Nick tried to eat the fish with some Poi and was impressed by the taste. He conveyed his positive remarks to a smiling Kumana, who was clearly having the time of his life.

'This is what life is all about – living in the present and being thankful for what we have.'

'I couldn't agree more, Mr. Kumana. What other stories do you have up your sleeve, if I may ask?'

'Oh, you'll like this one. In fact, it's about myself and one of my good friends, Biaku Gasa. God rest his soul. Let me get us something to drink, and I'll tell you this story.'

After fetching them a jug of water, Kumana began retelling the story of his and Gasa's experience during World War II. They worked together with the Coastwatchers, a network of agents based across the Pacific islands during the war, tasked with monitoring the enemy and reporting back to the Allied forces. Nick felt like a kid again, listening to the stories of his grandfather from World War II. The story reached its climax when he learned about who Kumana and Gasa had stumbled upon during their daring adventures around the islands.

'So, without a coconut and you two, Kennedy would've never become the president of the US,' Nick said in total awe of what he just had heard. 'That's possibly the greatest story I've ever heard, Mr. Kumana.'

'Well, we were just two kids doing what we had to do for our country. We didn't know who this man was, only that he was an ally in command of the PT-109 boat. Great things from small things, I guess.'

The man was right – 'sic parvis magna', greatness from small beginnings. Nick had to give it to him; he had figured out life and what made him happy. He could've been out there, portraying himself as an unsung war hero all his life, clinging on to the past. Instead, he lived in this remote village and enjoyed every day like it could be his last.

Nick checked his Squale and realised that time had flown by. He thanked Kumana for his hospitality and promised to send him an OMIA baseball cap. They exchanged a heartfelt hug before going their separate ways.

It took him a few minutes to return to the RIB, but after that, everything happened fast. The sun was setting as he approached the RV Solander. Jason and Santini, who were chilling on the deck, waved at him.

'There he is! Nick Diamantis, the cultural explorer!' Jason called out as Nick stepped on the deck. 'Please, welcome aboard our ship, your excellency.'

'I see you haven't lost your sarcasm,' Nick replied with a smile.

'How was it? You were gone for a good while,' Santini asked.

'It was amazing, to be honest. I mingled with the locals and even met an important historical figure.'

'Wait, what? Who was it?'

'I met Eroni Kumana, the man who helped save John F. Kennedy back in World War II.'

'No way! He lives here? That's crazy. My father loved telling me this JFK story,' Jason said.

'What he did was heroic – the man swam like there was no tomorrow.'

'Besides the touristy stuff, did you learn anything useful we can use in our investigation? That's what I'm more interested in, considering our circumstances,' said Santini.

'Okay, Boss. For you, I will cut to the chase. I talked to Ramo earlier today about who could have the funds to smuggle drugs with narco subs in the Solomon Islands. We concluded that this has to be someone outside of the country. My next question was about where someone could do illicit activities uninterrupted in the Sandfly Passage. Ramo suggested that we check with locals about old tales or legends. Since the people here are highly superstitious and spiritual, these stories significantly influence their lives.'

'An interesting and rather original approach. And what did you find out?'

'All fingers point towards this island here,' said Nick, pointing to Mbike island on the map he was holding. 'Locals have been calling it the Island of Death for well over two hundred years now.'

'What do you suggest we do next?'

'I suggest we do a LiDAR scan with Jason's drone to get a lay of the land and see if we can spot any irregularities. It would be foolish to just waltz onto the island and get killed by drug smugglers.'

'I agree. Jason, please fire up the drone as soon as the sun has set. We don't want to alert anyone of our intentions,' Santini directed.

'Aye, aye, boss, I'll start prepping it.'

Jason headed inside to set up the drone, while Nick and Santini waited outside, watching the sunset. Nick tried to keep his expectations realistic regarding this search. The island was in the middle of the passage, and those on it could get a 360-degree view of their surroundings. Sneaking in and out of the island was thus challenging. Add the smuggling of drugs to it, and the probability percentage dwindled. Nevertheless, Kumana's Island of Death story had a certain allure that kept him believing.

30

A LITTLE PAST midnight, the night sky covered the earth like a dark veil. A black-to-navy gradient was the backdrop for the full moon, and the night sky was so clear that almost every single crater could be seen. The moon, with its yellowy-white glow, loomed large over the Sandfly Passage, surrounded by an ethereal glow. Millions of stars were sprinkled around it, with a few large ones but mostly a multitude of minuscule white pinpricks. The ocean waves lapped lazily at the hull of the ship, a mosaic of navy and royal blue that glistened in the night.

Nick was patiently waiting for the results from Jason's LiDAR scan. The others were in the op centre, crunching on their computers and analysing the data, while he preferred to be alone with the night sky rather than sit in a room full of sweaty people high on caffeine.

A door opened behind him, and he turned around to see Jason, gesturing for him to come inside.

'The results are in.' said Jason.

Nick took a second to stretch his back before walking inside towards the op centre. The lights were off, and a map of Mbike Island and its surrounding sea floor was projected on the wall.

'Okay, Nick, this is how the island looks when we peel back its layers. As you can see, the island appears to be a typical one with a dense jungle and a sandy beach encircling it. Nothing special, right? Here's what the LiDAR scan has revealed,' said Bakke, pressing a few buttons on his keyboard. 'Ta-da! Look at it now. It has revealed a lake in the middle of the island that is probably covered by all the trees and dense jungle vegetation.'

'The lake doesn't look natural, though. It's a perfect rectangle. Do you have the measurements of the lake?' Nick asked.

'Give me a sec,' said Bakke, clicking around with his mouse. 'Aha, the lake is fifteen metres long and eight metres wide. A rectangle indeed.'

'That's about the size you need to fit two narco subs. Did the scan reveal anything else?'

'Yes, indeed. Look at this shape that's roughly seventy metres away from the island. That's an entrance to an underwater cave or tunnel.'

'So, that's how they enter the island undetected. Very smart. This has to be the location the smugglers use for resupplies.'

'You're spot on, Nick. This next thing, you'll definitely like,' said Bakke, pressing the enter key on his laptop.

Another overlay appeared on the map, showing human-like structures and various anomalies. Suddenly, a sausage-like shape appeared on the lake, alongside a square shape next to the lake. Nick gasped.

'Wow, so a sub is currently docked on the island? The other square shape on the land must be some sort of building, right?'

'That's correct. In the middle of a busy passage, these guys smuggle drugs without anyone noticing. Gotta give them some credit; if they hadn't crashed into the World Discoverer, no one would have noticed,' said Bakke.

'Anybody feel like paying them a visit? I just want to ask them some questions I have,' said Nick, punching his left fist into his right palm.

He slowly felt his anger simmer within. He hadn't forgotten the near-death experience he had had aboard the Liberian fishing trawler, Bonheur.

'We certainly will, Nick, but we must do it as smartly as possible. That's why I asked the Admiral and Agent Chapman to join us as well,' said Santini.

In a few seconds, the Admiral and Helen showed up and took their seats in the room, the Admiral in a suit and Helen in a black t-shirt and olive green khaki pants. This time, she had let her blonde hair down. Nick nodded and smiled as she settled into her chair.

'Now that we're all here, let's come up with a plan to approach this situation,' Santini said, addressing the entire room. 'I think we should do this as stealthily as possible. I don't want us to stir a hornet's nest. Anyone care to share their ideas?'

'I have an idea, Mr. Santini,' said Helen, rising from her chair. 'I propose that I and another person dive and approach the island through the underwater tunnel. We'll also need some people on standby with the RIB in case backup is needed. To operate a narco sub, you'll need at least four people, but I suspect there are more on the island acting as guards. I estimate they will outnumber us one to five or even one to six.'

'I can join the diving team,' Nick chimed in, looking around the room for reactions.

Jason raised his hand. 'And I can take the RIB as close as possible for a strategic striking position.'

'Our primary goal is, of course, to get the smugglers to surrender so that we can interrogate them for any intel,' Helen emphasised.

Santini looked at the Admiral to gauge his reaction. The Admiral had a distant look but momentarily broke out of character and nodded positively. Nick noticed a slight smirk on the Admiral's face.

'Well, that settles it then,' Santini said, concluding the meeting.

The room woke up to life with the buzz of excitement and caution. OMIA took up risky jobs all over the globe, but what they were about to do next was a unique venture for them. Santini's confidence and belief in each team member quickly spread to everybody on the ship. Their nervousness steadily diminished as the preparations neared their end.

Nick, now in his drysuit, walked out onto the deck, holding his SealLine drybag containing his mask and fins. People were rushing back and forth, ensuring Jason and Helen had everything they needed for the operation. A crew member showed him where his rebreather was, along with an assortment of gadgets.

He spotted a pair of night vision goggles, a silencer and his Heckler & Koch MP5 submachine gun. The weapon had a heather grey sheen on some parts because of its lithium-based coating, which helped increase resistance against saltwater corrosion. A magazine cartridge lay next to the gun.

Nick picked up the MP5, pointed the muzzle downwards and ensured the safety was on. He then grabbed the magazine and inserted it until the magazine caught and locked it into position. He tapped the magazine on the bottom to ensure the gun was safely loaded. He then used his other hand to retract and release the bolt using the charging handle. As the bolt travelled forward, it inserted the first round into the chamber. The hammer was now cocked. He picked up HUX-

WRX's RAD 9 silencer and twisted it onto the MP5's muzzle using its long configuration.

'Hold on there, cowboy. You forgot this,' said Helen, giving him an Aqualung Argonaut diving knife. 'Just for when things get messy.'

'I like to keep things clean, but thanks, I guess,' said Nick, throwing her a playful look as he examined the knife.

'Aren't you a charmer?' she said, laughing. 'Jason is waiting for us. Get a move on and we might finish this minor operation of ours before the sun rises.'

'Right back at you. I'm all strapped up; let's go.'

Nick mentally rehearsed all the scenarios that could unfold. He considered all the actions the drug smugglers might take to thwart their raid and visualised himself reacting accordingly to complete their mission. Although he felt sure about their skills, he kept a small door open for eventual surprises that they may face on the island.

The smugglers were a resourceful bunch, and he did not write them off as easy opponents. But the crew also had a few tricks up their sleeves. Helen had gifted him and Jason a set of molar mics they could use to communicate while diving and on land. It was a small device that could be clipped onto their back teeth. The mouthpiece turned incoming audio into vibrations that the inner ear translated into sounds that appeared to be coming from inside the head while still allowing external sounds to be heard. All three of them tested their molar mics as they moved to their diving spot. Nick and Jason could not keep it together and began laughing as they got used to the molar mics. To them, the molar mics blurred the line of reality, making it seem as if they had each other's voices inside their own heads.

'Boys will be boys,' said Helen, shrugging her shoulders.

Meanwhile, Jason had switched the RIB to the electric power unit, making it completely silent. When they were near the underwater tunnel, he signalled Nick and Helen to go ahead. They both nodded to each other and slipped into the black waters. It was go-time.

31

THE WATER WAS completely dark, and Nick could not see a thing. He tapped a button on the left side of his mask to turn on his night vision. Bakke and Johnson had come up with an ingenious way to integrate night vision into the mask without the need for the additional bulky gadgets most commercial divers used. Everything appeared in shades of dark grey, and it felt like watching the black and white footage of a CCTV camera.

Helen, a few metres ahead, swam towards the tunnel, and Nick followed. As they were swimming, Nick noticed a set of lights that had been turned off lining each side of the tunnel. He hoped they only used the lights when a narco sub entered the tunnel's dark confines. If they were rigged up to some alarm system, they would be exposed and turned into easy targets for the smugglers.

The tunnel was really long at about sixty metres, exactly as much as the LiDAR scan had estimated. The tunnel walls looked exactly the same, creating the impression that they were swimming in an endless loop. Their plan was to find a suitable spot to get out of the water and silently remove their rebreathers from their backs. From there, they could assess the situation and proceed accordingly.

After a couple of minutes, Helen abruptly froze, pointing towards the sub docked in the hidden lake. Nick slowed down and examined its hull. It was an identical copy of the sunken sub he had seen earlier that day. They knew the smugglers had a building next to the docked sub, so they swam towards the other side of the lake, hoping they could exit the lake undetected from there.

Nick turned off the night vision mode and signalled for Helen to stay underwater as he broke the surface with his head, slowly rising out of the lake's dark waters. He rose just enough for his dark emerald eyes to get a lay of the land. The coast was clear, so he crawled up from the lake and into the dense vegetation of the jungle. Helen soon followed his lead and crawled up beside him.

They took off their rebreathers when they were sure no one was around them, hoping the vegetation would not rustle from their movement and jeopardise all of their efforts.

'We're out in the open, Jason. Proceeding with our mission. Our next goal is to locate the smugglers here before going over to the next phase of our operation.'

'Roger that. I'm in position as well. Remember, this is a recon mission; we need our targets alive for interrogation,' said Jason, looking through the scope of his suppressed Remington 700 SPS Tactical AAC-SD sniper rifle. He had loaded the rifle with subsonic .308 ammo and was scouting the island for any potential threats to Nick and Helen. His right index finger was patiently stroking the trigger.

Thankfully, the sea close to Mbike Island was calm, and he could easily compensate for the waves that were lightly rocking the RIB. In case he needed to provide some covering fire, picking out a target would not be an issue. He had a double-digit number of confirmed kills with his trusty rifle while hanging out from the sides of helicopters during his time as a Rockport mercenary in the Middle East.

Helen rose to a crouching position and began moving through the dense vegetation towards the building on the other side. She pulled out her tranquilliser gun and kept to the shadows. Nick kept a safe distance and stopped the moment he saw her clenched fist.

Approximately five metres in front of them, two guards were patrolling the left side of the building. They were on the same walk they would do every thirty minutes, moving away from the building and into the jungle before returning to their starting point.

They heard one guard ask the other for a lighter, and the second guard obliged, helping him light up a cigarette by flipping open his Zippo lighter. As he exhaled the smoke and thanked him, they both went their separate ways. One went to check on an area close to the lake, while the other one moved towards a vantage point overlooking the beach.

'This is our chance; take out the one by the lake, while I put the other one to sleep.'

'Copy, I'm on it,' said Nick, pulling out a tranquiliser dart.

He waited until the guard had turned away before making his move. The moment he saw him pivot, he slipped through the leaves and stabbed the guard in the throat with the dart. Then, Nick covered the guard's mouth and slowly lowered him to the ground.

Meanwhile, Helen focused on her target and aimed her tranquilliser gun at his neck. When she was almost three metres away from him, she fired her gun, hitting the target under his right ear. The guard staggered and pulled out the dart from his neck. He only got a glimpse of what hit him before blacking out. Helen quickly moved forward to break his fall and gently ease him to the ground.

'Two down; that was smooth,' Nick said, watching her.

They zip-tied the two smugglers and regrouped.

'Let's move towards the building and see if we can spot where the rest of them are.'

Nick nodded, and together, they methodically carved their way through the jungle, circling over to the other side of the lake. Through their night vision goggles, they could see four smugglers talking in a huddle outside the building. The building itself was a makeshift wooden cabin that had been wrapped with a military camo net and various leaves, making it almost impossible to spot from a long distance.

One smuggler stood out, appearing to be their leader. He was pretty vocal and agitated about something, barking out orders to the other three. When he had finished his tirade, he entered the cabin and banged the door behind him. The remaining smugglers spread out and began combing through the jungle to look for the two missing guards.

'I think they're looking for their missing friends. They must have certain patrol schedules to follow. No wonder their boss is fuming.'

'Must be. What do you suggest we do?' Helen asked.

'I say we don't take any chances. Jason, are you there?' Nick asked and waited a few seconds for Jason's response. 'Shall we try a sync shot? If we take down these three, that leaves only the big honcho and his two lackeys. I think it should suffice since he likely has the bulk of the information.'

'I agree. Agent Chapman, are you with us on this one?'

'Totally. My target is the one on the dock next to the sub.'

'I can take out the one walking away from the cabin. What about yours, Jason? How are you gonna take out the last one?'

'What if I distract them with a light and get them moving towards me? When everybody is in sight, we count down and bang.'

'That's smart. If we move them away from the cabin, their boss won't hear what hit them. Let's do it,' said Nick.

Both he and Helen repositioned themselves closer to Jason, studying the guards' movements as they moved in the dark. When they had suitable positions, they signalled Jason to begin his distraction.

He flipped a switch beside the RIB's controls and pressed a button. A blinking red light began shining in the middle of the dark sea. It did not take long for one of the guards to react.

'Jason, the other two guards are also moving towards you. Switch off the lights when I tell you,' said Nick, waiting patiently.

All three of them aimed their rifles towards their respective targets, tracking them through their scopes.

'Now!' Nick whispered.

Jason switched off the light and zeroed in on the skull of his target with the sniper rifle. Nick started a countdown.

'Three, two, one...'

A simultaneous burst was heard from their three rifles. Soon after, the guards tumbled down, their bodies contorting on the ground with a hole in their skulls, courtesy of three subsonic bullets.

'Nicely done, team. Jason, get into position by the beach and prepare for extraction. Helen and I will have some words with their boss.'

Jason began moving the RIB closer to the beach as the others approached the dead bodies to look for any clues on them.

'There's nothing of interest in their pockets,' said Helen, looking over to Nick. 'Just cigarettes and pocket change.'

Nick, however, was curious and focused on their weapons, which looked like regular AK-47 rifles. He grabbed one and began examining it.

'Now, this is interesting. Look at this.' He traced his finger along the serial number engraved on the rifle. 'Chinese numbers.'

'Interesting. This is a type 56 assault rifle by Norinco, a Chinese-made variant of the AK 47. I wonder how they got their hands on these.'

'I'll bet their leader knows more about this. Let's rain on his parade, shall we?' said Nick.

They silently walked down a small path until they were within striking distance of the cabin. Nick crouched, slowly grabbed the door handle and looked at Helen, who was standing with her gun raised.

'Ladies first,' said Nick, ripping the door open, allowing Helen to burst through the door with her weapon held high.

'Freeze!' She aimed at the smuggler sitting behind an office desk.

The smuggler was so blinded by the flashlight in his face that he did not even pick up his gun. Nick quickly approached him and zip-tied his hands.

'Who are you? What do you want from me?' The man's voice trembled with fear.

'That's none of your business. We will be asking the questions,' barked Helen, pressing her gun into his temple. 'You got that?'

The smuggler nodded as cold sweat trickled down his face. He identified himself as James Ngelea.

'So, I see you have two narco subs, albeit one of the two has seen better days, Chinese rifles, and a hidden island base. Pretty hi-tech stuff for a couple of smugglers. Fill me in on your agenda. I assume you call the shots around here,' Helen interrogated, while Nick walked around the room, exploring the cabin's contents.

'I will. Please, don't shoot me.'

Helen lowered her gun from his temple. When he had caught his breath, he began talking.

'They paid me and my crew to pick up a drug shipment here at the Sandfly Passage using the narco sub. All we had to do was collect the shipment and transport it to Australia. Nothing more, nothing less.'

'I see. Where did you build these subs? This island is too small for that.'

'We manufacture them in the jungles of Buena Vista Island. It's an island north of us. I can show you on the map.'

'Ain't no need for that. And the shipment, where does it come from? You said you're picking it up from someone else,' asked Nick, joining in on the interrogation now.

'The drug shipment we picked up came from Honolulu, Hawaii,' James disclosed.

'Interesting. The same place from which the World Discoverer set sail more than a week ago. Tell me, was it you who removed all the evidence from the shipwreck, sank the ship, hacked our systems and tried to kill me by blowing up a fishing trawler?' demanded Nick.

'Yeah, we did everything except the hacking. Come on, man; it was nothing personal. We were just following orders and trying to get on with our objective.'

'No offence taken. It's just that I prefer to be alive than sleep with the fish. You said the hacking was done by someone else. Who?' Nick pressed, planting both his fists on the table.

'I only know him by his codename, Cobra. He's the Chinese guy who came to us and proposed this business opportunity.'

'Hmm...Chinese, you say. Interesting.'

'And this guy, Cobra, what was his role in the operation?'

'He helped us kick off this operation in Honolulu and provided us with the hardware.'

'Noted. And now, for the million-dollar question, was it your team that crashed into the World Discoverer, causing it to sink?'

'Unfortunately, yes. Things didn't go as planned. I'll explain everything to you.'

'Oh, please, don't mind if you do. I have all the time in the world,' said Nick as he sat down on the table and pressed the record button on his digital voice recorder.

32

HONOLULU HARBOUR, HAWAII
A WEEK AGO

THE DIVING VESSEL Blue Descent was entering the Honolulu channel and making its way towards Pier 24, where it was about to dock. The Aloha Tower, a retired art déco lighthouse that had been welcoming ships to Hawaii since 1926, greeted it on its starboard side. Behind the Aloha Tower and its surrounding marketplace, the modern skyline of Honolulu was taking shape, with a wide variety of modern-looking skyscrapers setting the scene and mirroring the orange hue of the afternoon sun.

A skeleton crew with divers and smugglers from the Solomon Islands had been a part of the ship's week-long trip from Honiara. They intended to follow the instructions of a mysterious character called Cobra, who had met up with their bosses in their HQ in Honiara. Their objective was to attach a torpedo, which they had picked up offshore through their moon pool, to a Norwegian cruise ship, the World Discoverer.

Cobra, whose real name was Lei Cheng, had arranged the offshore delivery of the torpedo and the acquisition of the diving vessel through his contacts in the Chinese government. Unaware of his government ties, everybody onboard Blue Descent viewed him as a high-profile crime lord from Shanghai. The torpedo was not of the typical kind made for military use. Au contraire, the torpedo was used to smuggle cargo. Inside the torpedo was seven tonnes of crystal meth and cocaine, with an estimated street value of five billion dollars if it reached the Australian markets.

The stakes were high for B squad leader James Ngelea, and he was feeling the pressure. To divert any suspicion, his ship had been painted

144

to replicate the American-registered diving vessel of the same name and proudly waved its star-spangled flag. Ngelea and Cheng planned to use it as a decoy, should the authorities look for any suspects if they failed their mission in Honolulu. When the port authorities searched on Vesseltracker, they would only find that the Blue Descent was south of Los Angeles, researching marine life with the Catalina Island Marine Institute.

Ngelea's phone rang in his pocket, and he answered the call.

'Hello, James, ready for tonight's mission?' It was Cheng on the other end. 'I will be in position in approximately one hour.'

'We should be good. Everything is proceeding fine on our side. By the way, how are you gonna transfer the torpedo to the World Discoverer at its location?'

'That's none of your concern. I've arranged everything and meticulously thought over every last detail. I have a device that allows me to steer the torpedo. It has a limited range but is enough to move it unnoticed to the other side of the harbour. All I need from your B squad is for your divers to accompany the torpedo with our magnetic cables. When the torpedo is right under the World Discoverer, the divers should swim up to the ship's hull and attach the magnets to the ship. This is where you come into play, James, and activate the magnets with the encrypted app I asked you to download. Then, your divers should move down and attach the two cables to the respective attachment points.'

'And the captain won't notice the added weight on his ship when they set sail from here?'

'Nope, not at all. I will board the ship as a passenger and mount a device inside the engine room. In this way, it can stay in range to the torpedo throughout the trip. The device will override the ship's system, gather data and adjust the speed of the torpedo's thrusters. By doing so, the torpedo will not slow down the ship in any noticeable way. It'll be like taking a small dog for a walk at the park without it tugging on the leash. They won't notice a thing.'

'Got it. I won't ask how you'll enter the engine room. I'm guessing you have that under control as well.'

'That's right, my friend. I better keep the secrets of my trade to myself,' Cheng replied, knowing his ticket had been booked with an untraceable fake identity. 'I'll call you when I'm in range.'

The next fifty minutes passed by in a blur as Ngelea's crew readied themselves for their mission. Cheng parked his rented BMW M3 and walked to the passenger terminal, where boarding was in progress for the World Discoverer. When he finally entered his cabin, he signalled the B squad to proceed.

Ngelea was down by the moon pool when he received the call from Cheng. After the brief conversation, he ordered everybody to commence the mission. They lowered the torpedo into the water, and as soon as they released it free from the gantry crane, Cheng remotely controlled it with his device. The torpedo had cameras on every side, allowing him to steer it underwater. His device had a small screen, and he could effortlessly switch between cameras with the press of a button.

To match the torpedo's speed underwater, the divers were equipped with underwater scooters. The ones carrying the magnets and cables had already dived and were well on their way towards the World Discoverer. When Ngelea saw from the divers' camera footage that the magnets were touching the ship, he activated the magnets, making them stick to the hull. Satisfied with that, Cheng carefully navigated the torpedo right underneath the docked cruise ship and let the divers finish the job. It took them four minutes to fasten the cables to the specific attachment points. The crew onboard the Blue Descent burst into celebration as they completed their part of the mission. It did not take long for Ngelea's phone to start buzzing again. He went to a quieter area and answered Cheng's call.

'Excellent job, James. I will infiltrate the engine room and mount the device there. A Harbin Z-20 helicopter will pick you up three hundred nautical miles from the Solomon Islands and transport you to Mbike Island. They will also scuttle the ship for you to hide all evidence. When everything is done, you and your crew will get your share of the money wired to your accounts. Please don't use everything at once; we're talking big bucks here.'

'Thanks for that, and good luck on your end. Pleasure doing business with you,' said Ngelea, envisioning dollar signs.

Cheng hated when people wished him good luck, so he aggressively hung up the call. Luck had nothing to do with everything he had achieved in his career as a spy for the Chinese government. Luck was an idea weak-minded people embraced to fulfil their goals.

'Pathetic,' He mumbled as he shut his cabin door behind him.

33

'THAT'S QUITE AN endeavour. You hear that, Helen?' Nick cast a glance at Helen, who was still aiming her suppressed Glock 22 at Ngelea's face.

'Our smuggler is quite talkative tonight, but I believe he hasn't answered all of our questions yet.'

'I kinda feel the same way,' said Nick, stroking his beard stubble. 'So, James, what happened here at the Sandfly Passage when you crashed into the World Discoverer? That couldn't have been part of the plan, right?'

'Can I please get a bottle of water? My mouth is dry from all the talking. I'm begging you,' Ngelea pleaded, looking exhausted.

After giving him a deadpan look for a few seconds, Nick stood up and took out a bottle of water from a small fridge in the cabin.

'No funny business, alright?' he warned, and Ngelea nodded silently. 'Open your mouth.' Nick poured him some water. 'Now that you're all hydrated, let's continue where we left off.'

'Yes, crashing into the ship was definitely not part of the plan. All we had to do was wait for the ship to pass the Mid Reef section of the Sandfly Passage. Cobra would release the torpedo by deactivating its magnets, and we were tasked with picking it up and bringing it to our hidden base here.'

'Okay, so what happened with your first sub that led to the crash?'

'We had a deviation problem with our GPS signal, making us come far too close to our target. Also, since our sub was facing the wrong way, we did not have a clue where the ship was coming from. When we finally got a visual, it was too late. We pulled away, but the damage had already been done.' Ngelea's disappointment was written all over his face as he lowered his head. The money he would have received for this job would have changed his and his family's life. Now, all he faced was a life in prison with the worst criminals on the islands.

'Okay, now that we've got that part out of the way, I have another question: where is the body of the crew member who, I assume, was killed by Cobra?'

'We stashed it on the fishing trawler along with Cobra's device from the engine room. In a way, you could say that we cremated him,' said Ngelea with a chuckle, his black eyes glowing sinisterly.

'You sick bastards! You didn't have the decency to bury the man,' yelled Nick, banging the table with his fist in anger. 'But what else should I expect from low-life criminals like you in the first place?'

'Come on, man. Life is cruel in these parts of the world. It's the survival of the fittest. We're not like you, especially you,' said Ngelea, pointing at Helen. 'The Australians come here, prancing around on their white horses, trying to help our nation. It's bullshit. All you care about is looking good for the US and the Western world. Who has ben-efitted from your security agreement in recent years? Certainly not us. Jobs are still scarce, people are divided and the police force is corrupt and in a state of decay.'

A heavy silence settled in the room as Ngelea's words loomed over Nick and Helen. Nick suddenly realised that the man sitting opposite to him had presented a valid point. The feelings of injustice and pent-up frustration he harboured were justified. A lack of jobs could force anyone to bend their moral boundaries and resort to crime. Some-times, putting food on the table for your family may outweigh the risks of solitary confinement or a lifetime of poverty. Sadly, this wouldn't be the first or last time someone like him would be put in this position. He realised that life on earth could be both a paradise and a hell, depend-ing on the set of cards fate dealt you with at birth.

'Okay, before we wrap things up, do you have any information you can share about this person called Cobra?'

'Nothing. I've never met the man. Only spoke to him on the phone. All I know is that he is from Shanghai, is loaded with cash and has con-nections everywhere. My bosses met him in Honiara.'

Nick sensed that Ngelea's patience was running out, so he pressed more directly for any new information.

'Where are the drugs right now?'

'Ah, they're probably getting smoked and sniffed by the brightest minds in Australia as we speak.'

'Keen to share any names? Any help we receive in this interrogation will be greatly appreciated,' said Helen, strafing around the room with her gun pointed at Ngelea.

'I ain't no snitch, bitch. You can stick that up your privileged...'

Before Ngelea finished his sentence, Nick stopped the recording, jumped over the desk, kicked him down on his chair and choked him.

'Never speak to a woman like that,' Nick snapped, staring right into his eyes.

'Alright, I give up! Samuel Samani, his name is Samuel Samani,' Ngelead wheezed out, gasping for air.

Nick bent down and whispered into his ear.

'Now that was easy, wasn't it?' He removed his hand from Ngelea's throat. Though his instinctive outburst was unexpected, he felt it was necessary. Ngelea's crew had created such a mess for OMIA and had been seconds away from killing him. This was the least he could do to get the answers they needed.

'Jason, this is Nick. Do you read me? I need immediate extraction of three smugglers. Please inform the doc that he needs to prepare three body bags for the smugglers we took down.'

It did not take them long to finish things up on Mbike Island. When all the smugglers had been transported back to the RV Solander – Nick had fine-combed the hidden base on the island and the second narco sub – they returned to the ship with Helen. Nick had one thing on his mind now, a meeting with the Admiral, Helen and Santini. If the drugs were already in the streets of Australia, the brains of the operation would have likely tasted a small portion of the billions involved in this shipment. If they wanted any chance of catching those on top of the food chain, they had to act fast and methodically.

'I know that face. What do you need, Nick? I'll set it up for you,' said Santini when he reunited with Nick onboard the RV Solander.

'I need the Australians and you in a private meeting. Can you arrange it?'

'Say less. Find out anything?'

'A lot.'

After pulling the strings in classic Santini fashion, all four of them were sitting inside the op centre, ready for a meeting. He had allowed Helen and Nick to grab something to eat before starting their conversation. Nick brought out the voice recorder and began playing Ngelea's interrogation for everybody. When the recording ended with a click, he put it back in his pocket and had the first word.

'I'm cutting right to the chase, folks. I will need your help and that of the Australian Intelligence, Helen, to look up everything you can find about Samuel Samani. He seems to be the brains behind this operation. Please try to look up Cobra as well and see if anything comes up; it's worth a try.'

'I'm passing along the information about Samani to my colleagues in Canberra as we speak,' she replied while typing on her laptop. 'For Cobra, I'll see what we can extract from our informants in China.'

'Good. Admiral, could you alert all port authorities in Australia and the coastguard to step up their patrol routes and inspections?'

'Certainly, Nick. I won't allow such a huge shipment to enter my country.'

'Okay, not to be a total killjoy here, but we have now solved the case of why the World Discoverer went down. As OMIA, we've finished the job given to us,' said Santini, looking around the room for a response.

'Yes, you have, Santini,' said the Admiral, 'but if you pull out of this now and leave, we will still have a lot of loose ends to go through. Five billion dollars in the wrong hands could be catastrophic.'

'Exactly, Boss. The Admiral is right. The shipwreck was just the tip of the iceberg.'

'So what do you suggest, Nick?'

'For now, I have nothing specific to suggest. But I would like to know what the deal is between you and the Solomon Islands. Ngelea mentioned something about a security agreement. He did not look exactly thrilled about it, to be honest.'

'That's correct. We signed a bilateral security agreement back in 2017. It gives our Navy access to all the ports in the Solomon Islands to resupply. We can also freely sail through their waters, do military exercises and take part in operations like this one. A similar deal was signed last year in 2021 with their neighbouring country, Papua New Guinea. We plan to build a naval base on Manus Island for the Papua New Guinea Defense Force. We estimate it can create three hundred and fifty jobs for the local population.'

'Interesting. Any similar plans for the Solomon Islands? They could certainly use the jobs.'

'Tulagi Island has fantastic potential for a navy base, but if we do not handle the internal turmoil in the country, it's a risky move. We need a stable government to complete a lengthy project like that.'

'I imagine China is not a big fan of these moves. They've spent years turning islands and reefs in the South China Sea into military bases and airstrips to expand their maritime borders,' Santini interjected.

'And don't forget about what they did in Djibouti in 2017. They set up a whole naval base near the entrance of the Red Sea. It's capable of housing two thousand navy personnel and boasts a twenty-three thousand square metre underground space and a three-hundred-and-forty-metre long pier. They can dock aircraft carriers, warships and nuclear-powered subs, and they are still expanding the base as we speak. All of that is a stone's throw away from one of the most popular maritime routes in the global trade of oil and goods.'

'Impressive, Nick. You really know your stuff. The Suez Canal, the Mediterranean and the Persian Gulf are key routes for the import of oil into China – oil that is vital for their military and shipping industry,' the Admiral acknowledged.

'The next choke point has to be the Strait of Malacca,' Nick stated matter-of-factly.

'Yes, and that's why we're trying our best to get most of the countries in the Oceanic region under our influence,' Helen commented.

'Any countries that stand out in particular?' Nick asked.

'For sure. Taiwan and the Solomon Islands are highly significant at this moment. Both countries are in pivotal positions regarding the future of the region. Losing them to China would create a big shift in the geopolitics of the entire continent, drastically minimising the presence of the US and Australia. Taiwan, especially, has really benefited from the trade war with the US and the recent pandemic, when compared to other countries. Just to put things into perspective, their GDP per capita in the last couple of years was comparable to that of Switzerland.'

'Impressive for such a small nation. Let me guess, the Americans have ambitions to build a base there like you do in the Solomon Islands? To further cement their presence, of course.'

'Yeah, I think it's on their agenda for 2024.'

'I've been listening to you for a while now, and I've come up with a rather far-fetched idea. Could Breland be involved with the Chinese? He's the only individual I know of with the budget to undertake such a huge smuggling operation,' Santini remarked.

The others were shocked by this idea and cast questioning looks in his direction.

'Why not? It's a win-win. He can cash in on the drugs and provide them with a sustainable form of power. What's not to like about that? The world is changing, and we can't forever depend on oil and fossil fuels.'

'But, Boss, why hire us specifically for the job then? It doesn't make a lick of sense,' Jason pointed out.

'That's the part I'm trying to figure out too. Maybe that's the genius of his move so that we don't consider him a suspect.'

'Could be, but even so, it's very far-fetched,' the Admiral concluded.

'Okay, since we're just speculating now, hear this: what if the Chinese are after what Breland already has on this island?' Nick paused to formulate his next sentence. 'If they could take this island under their wings, they could probably squeeze him out of the country by bending the laws in their favour. In this way, they gain a new ally in the Pacific Ocean and save themselves the burden of setting up a Geothermal energy plant.'

'It seems we could spend all night speculating about this matter. So, what's your call, Santini? Are you willing to see things through, or shall we call it a day?' said the Admiral, whose patience was waning.

Santini was thinking hard, drumming his fingers on the table.

'It seems we're caught up in a matter that can have serious repercussions for many. If OMIA can be of service to the Australian Navy and contribute to the stability of the entire region, we will certainly see things through, Admiral. You've got my word.'

'Nick, I can give you forty-eight hours to see what this Samuel

Samani guy can reveal. When those hours pass, we must ensure that the fuel from the World Discoverer is completely removed and the local marine life is not harmed in any way. Then, we contact Breland, finish this operation and return to Norway.'

'I truly appreciate it, Mario. I will not forget this the next time our paths cross again,' the Admiral affirmed.

'Thanks, Boss. Any news from Canberra, Agent Chapman?'

'Not yet. They are working on it with all their resources.'

'Alright. I say we inform Captain Clark to set course for Honiara, where we will continue our investigation from tomorrow.'

'If anything urgent pops up, Agent, just wake us up. We can take the RIB to reach Honiara faster.'

'I'll keep that in mind, Mr. Santini.'

Everyone agreed with this decision, and one by one, they left the op centre to return to their cabins. Nick, however, had an ace up his sleeve and needed to do one more thing before sleeping. He intended to call Ramo to see if he could help him come up with any info about Samani. The guy knew the underworld in Honiara like the palm of his hand. Right now, any lead could go a long way.

*

Ramo could not sleep at all that night. He had been staring at his ceiling fan for over an hour, thinking about his wife and daughter. Just then, his phone began vibrating. Fumbling around in the dark, he located his smartphone and answered the call. It was Nick.

'Nick, what's going on? I hope none of us is in danger, given that you're calling at this ungodly hour.'

'Nobody's in danger. I'm just in need of any information you might have about a certain Samuel Samani. Does this name ring any bells?'

'Oh, that guy. He was the leader of one of the main militant groups during The Tensions period. The militant group was GRA, the Guadalcanal Revolutionary Army, and they were fighting against the MEF, the Malaita Eagle Force. Those were some really dark times for our islands.'

'And when was that, so I can get an idea of his age now?'

'That five-year period started in 1998 and lasted until 2003 when international efforts restored peace in the country. Samani should be close to fifty years old now. He was ruthless in combat, responsible for hundreds of deaths through his militia.'

'Sounds like a man who must have fallen out of favour in modern times.'

'There, you are wrong, my friend. After serving a brief jail time, he distanced himself from the GRA and began working as a black-market arms dealer using his vast network. Although everyone is aware of his illicit activities, the police are afraid to investigate his organisation. They fear he might go totally berserk if his weapons imperium is threatened. It certainly helps that most of the police are on his payroll.'

'The thing is, Samani and a mysterious Chinese man with the codename Cobra orchestrated one of the most impressive drug smuggling operations ever.'

'Tell me more,' Ramo said, sitting upright in bed.

Over the next ten minutes, Nick provided a comprehensive account of how Samani's crew used the World Discoverer as a ferry for their huge drug shipment. Ramo paused Nick's retelling every time he had a question or a tidbit of information related to Samani. When Nick finished his retelling of the story, he shared his concerns about Samani.

'To be honest, John, with what I'm hearing from you, I'm feeling deeply troubled about someone like Samani potentially gaining access to billions of dollars.'

'As you should. If he has involved the Chinese as well, I think he's going back to his old ways. I suspect the motive behind all of this is political, even though money is an excellent incentive on its own.'

'I imagine his crew must working non-stop as we speak. Is there anywhere you could go to look for clues?'

'I could take my car and have a stakeout near one of his warehouses down by the sea. It's around three kilometres south of the Port of Honiara, down Kukum highway. If they've received the shipment from their second narco sub, it should've made a stop there.'

'Please do that, and if you need any help or backup, call me. We should arrive in Honiara at the break of dawn, but I could hop on the RIB and speed the process up if needed.'

'No worries. I'll change and get there as fast as I can.'
'Perfect. We'll keep in touch. Stay safe, John.'

34

NICK HAD JUST disembarked from the RV Solander and was moving towards Ramo's parked Toyota RAV4. His Squale showed it was 7:14 in the morning. Captain Clarke had docked the ship at the Port of Honiara a few minutes ago after sailing from Mbike Island through the night.

The port had returned to normal again. Gone were the ferries, the passengers from the World Discoverer and the makeshift tents of the RSIPF. Instead, they were replaced by a hundred-and-forty-metre-long Handysize bulk carrier transporting rice from Port Klang in Malaysia. Dock workers dressed in oil-greased orange coveralls were busy offloading the ship's cargo under the scorching sun.

'Morning, John! How did your stakeout go?' asked Nick as he settled into the co-driver's seat.

'Things are quite serious. Let me take you on a drive, and we can discuss it along the way.' Ramo shifted his car into gear and made a sharp U-turn to begin his drive toward the port's exit.

'Take this. You'll need it for later,' he said and tossed Nick a pair of binoculars. 'After our call last night, I moved to a vantage point overlooking the warehouse Samani uses to store weapons and armaments. I examined the location for two hours.'

'What did you see?' Nick asked eagerly.

'First of all, there was a lot of activity in the parking lot. I counted five trucks entering and exiting in just those two hours. All of them were loaded and sent in different directions as soon as they hit the highway. Three of them drove towards Honiara.'

'Did you get a glimpse of what they were moving around?'

'Oh, I'm sure it is weapons and ammunition. Most of the pallets contained wooden crates.'

'Interesting. How is the security there?'

'They have a tall metallic fence with barbed wire covering the warehouse. Four security guards armed with rifles watch the trucks come and go through the main entrance, and another set of guards coordinate which gate each truck should use to collect their cargo.'

'So the warehouse has open access from the seafront, correct?'

'Yes. You will see it later when we park the car. They have a small wharf there to dock ships similar to the size of the one you were on.'

'Okay, got it.'

They continued their drive down Kukum highway until Ramo turned on his flashing lights and pulled out of the highway and onto a dirt road on their right. He stuck to the ruts and carefully manoeuvred the car on a winding road up the mountain. The ride was bumpy, but since the weather had been so nice the last few days, they made slow and steady progress. If they had tried to drive up this road after a tropical rainstorm, they would have probably been stuck in the mud.

'We should be close to the vantage point now,' Ramo said as they broke out of the dense jungle and into a clearing.

The clearing was next to a sharp right hairpin that continued further up into the mountains and ended in one of the many villages outside Honiara. Ramo brought the car to a stop on the side of the road. Nick grabbed the binoculars and followed Ramo to the edge of the cliff. They were about five hundred metres away from the warehouse.

'Alright, let me guide you as you use the binoculars.'

Nick pulled up the binoculars and focused on the main entrance outside the warehouse.

'I'm looking straight at the warehouse entrance right now.'

'Okay, good. See the four guards I mentioned earlier in the car?'

'Yes, I see them.'

'Great, now focus on their outfits. See the patches on their arm sleeves?'

Nick steadied his hands and zeroed in on their uniforms. Three white letters stood out on the patch – GRA.

'They are all wearing GRA uniforms?'

'That's right. Seems to me that Samani is warming up to the idea of reviving the GRA once again.'

'What would he gain from that?' asked Nick, lowering his binoculars, as he had seen enough.

'Multiple things, if you ask me. The first thought that comes to mind is to awaken the animosity once again with the MEF.'

'And to throw the islands into a civil war again? Now that you mention it, he could provide both sides of the conflict with weapons. With the billions in his pockets, he could fuel this war for a substantial period.'

'He has enough cash now to set this already struggling country back a hundred years. We need to stop him.'

'I agree. If that's his plan, we can't let him succeed. I'll inform the Australians about Samani and see if they were able to dig up any information last night.'

'Perfect. I'll take you back to your ship,' said Ramo, opening the car door for him.

The downhill drive back to the port took them half an hour due to the morning rush-hour traffic. When they had finally arrived, Ramo parked the RAV4 under a roofed parking space. Nick asked him to lie low and be ready if they needed his help again during the day.

Inside the ship, Nick looked for Jason, Santini or Helen. He found Jason outside the op centre.

'Morning, partner. Where have you been? I didn't see you leave the ship this morning.'

'I had to follow up on some intel I received from Ramo.'

'I like that fellow. How did it go?'

'Let's find Helen and Santini so we can go through this together.'

Jason agreed and moved into the crew mess to find the rest of the team discussing around their table.

'Nick's back and has some interesting information. He's waiting for us in the op centre.'

They all picked up their empty plates and cleaned the table before making their way to the op centre. Inside, Nick had prepared the photos he had taken of the warehouse and was projecting them onto the screen. When everyone had grabbed a seat, he began explaining about Samani's ties to the GRA and the position he held at the moment. He emphasised the potential revival of The Tensions from 1998 and how Samani could make the most out of a situation like that. In his concluding remarks, he asked Helen if the Australian Intelligence could corroborate the intel and if they had made any progress on their end.

'Most of the intel I received from Canberra perfectly aligns with what Nick just told us. However, they also came up with a few viable leads that looked quite interesting,' said Helen, taking over from Nick.

'This particular warehouse Nick scouted earlier today has been funded and built using money from a Chinese shell company that we traced back to Shanghai.'

'The same city where Cobra is rumoured to be from.'

'Exactly. Although we couldn't dig up anything else on Cobra, it was an interesting connection nonetheless.'

'What's the other lead?'

'The same shell company has also made sizable investments in the local football team of Honiara, known as Central Coast FC, and in a Chinese hospitality investment group.'

'Who has ties with the football team and this particular investment group?'

'One name kept popping up – Moses Sikua.'

'I assume you've looked into this gentleman?' Santini asked.

'Of course, Mr. Santini. Moses Sikua is a well-known businessman from Honiara. Besides owning the city's football team, he also owns the five-star Coral Sea Resort where you were staying and a seafront casino called Queen of Hearts. He comes from a family of farmers who have been producing palm oil for hundreds of years. When he took over from his parents, he immediately aimed higher and began exporting to global markets, with China as his primary customer. He finished his bachelor's degree in Financing and Banking at the University of Honiara, and back in 2010, he moved to Hong Kong to take a master's degree. In 2012, he completed his degree at the Hong Kong Polytechnic University with an MSc in Hospitality and Business Innovation. From that point on, he financed his childhood dream of building the Coral Sea Resort in 2015, and in 2018, he opened up his own Casino. He bought Central Coast FC in 2019 and recently completed a total renovation of the club's home stadium, making it the most modern stadium in the Oceanic Region. He publicly stated that his dream is to arrange the Pacific Games in 2024 and help improve people's lives on the islands. He spends most of his free time in his mansion outside of Honiara, taking his private seaplane for a spin or polishing his Kung Fu skills. I forgot to say he's a certified Sifu in martial arts, accredited by the Hong Kong Martial Arts Association.'

'Back to business, though, Sikua and Samani look like two people who could benefit greatly from working together.'

'What do you mean by that, Nick?' the Admiral asked.

'I mean, Samani is the perfect guy to kick off a wave of social unrest, leaving the door open for Sikua to take over the nation with a fellow swoop. To me, he seems like a future prime minister, and his moves are very strategic. First, he cemented his family's legacy and well-being by turning the family business into a profitable one. Then, he widened his network abroad – in our case, China – and slogged his way into a position where he could realise his dreams and enter the elite status in his country. Along the way, he constantly improved his own knowledge, becoming a more savvy businessman. The cherry on this cake is buying the city's beloved sports team and doing all this charitable work for the local communities. What is the current consensus of the people about their government? Not good. Every individual we have encountered on our trip has commented on that fact. A bout of social unrest where blood is spilt would be the end of this government, and you all know it. With the right timing, Sikua could take over the country.'

Everyone took a second to process what Nick had said, absorbing all the information. Santini was the first to reply.

'Let's not forget that the current government has taken Australia's side since 2003. Although they may not have stabilised the country, they are technically on your side, right, Admiral?' Santini asked, and the Admiral nodded. 'And it's obvious that Sikua would take the Chinese's side if he ended up as prime minister, right?'

'That's right, Mario.'

'And if that happens, you will have no access to this part of the Oceanic region. Plus, they would nab a Geothermal plant and a prime location for a new naval base in Tulagi right under your nose.'

'I believe this is a highly plausible scenario,' said Helen. 'My fear is this: what if Samani gets addicted to the thrill of guerrilla war again and decides not to pull the plug for this conflict, consequently sabotaging Sikua, who will definitely look to step in as a saviour for the local population? Samani was a brutal killer back in the day with no regard for human life. He doesn't strike me as someone who likes to follow orders.

'That's a question I'm not willing to sit and wait around for an answer. To me, it seems easier to approach Sikua than Samani at this point. Any ideas?' asked the Admiral.

Nick was scrolling on his iPhone, checking when the next game of Central Coast FC would be. 'Folks, I think it's our lucky day. His team is playing later today at their home stadium. What if I approach Sikua as a potential sponsor for his club? I can pretend to be some rich British-Greek expat with lots of money. I can suit up, put on a cheesy Greek accent and take it from there?'

'Anyone with a better idea?' Santini asked, fishing for someone else to chime in with a better suggestion. 'Nobody?'

Nick sized the opportunity and ran with the idea.

'Well, what if I go to the stadium and have Jason shadow me in case something should happen? Meanwhile, Helen can keep an eye on Samani's moves down by the warehouse throughout the day?'

'We can totally do that,' Helen replied, receiving a nod of approval from the Admiral.

'Very well, Nick. Get your ass in gear. Find a proper suit and come up with a damn good cover story for tonight. I'll see what I can do to get you a VIP ticket for tonight's football match,' said Santini before ushering him out of the op centre.

'For sure, Boss. You're talking to Dinos Nikolaou of Mediterranean Investment Holdings, specialised in global deep-sea, coastal and inland water transportation and maritime asset management. My aim for tonight is to get my shipping company, Phos Shipping, on the shirt of Central Coast FC.'

With that, Nick excitedly departed from the op centre, waving goodbye to everyone.

35

NICK KNEW HE wouldn't have to visit a tailor, as he was always prepared when it came down to clothes, accessories and outfits. A tailored white shirt, with the top two buttons left unbuttoned, was tucked in his high-waist white Casatlantic pants. A baby-blue linen jacket rounded it all off, with "spalla camicia" shoulders, as the Italians would say – a shoulder type that followed the natural lines of the body and produced a gentle, flowing shoulder, perfect for a more casual setting like this football match.

To completely sell the look, he printed a couple of business cards with Johnson's help. He also went the extra mile by setting up a simple website for Phos Shipping in case Sikua decided to look him up. Johnson and Bakke had a lot of fun with that and used their downtime to populate the site with various information and photos.

'Splendid outfit, Mr Nikolaou,' Jason commented. 'The transportation is ready and waiting for you. You have a big game coming up.'

'The time is ticking, Jason. Let's get going.' Nick said, tapping his finger on his watch.

Jason had parked a rented racing yellow Porsche 986 Boxster next to the ship's gangway.

'Wow, you've outdone yourself, partner. This car's a beauty, and you've picked the one with the convertible top,' said Nick, stroking the car's bonnet.

'Yes, sir. I always nail the assignment. A 2002 model post-facelift. The keys are in the ignition. Don't you worry about me. I'll pull up in a banged-up pickup truck and park somewhere around the stadium.'

'Thanks, man. We'll stay in touch through our molar mics if needed.'

Nick jumped on the throttle and smiled at the engine's sound. The rear tires spun, leaving the smell of burnt rubber in his wake.

When he was nearing the stadium, he almost wished the drive had lasted longer than the five minutes it had taken him. The car was a blast to drive and had clearly stood the test of time. As he drove to the parking lot entrance, a security guard stopped him and asked for his ticket. He pulled out the ticket from his breast pocket and flashed it at the guard. Santini had arranged for the best seats in the house so he could mingle with Honiara's elite.

'The VIP parking section is straight down and to the far right. Enjoy, sir!'

Nick tipped his invisible hat at him and drove the car to the VIP parking spot. An interesting assortment of late 90s and early 2000s sports cars were lined up. The stadium looked impressive from the outside and reminded him of a miniature version of Udinese's old stadium, Friuli, before the 2013 renovation.

His initial impression of the stadium was confirmed when he stepped out of the lounge area and into the stands. A curved roof covered the short side, where the press, VIPs and locker rooms were located. The rest of the uncovered stands circled the pitch, separated by a running track and field. Although he did not like such stadium layouts since he preferred being close and personal to the action, he completely understood the decision since Sikua wanted to host next year's Pacific Games. He grabbed the match programme and began reading it to understand what was at stake in tonight's game. Nick occasionally cast a glance back at the lounge's entrance to see when Sikua would arrive.

The fans slowly filled up the twenty thousand available seats, and the speakers began blasting pop music as the teams warmed up. Amid the rhythmic chanting and drum sounds, the crowd's clapping suddenly intensified. Nick turned to look behind him and saw Moses Sikua entering the building, waving to the fans.

He had a towering presence because of his height and athletic physique. Nick sized him a little under two metres. Sikua was wearing a white shirt, navy blue dress pants and an eighteen-carat yellow gold Rolex Yachtmaster II with a blue bezel on his left wrist. He looked towards the pitch through his golden Cartier prescription glasses and made small talk with some people from his entourage. His fade and goatee were extremely crisp, making it seem as if he had just visited his barber. In Nick's eyes, he evoked the aura of Russell 'Stringer' Bell from The Wire, but he struggled to imagine him practising Kung Fu. His physique was more akin to that of an NFL linebacker or an under-sized NBA centre. Either way, this was not a man to engage with in a fistfight.

Nick checked his Squale and noted there were around forty minutes until kickoff. When Sikua's entourage went about their business, Nick stood up and approached him.

'Good evening, Mr. Sikua! What an atmosphere the fans have set up for the team tonight. I'm Dinos Nikolaou, CEO of Mediterranean Investment Holdings. Love what you have done with the stadium. And the new coach looks exciting on paper. I know him from his short stint back in my home country, Greece.'

'Pleased to make your acquaintance, and thank you for your kind words. Greece, you say, Mr. Nikolaou? I've never been there, but it looks magnificent. I'd like to go to Mykonos and Santorini.'

'You certainly can't go wrong with those two. I highly recommend them.'

'Maybe I need to squeeze a visit into my schedule for next year. How did a Greek like you end up in Honiara? I hope you're enjoying your time on the most beautiful island in Oceania.'

'It's my first time here, but I quite like it. I'm a British-Greek expat from London on a business trip, actually,' Nick replied. 'I had a meeting with Gustav Breland – I'm sure you know of him – about some potential business opportunities.' Nick wanted to check Sikua's reaction when he mentioned Breland's name.

Sikua livened up, but there was nothing suspicious about his reaction. 'How can I not know him? Of course, I know him. He is an excellent person and a forward-thinking businessman. Pity about his ship, though; I hear it's unsalvageable.'

Nick made a mental note of that remark.

'I don't know for sure, but if you say so. Poor guy, though. Things were incredibly hectic for him. It was pure luck that I got to meet him yesterday.'

Nick had warmed Sikua up enough with the small talk, so he got straight to the point. 'By the way, on this trip, I had a second mission I wanted to accomplish, and that was to propose a potential cooperation with you, through my shipping company.' Nick handed him the fake business card.

Sikua always enjoyed discussing new ideas that could result in financial gains. He consulted his Rolex to check how much time he had before kickoff and quickly opened up a tab on his phone to check the website on the business card and verify Nick's legitimacy. After scrolling through it for a bit, he looked back at him.

'Your luck still runs strong. Let's go into my office and discuss this over a drink. Come.'

Nick followed Sikua as he parted the VIP crowd like Moses parted the Red Sea. On the way, he ordered a drink called Chuan Energy. It was a vodka-based cocktail infused with vanilla, lychee liqueur, and Sichuan pepper honey, all topped with a splash of lime. It was Sikua's favourite drink from his time in Hong Kong, back when he was a regular customer at the Hutong restaurant.

'What would you like to drink?' Sikua asked Nick.

'I'll have a negroni.'

'A classic choice. Make the gentleman a baijiu negroni, Hong Kong style.'

The bartender prepared the negroni as usual but replaced the gin with baijiu, a white liqueur distilled from fermented sorghum. It had a funky, sweet, fruity flavour with a touch of nuttiness. Baijiu could also claim the title of the strongest Chinese alcoholic drink. Nick watched closely as the barman did his thing, ensuring that he didn't get spiked. God knows what Sikua was capable of. When the barman finished mixing up the cocktails, they moved into Sikua's office.

His private office was more like an enormous living room that overlooked the pitch. Calling it an office was an understatement. Plush decorations and classic art pieces adorned the walls alongside a trophy cabinet with the club's accomplishments. A wall-mounted 8K TV displayed the live feed of the game, allowing Sikua to multi-task or retreat to his private quarters if the match wasn't going his team's way. Sikua leaned back into his armchair and crossed his legs.

'So, now that we have some privacy, I'm all ears. How can I benefit from your shipping company?'

Nick took another sip of his negroni and lowered his glass. It tasted funny, but out of politeness, he tried not to grimace.

'For many years, I have looked into getting involved with football in this region, but I was always hesitant. I never seemed to find the right project to match my ambitions. When I saw what you were doing with your team, I realised I had to reach out to you. With the Pacific games on the horizon next year, I think it's the perfect timing.'

'I'm always on the lookout for anyone willing to invest in my club. My big dream is to merge the Oceania Football Confederation with the Asian Football Confederation so that Central Coast FC can be the first team in the nation's history to compete in the AFC Champions League. I believe we are closer than ever to making it happen. I'm tired of being on the outside looking in,' Sikua replied.

Nick seized the opportunity. 'I didn't know about that, but you've just given me another extra reason to invest in this team now. Lofty goals like that are only set by real winners.'

'Let's cheer to that.' Sikua raised his glass. 'So, what were you thinking in particular?'

'I was thinking of a main sponsorship for the jersey and setting up a cooperation with a network of lower division clubs in the UK to share experiences, player development and resources to elevate this club to where it truly belongs.'

He could see in Sikua's eyes that he was sold on his sales pitch.

'You know what? Why don't you come to my casino and discuss numbers with my associates? I have a charity event happening later today, and the proceeds will go towards building a children's hospital in Honiara.'

'For sure! Let's enjoy the game and talk business later,' said Nick, proceeding to shake Sikua's outstretched hand.

'Pleasure to meet you, once again. I think we can do great things together.'

Satisfied with how the meeting had gone, Nick returned to his seat. He watched the entire game and only left his seat when the referee had blown his final whistle thrice. Sikua's team had won with three goals to zero, and the atmosphere in the stadium was electric. Thanks to Santini's VIP ticket, he squeezed through the traffic ahead of the regular crowd.

Nick had a clear plan: he had to break into Sikua's office in the casino.

He was sure that any dirt on Sikua could only be found locked up inside in the safest room he had. The only thing he had to do now was to convince Helen and Jason to tag along with his plan. He pressed a few buttons on his iPhone and put Helen on speaker as he drove his Porsche.

'Listen carefully,' said Nick, 'I'll need your help tonight with raiding Sikua's office. Find the most beautiful dress you can and join me at his charity event.'

'If breaking into a millionaire's office right under his nose is your idea for a date, count me in. Samani mentioned something about Sikua being in charge of things when I looked for clues down by his warehouse earlier today.'

'Interesting. How did it go with your infiltration of the warehouse? Stupid of me to ask. You're probably okay since you've answered my call.'

'Yeah, it took some time, but I managed to sneak in from the sea when it got darker. If you have a spare minute or two, I can tell you exactly what happened.'

'By all means, do tell. I'm stuck at a red light, and the traffic is picking up. I have more than enough time to listen to your adventures,' said Nick, turning the phone's volume up a few notches.

'Alright, so this is how it all played out,' Helen began.

36

HELEN METICULOUSLY SCANNED every single inch surrounding Samani's coastal warehouse through a pair of night vision binoculars. After two hours of observing guard routines, camera placements, patrol routes and possible entry points, getting familiar with the lay of the land and waiting for the night shift to commence, she was now ready to proceed with the more practical part of her infiltration. Without raising any unwanted eyebrows, she had haggled herself onboard a small purse seine vessel to get within Samani's orbit. The vessel was due for a late evening fishing trip along the coast of Honiara, and after Helen's instructions, the crew had decided to divert from their usual course and drop their nets close to the warehouse. She genuinely hoped they would still be able to reel in a good catch despite not fishing by their regular spot.

The family of five that used this boat to earn their daily bread had been kind enough to let her come aboard. They hadn't asked any intrusive questions, which was how she preferred things when operating undercover. It may have had something to do with Ramo's kind gesture of vouching for her in the presence of the family's father. She told them that by accepting her as a passenger and taking the bundle of cash she had brought with her to the captain, they were doing their motherland a big favour in combating the illicit trade of tobacco. The amount they had negotiated was more than enough to sweeten the deal for the head of the family. Whether they actually believed her narrative was purely their decision to make. She felt she had done all she could on her part to shield them from the hard truth. It was imperative for the mission's success that they didn't flake on her. And if a white lie was all it took to provide her with a coastal vantage point and a safe getaway, she would gladly fabricate a convincing one.

For the first time during her whole stay in the Solomon Islands, she would get a chance to branch out on her own. She experienced a new-found sensation of freedom and danger boosting her alertness. Though she did not have to prove anything to anyone, she would finally be able to show the Admiral and OMIA what she was really capable of. At the same time, though, she didn't want to cast any doubt on her tobacco smuggling cover story, especially for the younger ones, who were unaware of the malevolent forces at play.

She had, therefore, chosen to run this op with the most spartan equipment set possible, opting not to showcase any visible weaponry with her tactical outfit. Even though she knew that being fully kitted would make her infiltration less cloak and dagger, her moral compass compelled her to do otherwise. The only items she could count on if things went sideways were her trusty little sidearm and knife, which were appropriately silenced and concealed for the occasion. Both were strapped onto a black ankle holster that blended in with the rest of her outfit.

The circumstances had finally compelled her to go in without backup. It felt like ages since she last pulled a stunt like this. Sinking deep into her pool of memories, she remembered the last time to be around the period she worked as a vice detective for the Sydney Police Department. Back then, she had spent endless nights all by herself, trying to pick apart a human trafficking and prostitution ring that had terrorised the streets of Sydney. She had barely managed to come out alive after a reckless raid on the traffickers' headquarters. Looking back from a more mature outlook, she didn't have any qualms about how she had handled that situation. Despite being heavily reprimanded for her course of action by her commander in the PD, she did what she had to do to disrupt the traffickers' network, sparing any life she could from a future of mental trauma, uncertainty and physical abuse.

Despite her family's beliefs, she believed with a steely conviction that putting the public's lives ahead of hers was the only way to properly go about her job. Although the stakes were different now, the flame of justice inside her still burnt with fervour – the same one she felt the first day she crossed the police academy's doorstep.

Tonight, she had to break into a warehouse and gather incriminating evidence on Samani and Sikua. The catch was that she needed to do so without leaving any proof of her presence. If not, then the next couple of days could turn 'The Tensions' period from the late 90s into a more romanticised era than previously assumed, but for all the wrong reasons.

Just by visualising the challenges that lay ahead, her current mission seemed increasingly insurmountable. But the deeper she kept looking for answers, the more she leaned on it being doable. And the sooner she got going with her infiltration, the faster the foggy clouds of doubt would disappear from her mind.

When the warehouse guards had around ten minutes left before rotating their crew for the night shift, she put on a pair of fins and her mask and silently slid into the dark sea from the stern part of the vessel. She reckoned she could make the swim towards the warehouse and get to land at around the same time as they exchanged shifts, and she hoped to catch someone slacking or slightly deviating from their routines.

Using the textbook form of a freestyle stroke, she swam like a seal, approaching the long stone-built wharf sticking out from the land, connecting with the rest of the facility. Her body glided through the sea without much resistance, while she alternately anchored her hands to move forward. The current was pushing her towards land, helping her cut down on valuable seconds. A trio of RIBs with Yamaha outboard engines were tied to the wharf, the same ones she had previously observed from the fishing boat. There was no guard activity near the wharf, so she decided to approach the opposite side from where Samani's guards had docked their patrol boats. It was much darker there, and the few light sources that could be found were solely focused on the boats. In case a guard veered off his patrol route and checked out the wharf, she would be impossible to spot unless he stood right over her.

The lapping waves of Iron Bottom Bay struck the shore with the steady pulse of the sea, overshadowing the sound of her swimming. When her feet finally touched the sandy bottom, she decided to remove her fins and silently waddle her way until she was on dry land. She quickly dug up a shallow hole to hide her fins and mask as the salty water from her face dripped down onto the soft sand.

Looking ahead, she could see the warehouse, beckoning her to explore it like it was a haunted mansion in the middle of nowhere. The mountains east of Honiara rose like dark shadows behind them; the darkness felt as ominous as Samani himself.

While staying in a crouched position, she snuck her way closer to the warehouse until the metal fence circling the property stopped her dead in her tracks. A short barbed razor wire with central reinforcement ran along the top of the fence. Keeping her head on a swivel, she studied it to see what options she had. Climbing was risky and could turn her into easy pickings if someone caught a sniff of her. Even so, the razor wire on top was impossible to climb over with her average body stature. She saw no point in handing herself an even bigger handicap than what she had at the moment. Precious seconds ticked away the more she studied the fence. It was at that moment her thoughts were interrupted by the sound of a large vehicle decelerating. The sudden wave of commotion coming from the inbound area of the warehouse caught her by surprise. And then, it actually dawned on her.

'The guards are rotating shifts,' she whispered to herself. 'Time to move.'

She took a deep breath to refocus, and then, she noticed something she hadn't seen before. Her eyes had finally adjusted to the darkness of the night and things seemed way sharper than before. The metal fence in front of her had clear-cut signs of rust from the constant exposure to the sea. She traced her fingers along the coarse metal. It didn't feel as secure as Samani's guards considered it to be. But still, even with the help of her diving knife, it would take her far too long to cut through the fence. It would also most definitely announce her position to the nearby guards. No, she had to find another way. Looking to her left and right for another solution forced a brand new idea to form in her mind. The sand underneath her was still very soft, so she instinctively began to dig like a dog, searching frantically for its buried bones. When she had managed to dig out a decent enough opening, she quickly laid down on her stomach and pressed herself underneath it, making her body as small as possible. The fence ripped the diving suit off her back, cutting her in a few places. She quickly placed her hand on the fence to make it stop vibrating. Next, she checked the wounds on her back and saw some of her fingers turn slightly red with her blood. She shrugged it off as a minor inconvenience. At long last, she was safely inside the warehouse's perimeter with only a few scratches to bear. No one seemed to have caught wind of what she was up to, judging from the commotion that was still going on strong in the warehouse's parking lot.

Her eyes were now fixated on the nearest entry point she could see. It was a small side door with no cameras in sight. She increased her pace and made her way to the door while simultaneously casting cautious glances around her in case a guard should appear. A gentle push of the handle was all it took for the door to open. Fast as the wind, she entered the warehouse, gently locking the door behind her. The room was pitch black, and she initially couldn't make out what it was used for.

The room emitted a strong odour of metal, booze and oil, causing her to grimace as she took her first breath inside the warehouse. When her eyes skimmed the small room, all she could see were steel ammo boxes, neatly stacked in towers of five. On her left, a tidy shelf crammed with small gun solvent bottles stretched along the wall. This is the storage area for everything but weapons, thought Helen as she silently navigated the overfilled room. On her way to the door, she passed boxes full of cotton rags and a half-pallet laden with illegally imported vodka bottles. She noticed the boxes were marked with packaging labels addressed to the port of Vladivostok. It seemed that Samani's drink menu featured only one cocktail, the old-fashioned Molotov.

Leaving the revelations of the tiny armoury behind, Helen edged closer to the door to see what was hiding in the next room. The door was wooden and had a small frosted window that was impossible to see through. Suddenly, the lights went on, lighting up the room behind the blurry window. Helen instinctively reacted to the lights by stepping to the side and placing her back against the wall, turning into one with the shadows. She heard a door creak shut, followed by multiple footsteps and an indistinct chatter slowly approaching her. The voices became louder and clearer as they inched closer to her position.

'So, Mr. Samani, when are we going to launch our assault? My men are getting restless from all this thumb-twiddling,' a gruff voice said with a markable annoyance.

'Soon, my general, soon. If it were up to me, we would have taken over Honiara by yesterday. But, as you already know, Sikua has the last word in this matter.'

'Damn, so be it then.'

'It's rather unfortunate, I know. On top of that, he has a charity event happening at his casino. I'm afraid we need to stay put for the night before we get any further updates from him.'

The general chuckled. 'I never thought this day would come when Samuel Samani, the legendary rebel himself, would speak so fondly of a capitalist.'

Samani laughed loudly, clearly entertained by the general's reply. 'Times change, people get older, and I like to convince myself that I'm getting wiser each year.'

'On the last two points, I can agree with you. But the first one, I don't think so.'

'Oh, how so?'

'Come on now, boss man; we're in the Solomon Islands. Open your eyes and you'll see that nothing has really changed since we were young rebels.'

'I can see where you're coming from with this. But, hey, let's be the ones to change that then. I hope you haven't lost faith in Sikua. If you have, I might have to send you in here to count how many bullets we have left.' Samani's strict military voice made it clear to his general that he wasn't joking.

Helen could sense that they were quite close now and that Samani had his hand on the door handle.

'No, not at all. I fully trust him,' the general backpedalled.

'Alright. But, then again, when was the last time someone checked that room? Our firepower ain't worth nothing if we don't have the proper amount of ammo.'

Samani couldn't afford any discrepancies at this stage of their plan and needed to ensure that everybody had proper ownership of their tasks. Helen could feel the tension building in her chest like a boiler. She mentally prepared herself in case she needed to pull out her silenced gun. They were standing right outside her room now, and if that door opened, all of her stealthy efforts would be for nothing. The seconds passed painfully slowly as she waited for the general to answer.

'I can assure you that we have everything we need. Me and a couple of my best guys handed over the last ammo shipment yesterday. Everything is under control and accounted for down to the last bullet.'

'Very well. Don't take it personally, my general. I'm just making sure everyone's on the same page.' Samini's hand let go of the door handle, much to Helen's relief.

The general grunted in response and continued walking further down the corridor with Samani until a sliding door was heard closing shut behind them. The lights went off and everything turned peacefully silent again, except for a soft beeping sound. Helen presumed it was an alarm dedicated to that area of the warehouse.

She exhaled a huge sigh of relief as she stood there, like a fly glued to the wall, lurking in the dark. Two things were clear from the brief interaction she had overheard: Sikua was the one calling the shots and pulling all the strings at the moment. Samani respected him so much that deviating from their plan, just to satisfy his rebels' gung-ho needs was completely out of the question. That wouldn't have happened two decades ago, as it clearly contradicted the modus operandi that had earned Samani a name for himself. The ball was now in Sikua's court. And if he were even half as good as his team, it wouldn't be long before he made a game-changing move.

Well, it was time now to gather some evidence. She unzipped her dive suit's calf zip and pulled out a tiny waterproof camera. It resembled any other USB flash drive you could buy at your local electronics store. On top of its flat surface was a small button that Helen pressed to snap pictures of Samani's armoury. An internal debate began in her mind. She wondered if the rest of the warehouse was worth investigating. She had concrete proof now that Samani and his rebels were arming up for something big, but still, she had nothing she could pin on Sikua. That would be Nick and Jason's responsibility. It was time to return to the fishing vessel and calm the worried crew onboard.

Before leaving, she checked if the door was equipped with a sensor or some kind of landline alarm. And indeed, it was. Right over the door frame, she noticed a small box with some cables linked up to it. A red blinking light indicated that the alarm was on. Helen checked which one of the colourful cables was the phone line before ripping it out of the alarm sensor.

As she exited the door, she came face to face with the guard assigned to watch over the warehouse's seafront. He had just turned around, curious to see who had emerged from the door behind him. No one was supposed to be inside the warehouse during his shift, so naturally, the sound piqued his interest. Helen had the advantage of standing on top of the short staircase that led out of the building. The guard couldn't move as swiftly as her since his shoes were planted in the sand.

Without letting him utter a single word, Helen surged forward and jumped into the air with her knee sticking out. She struck him right in the abdomen, causing the surprised guard to double over in pain. His AK-47 rifle clattered down beside him, and the guard was left winded and vulnerable as he tried to reach for his knife. In one fluid motion, she followed up with a thunderous roundhouse kick to his jaw, sending him sprawling backwards. Seizing the opportunity, she swiftly disarmed him, throwing the knife high over the fence. Undeterred, the guard fought back with wild swings. Helen evaded the guard's reckless onslaught of punches with the nimble fluidity of a ballerina.

When the guard slowed down to regain his balance, she countered with a barrage of lightning-fast strikes aimed at his upper body. Her last strike hit him right in the temple, causing him to collapse on the sand like a toppled statue. His eyes were wide open as he lay there, staring into the nothingness. As she walked away from him, she thought he looked like a house where the lights were on but nobody was at home.

If the guards stuck to their schedule, it would take one to two hours before they noticed somebody was missing. By then, she would be long gone, freshly showered and wearing one of her favourite gala outfits. Her job here was done, but the night was young and could still deliver some even bigger thrills.

37

NICK HAD CHANGED into a more formal, dark-coloured suit and was waiting inside the Porsche. He drummed his fingers along the steering wheel in time with Larry June's newest song. His hair was neatly slicked to the right with a crisp side part. The temperature had dropped as the sun had been swallowed by the horizon, and a cool breeze was making it easier to cope with the suit he was wearing.

Good job, Agent Chapman, he thought as he made eye contact with Helen, who was walking down the gangway of the ship. She looked absolutely gorgeous in her Michael Lo Sordo Alexandra navy blue silk satin cocktail gown, with her hair in a slick back ponytail. A matching set of Messika diamond necklaces, bracelets and earrings made her shine bright in the tropical night. She was holding a YSL leather clutch with an embossed gold monogram of the brand on its side. A slit on the right side of the dress showed off her delicate curves and most of her right leg, leaving little to the imagination. A deep V-neck accentuated her cleavage.

'I think my cavalier for the night has arranged for my safe transport,' she said as Nick quickly exited the car to greet her.

'That's right, madame.' Nick bowed slightly and kissed her hand. 'Here, grab a seat and get comfortable.' He gallantly opened the door for her. 'Please fasten your seatbelt and enjoy the ride. And who knows, if we come out of this night alive, maybe I can take you out on a proper date.'

Sikua's casino, the Queen of Hearts, was an impressive feat of architecture, easily visible from anywhere in the city. It rose taller than any other building in town, and its rooftop lounge area lit up Honiara's night sky with lots of vibrant colours. A seafront beach club and marina had attracted the finest yachts in the area for tonight's charity event.

'They will surely collect enough money tonight to build not one but

177

two hospitals,' Helen commented as they waited to hand over the car to the casino's valet.

Two car lengths in front of them, Sikua was stepping out of a silver Bentley Continental T Stratton, a one-of-a-kind car he had acquired at a Sotheby's car auction. He greeted his employees and headed straight for the entrance, where lots of guests had gathered. Waiters in classy outfits were walking around, handing out welcome drinks at the casino's entrance.

'We're out of our car and moving into the casino. Where are you now?' Nick asked through his molar mic.

'I bribed one of the marina's dockworkers to find a spot to dock the RIB. I will be here when you need exfil. I see a lot of armed guards tonight among the crowds.'

'That's good to know. Send us your location in a message so that we can easily get to you.'

'Alright, I'll do it. Stay safe and let me know if you need anything on the way,' Jason said.

As soon as Nick and Helen walked through the golden revolving door of the casino, they were transported to a different world – a playground for adults bathed in neon and strobe lights. A world where the murmur of crowds was drowned by the bells and whistles of slot machines and the clatter of their levers being pulled. People were glued to their seats, intoxicated by the spinning roulette wheels and the way the red and black collided as it spun on its axis. High rollers glided from table to table in their extravagant suits, with the occasional sobbing man in the corner, having lost everything on the craps table. Sometimes, the exalted shouts of a winner could be heard, followed by applause from the bystanders. A handcrafted golden statue of a queen holding a queen of hearts card inside an exquisite fountain was the pièce de résistance of the casino's main hall.

'Ah, I see you found your way to the event,' Sikua said to welcome Nick. 'And you've brought some wonderful company as well. Welcome to the Queen of Hearts! My name is Moses Sikua.'

'Nicole Pereira, I'm Mr. Nikolaou's personal assistant. Nice to meet you, Mr. Sikua.'

Sikua mentally undressed Helen with his sleazy eyes before turning his attention back to Nick.

'Care to join me on the main table for some blackjack?'

'Of course, it would be an honour. How has the turnout been to-night? The place is buzzing.'

'It's been amazing. I think we're easily gonna surpass my initial expectations. The silent and live auctions tonight have been a tremendous success. Various raffles and the poker tournament are also going pretty strong at the moment with lots of money being generated.'

'That's awesome. Let's make some money for these kids.'

Nick took a seat and ordered a negroni from one of the waiters. Helen stood beside him, her right arm around him, while her left hand expertly lit his Rocky Patel cigar. He inhaled the wooden fragrance of her perfume, with a hint of fresh floral notes. Without letting the flame touch the cigar, Nick gently puffed a few times without inhaling until he felt the smoke in his mouth. He briefly checked the cigar to ensure it was evenly lit and continued smoking it, without inhaling, puffing in consistent one-minute intervals. When the ash grew to about two and a half centimetres, he gently tapped it along the ashtray's edge.

Sikua was sitting on the opposite side of the table, acting as the croupier. The minimum amount to play at the VIP table was ten thousand dollars, which Nick had withdrawn from OMIA's emergency account after receiving Santini and Rousseau's blessing.

Although it was for charity, Nick felt a fierce competitiveness emanating from the gentlemen playing at this table. Around him were lawyers, industrialists, politicians and celebrities. It was funny how men always made everything a competition.

The momentum on the VIP table ebbed and flowed back and forth, with the chips constantly changing positions. As time passed, more and more people left the table since Sikua had taken all of their chips. When Nick was the only one left, Sikua came up with a proposition that woke everybody up. Nick had around seven thousand dollars worth of chips at that moment, while Sikua had collected approximately sixty-three thousand dollars from the other players.

'Since it's just you and me, let's play a round of winner takes it all,' Sikua proposed.

Suddenly, the crowd got into the game again and pulled closer to the table so that everybody could have a clear view of the cards. Nick dramatically paused to make the scene extra tense.

'All in,' he replied, pushing all of his chips to the centre of the table.

Sikua handed Nick two clubs and two hearts. The crowd oohed and aahed because of the bad hand that had been dealt to Nick. Sikua smiled and handed out a king of spades to himself. The second card, he placed face down and slid underneath the previous one. He checked it through his peeker, a mirror that revealed what type of card it was. Next, Sikua quickly lifted his head back up and asked Nick for his next move. Sikua had the upper hand, so Nick had to go on the offensive to have any chance of beating the house.

'Hit me.'

Nick anxiously waited for the next card. Sikua looked around the table before placing a ten of spades beside Nick's cards. He was up at fourteen now, not a favourable spot to be in after having been dealt three cards.

Then came the critical decision. Should he hit for another card or stand at fourteen and pray that Sikua would overshoot it by coming over twenty-one? Helen winked and, with a kiss on the chin, whispered into his ear, 'If the croupier slowly brings his head back up, they have a blackjack. The quicker their head moves up, likely they don't have it.' She masqueraded her words with an angelic smile.

Nick immediately remembered that Sikua was rather quick to lift his head.

'Hit me,' Nick said, and the crowd fell silent in anticipation of the next card.

He took a big sip of his negroni and waited patiently. Sikua placed the card face down and pushed it excruciatingly slowly over to Nick's side of the table. When he felt he had everyone's attention, he flipped it. It was a seven of spades, exactly what the doctor ordered.

'Blackjack for Mr. Nikolaou.' Sikua said.

He immediately tensed up in his chair, and sweat stains began to form on his shirt's armpits. The only thing that could save him now was getting a blackjack with the third or fourth card. He handed himself the third card, an ace of hearts. Nick lived to fight another day. It would all come down to his fourth and last card. If he got an eight, they would tie and would need to play another round.

Sikua did not waste any time and nervously flipped his fourth card.

It was a nine of hearts. Nick had won by blackjack, and he stood up from his chair to celebrate. Many people in the crowd high-fived him. Sikua, in a noble act, clapped and pushed all the chips across to his side of the table.

'Thank you, everybody, but I want to donate all the money to the children's hospital.'

The crowd erupted with more cheering, and even Sikua came up to him to thank him for his generous gesture.

'You didn't have to do it, but I deeply appreciate it. Would you excuse me, Nicole? I'd like to borrow your plus one for a while. He and I have some business to attend to. It shouldn't take long.'

'By all means, do your thing. I'll take a walk and explore the rooftop lounge,' Helen replied.

'Do that, honey. See you later.'

When she was out of hearing range, Sikua commented, 'You are really lucky, my friend. She looks like a fine woman.'

'She is indeed,' said Nick, admiring her backside, 'but she is only my personal assistant.'

'Isn't that what everybody says?'

His indecent remark annoyed Nick, but he kept his composure and calmed himself down. They took the private elevator together with his bookkeeper and a pair of guards. Somewhere along the top floors, the elevator stopped, and they walked towards Sikua's private office.

'Gentlemen, could you point me in the direction of the lavatory? I need to empty my bladder. Wouldn't want to interrupt our meeting for such a mundane reason,' said Nick.

The guards pointed him the right way before heading to Sikua's private office. He thanked them and began separating himself from the entourage. When he had safely locked the toilet entrance behind him, he began speaking into the molar mic.

'Helen, can you hear me? I have a few seconds on my own.'

'Yeah, of course. I'm at the rooftop lounge. Where are you?'

'I'm right under you, I think. His office seems to be right under the rooftop. I can hear the music from upstairs. What I wanted to say is that I will be locked inside his office with all of his entourage. When I clear my throat, could you please make a scene in the lounge so that his guards can go up and check the commotion? If it's just him and his bookkeeper, I can try to take him down with a tranquiliser dart. I'll need to come up with a good distraction, though. If all goes well, I'll try to look around for any incriminating evidence, and then, we can meet up at the main staircase in the casino hall.'

'That, I can handle. Sure you don't want me to give you some backup?'

'No, it's fine. Hey, Jason, are you there?'

'Copy, partner.'

'For precautionary measures, could you please disable the guards' powerboats in the meantime? I plan to use our RIB as a getaway vehicle.'

'Smart move. I can take care of that. The marina is silent at the moment. Seems like everyone has moved inside.'

'Alright, let's do this,' said Nick, ending the transmission.

38

THE OFFICE BOASTED a panoramic view of the entire Honiara coast-line. Sikua was standing behind his window, looking out at the city.

'I can remember those days at the palm tree plantation as if they were yesterday. It's surreal to look at the life I've created for myself now. Two things have stayed the same since then: my drive and work ethic. You can't be a successful man without intention or purpose in life,' said Sikua, taking a seat. 'I'm sorry. I got a little carried away. Let's talk numbers, my friend. Are we ready?' he asked and glanced at his bookkeeper.

The bookkeeper was an odd-looking character – short in stature and built like a tank. He introduced himself as Mr. Cheng from Hong Kong. He must work out eight days a week to maintain a physique like that. When Nick commented on it, he politely laughed it off.

The guards had been stationed outside the office's entrance, watching out for any uninvited guests.

'Alright, we're ready. What was your official offer again?' Sikua asked.

'Okay, here goes. I'm offering you five million dollars over two years in exchange for a main jersey sponsorship and billboards around the stadium. The total amount will be paid out quarterly to the club in even sums.' Nick paused and pulled out a paper. 'Here's the network of the teams and personnel we can work within the UK to strengthen your team and bolster the international exposure of your team and my company, Phos Shipping.'

With that amount of money, Sikua could cover the wage budget for the next three years. He would have been a fool to renegotiate this offer.

'I think we have a deal,' said Sikua, raising his head from the paperwork and shaking Nick's hand. 'Oh me, oh my, that has to be the fastest negotiation we've ever done in this office. Mister Cheng, would you be so kind as to start the paperwork?'

The bookkeeper nodded and buried himself in stacks of paperwork, filling in the information and stamping the documents in front of him. Sikua had stood up and was lost again in his thoughts as he watched out of the window.

Now it was Nick's chance, and while the bookkeeper was occupied, he would stab Sikua with the dart and put him out of the equation. Afterwards, he would deal with the bookkeeper alone. After all, he was just a bookkeeper. How tough could he be?

Nick cleared his throat, using his fist to muffle the sound, and walked up to the window, feigning interest in the views below. Instead of patting Sikua's shoulder like a friend for their newly signed deal, he plunged the tranquilliser dart between his shoulder blades.

'Hey, what's this all about?' Sikua exclaimed in anger, trying to push Nick away. Nick evaded the push and watched as he slowly lost his senses and staggered as he attempted to move.

'Cheng, help me,' said Sikua, gasping for air before falling face down on the floor like a sack of potatoes.

This entire sequence played out in a few seconds, with Cheng only reacting when he heard his name being called out.

Meanwhile, on the rooftop lounge, Helen was busy getting two rich men to fight. After spilling red wine on both of them and tapping their shoulders, the two men began making a raucous in front of the bar, each thinking the other had spilt the drink on them. When both of their intoxicated entourages joined the fray, it escalated into a full-blown bar fight, like the ones you read about in the pulpy Morgan Kane novels of Louis Masterson. The few guards on the rooftop were out of their depth and began calling for reinforcements to contain the fight. More guards, including Sikua's two private guards, began flocking to the rooftop to help with the situation.

Down at the office, Nick had slid over the desk and tackled the bookkeeper, hitting him in the chest and knocking him over. After he dusted himself down, Cheng grabbed a pair of nunchaku that were hanging on the wall as decoration. He began deftly spinning them around in figure-eight motions as they measured each other like lions in the savannah.

'You're stupid for even trying. You ain't leaving this room alive,' Cheng warned.

'Says who?'

'I'm Lei Cheng, but you can call me Cobra,' Cheng declared, throwing away his blazer.

Slithering on his right arm was a realistic-looking tattoo of a cobra.

There he was, standing in front of him, one of the orchestrators of this mess, a person who had no qualms about endangering the lives of so many innocents. Nick felt his blood boil, but he had to move smartly. What little Nick knew of the martial arts, he compensated with his athleticism and unrelenting willpower.

Cheng lunged forward and slashed ahead with the nunchaku. He had telegraphed his movement, so Nick ducked and slid to the side. All Cheng did was smash Sikua's desk into pieces.

Nick backpedalled and stayed light on his toes. Cheng re-centred himself and turned towards him. He began closing the distance until he pinned Nick to a bookcase. When Nick didn't have anywhere to go, Cheng did a horizontal strike and hit him straight in the ribcage. Nick groaned and crouched as the wind got knocked out of him. Through the corner of his eye, he saw Cheng try to do the same, but he wouldn't let him land a second blow.

Suddenly, Helen burst into the room and began throwing multiple hardcover books, one after another, to startle him. Cheng had to prevent the books from hitting him by covering himself with his arms. Nick was glad to see her and used that moment to launch an offensive barrage against his opponent, knocking the nunchaku out of Cheng's hands.

Time was running out, and Nick saw no easy way to take out Cheng or break open the vault. They would have to come up with a new plan after tonight. The most important thing for now was that he had established a connection between Cheng and Sikua.

'It's pointless. We need to exit the building now,' Helen shouted as she saw Cheng picking up Sikua's revolver from the floor and loading it with bullets.

It was the one Sikua had stored inside his desk drawer.

With a rapid movement, she grabbed the nunchaku and sprinted towards the office's exit. Nick followed suit, quickly closing the doors behind them while she secured the nunchaku between the two door handles. Cheng tried to push open the doors, but they wouldn't budge. Nick then pushed a low shelf with some coffee table books and flower vases to block the door. They had to duck to avoid being hit by Cheng's bullets, which pierced through the wooden doors. Together, they sprinted towards the elevators.

'Jason, I'm with Helen. We made it out of the office, and we're taking the elevator down. We need to get out of here as soon as possible; they are onto us.' Nick put his hands on his knees to catch his breath.

'I'm starting the engines and waiting for you. I will contact Santini and let him know we are returning to the RV Solander.' Jason pulled out his phone to make the call.

When the elevator doors opened, Nick and Helen sprinted towards the gold revolving doors in the entrance. Time seemed to stretch as they waited for the doors to rotate and provide them with an opening to walk out. He turned around to see three guards pointing at them, probably concluding that they were the ones Cheng was looking for. When Nick and Helen exited the casino, they sprinted in the direction of the marina. Their chasers had exited through the employee door, saving them a lot of valuable time and helping them close the distance between them.

When Nick sensed them breathing down his neck, he increased his pace. Helen held her own and was not far behind. The marina was not far away now, and he could see the RIB with Jason waiting for them. When they arrived at the marina, the guards started shooting at them. The bullets whizzed by them, kicking up clouds of dust every time they hit something.

'Go!' Nick yelled as they jumped onboard the slow-moving RIB.

Handgun bullets were hitting the RIB in various spots, but without causing any significant damage because of its bulletproof construction. As Jason sped up out of the marina, Nick could see the guards trying to start their own powerboats. When they realised Jason had disabled them, their body language clearly showed their frustration and anger, even from a distance.

They may have lived through the night's escapades, but Nick was certain that Sikua, Cheng and Samani's crew would hit them back twice as hard. He only hoped that they could be one step ahead of them next time to confront them with the scales of justice.

39

'HEY! WE NEED some help over here! Anybody hear me?'

Cheng had finally broken open the office doors and was now seeking aid. When he saw a few guards responding to his call, he went back in to check on Sikua, who was still unconscious on the floor and bleeding from his forehead, an injury he had picked up from his uncontrolled fall. With the help of the other guards, he lifted him and placed him on a couch inside the office.

Cheng crouched to check Sikua's pulse. Cheng was really stressed that Sikua might have been poisoned or sustained a fatal head injury. His heart was still beating, so he would just have to wait for the effect of the tranquilliser to wear off.

'Did you catch the people who did it?' Cheng demanded, standing up to address the guards.

'They… they… escaped,' one guard replied, trembling with fear.

'You useless, lousy excuse of a guard. How did they escape from the most well-guarded building in Honiara?' Cheng yelled, walking straight up to the guard's face.

'Well, there was a…'

'I don't care about your excuses!' He punched the guard right in his face, knocking a few of his teeth out.

The guard collapsed on the marble floor with a loud thud. Cheng used the fallen guard's shirt to dry the blood from his hands.

'You saw what happened to your partner, right?' The second guard nodded in fear. 'I want you to check all the CCTV footage and give me the real name of Mr Nikolaou and the woman he entered the casino with.'

'Affirmative…'

'I said now!'

After twenty minutes, the guard returned with a folder in his hand containing photos of Nick and Helen from the CCTV cameras of the casino. The Chief Security Officer had analysed their faces through a vast database to see if he could get any hits on them. Cheng was leafing through the folder until he paused halfway through. His eyes focused on the printouts of their passports.

'Aha, here they are, Nick Diamantis and Helen Chapman. What did you find on these two?' asked Cheng, closing the folder.

'All we could dig up on Nick was that he's a Norwegian marine investigator working for OMIA. We had a difficult time finding something on Helen Chapman, however. The only thing we found was a news story about her working as a vice detective for the Sydney PD a couple of years ago.'

'Maybe she's some type of special forces or naval intelligence officer. I heard OMIA are working with the Australian Navy, so it makes sense.'

'So, what do you want us to do next?'

'Regroup downstairs with the rest and find me a group of ten of Samani's finest rebels who can be on standby for a special assignment. I'll have to see if Sikua is awake first. Okay?'

'Yes, sir,' the guard replied and exited the office.

In the meantime, Sikua was regaining his consciousness. As the dizziness dissipated, he sat upright on the couch. Cheng was quick to offer him a towel and a bottle of water to clean the blood from his face.

'What happened after I passed out? Did we get him?'

'I'm afraid not, sir. But I have some information you may find useful. We have his and his partner's real names. Look, it's Nick Diamantis from OMIA and Helen Chapman, an Australian intelligence officer, it seems. They are the ones working the World Discoverer case.' Cheng showed him the photos of their passports.

Sikua took his time scrutinising their photos before responding. His head was still ringing from the hit it had taken.

'If they are onto us, they surely must have found out about our involvement with the ship's sinking.'

'Probably yes, but they don't know our ultimate goal. We still have the upper hand in this scenario, and our alibis are rock solid. Plus, without any incriminating evidence, the only one they can pin this on is Ngelea.'

'I see. Wasn't it Breland who hired them to look into the World Discoverer?'

'That's correct. He flew them in his private jet.'

'Oh, and he will pay for this. While on the subject, have you cross-checked that all of Samani's deliveries have reached their destinations?'

'Of course. All the weapon shipments have been delivered to each GRA hideout in Honiara. Everyone is armed and ready, awaiting your signal.'

'Hmm... Maybe it's time for us to enter the last phase of our plan. Before that, though, there's one small thing I want to take care of.'

'I think I know exactly what you're thinking of, sir,' Cheng said pointing at the map decorating the wall beside Sikua's bookcase. His finger was on Savo Island.

'Indeed. You can borrow my seaplane for this. Choose your best GRA men for this operation. We can't tolerate any mishaps from now on. The objective is to parachute onto Savo Island and infiltrate Breland's GEOrganic plant. Kill all the scientists there but leave the machines and facilities intact. When we have this country in the palm of my hands, your country will take over the management of this energy plant, as we agreed upon.'

'Roger that. The China National Energy Corporation is ready to send over its best scientists and engineers. Any message you want us to send to Breland?'

Sikua touched his mouth and debated the answer to that question really hard.

'You know what, Cheng? Burn down his villa, but let him live. I want him to be constantly tormented by the lives lost because of his actions. And who knows? Maybe he will decide to join his father in the afterlife. When we are done with him, give the green light to the rest of the GRA. Tomorrow, we will finally free this country from the shackles of our oppressors. It's about time we reclaimed our own destinies. My people have suffered enough. Mark my words.'

'Let's make history together,' said Cheng, shaking Sikua's hand. 'I will radio you a message when our mission at Savo Island is complete.'

'Perfect. I will be here with a bird's-eye view of all the mayhem that will take place on the streets. I considered going to my villa, but maybe I'll drive there a little later when everything has simmered down.'

'No need to worry about anything. We will handle it, sir. The Westerners and the Australians will never bother you again no more.'
'Amen to that.'

<h1 style="text-align:center">40</h1>

The pilot flying Sikua's seaplane signalled to Cheng that they were nearing their drop zone. Cheng moved toward the sliding doors and addressed his crew.

'Our drop zone should come up in a few clicks. Try to land in the designated spots we talked about. Let's go, boys. Lock and load.'

He slid open the door, and the air hit him right in the face. One after another, he watched his crew jump and disappear into the dark sky.

'Meet us down in the bay where Breland's villa is,' he instructed the pilot before jumping out of the plane himself.

He adjusted his arms and legs into the correct position and began his descent down to the island. With a few seconds between each jumper, he could see his squad opening up their parachutes and gliding towards GEOrganic's facilities. Cheng, a seasoned paratrooper, enjoyed the freefall, resting with the support of an air column that kept him airborne and slowed his descent.

When his mental countdown was done, he pulled the chord of his parachute and sailed towards the energy plant's glass roof. He planned to have five of them break in through the main entrance, while he and four others would carve their way in from the top floor.

As soon as he landed on the roof, he took off his parachute and began directing his crew to the right positions. The energy plant had people working there 24/7, but they only used the top floor for board meetings and certain corporate events, meaning it would have little to no security presence. Cheng pulled out a device and typed a few combinations on its buttons. He placed it face up with its suction cups sticking to the glass roof. When there was a safe distance between him and the device, he activated the detonator.

The device triggered a super powerful EMP blast that short-circuited everything inside the plant, including its alarm system. They had ten minutes before the backup generator kicked in and brought the plant back to life.

'Go!' He yelled at his crew, and they began using their circular laser cutters to make pothole-sized openings to break into the facility.

One by one, they jumped through the holes and regrouped inside the boardroom.

Back down at the main entrance hall, the rest of Cheng's crew had entered as soon as they felt the EMP blast go off. The confused receptionists thought it was their own security doing a drill at first until they saw the barrels of Type 56 rifles pointing their way.

The muzzle fire from the rifles lit up the dark room as the bullets shredded the flesh of the innocent receptionists. Blood spatters painted the wall red behind the reception counter.

When Cheng heard the first shots go off in the entrance hall, his group moved towards the main staircase. They were about to enter the office section of the facility, where most of the scientists, engineers and managers spent their time. A couple of startled security guards walked around with their flashlights on and got blasted in their stomachs with Cheng's twelve gauge Type 97 shotgun. Another person from Cheng's crew pulled out his QSZ-92 handgun and planted a bullet in each of their skulls to put them out of their misery.

Hearing the gunshots, many people began screaming frantically and sprinting out of their private offices and cubicles. All of them were easy pickings as the five-man team killed them off one by one as they progressed through the building. Cheng felt like he was skeet shooting as he aimed and pulled the trigger without a second thought.

Papers were flying in the air and glasses were shattering, drowning the screams of agony of their victims. Case shells rhythmically fell from each of their rifles, scattering all over the floor.

Cheng and his squad continued with their killing spree, dealing death to anybody who crossed their paths, until they met up on the third floor of the building with the rest of his crew. They had done exactly the same, moving up from the facility's entrance, leaving nothing but death and destruction in their wake.

'The first part of our mission is complete. Let's head back down through the main entrance,' said Cheng, reloading his shotgun with more shells.

The regrouped squad sprinted down the main staircase and, in a little under a minute, were outside the facility.

'Breland is two clicks away from the facility. We'll cut through the jungle and raid his villa head-on. Follow me,' Cheng instructed, and the rest of the squad followed his lead like a well-trained unit.

Circling Breland's property was a metal fence mounted on a stone wall. Two security guards watched over the main gate. When Cheng neared the edge of the jungle, he crouched to stabilise his aim and peered through the sights of his weapon. The guards were forty metres away. Two crackling sounds were heard in quick succession, and the guards fell dead on the gravel road.

The loud noises caught Breland's attention as he sat on his balcony. They seemed to come from the other side of the property. He stood up and walked through his living room to get to the opposite side of his mansion. When he opened the door to his bedroom and looked out of the enormous windows there, the sight he witnessed in the mansion's garden had the hair on the back of his neck standing up.

Ten shadowy figures were fanned out in his garden and walking parallel to each other, armed with rifles. Down by the gate, he noticed the silhouettes of two figures lying on the road. He quickly figured they were his own security guards since the alarm hadn't sounded. Breland swallowed his fear and moved back into the living room.

Most of his staff had retired to their private rooms. Only Iversen and his private chef were awake. Both of them sensed something was off when they saw him re-enter the room.

'Guys, we need to evacuate everyone from their rooms. I saw a group of armed men walking to the house.' Breland's voice was shaking with fear.

'Hey, hey, Gustav, hear me out now, calm down,' said Iversen, grabbing Breland by his shoulders. 'I'll go around the house with the chef and get everyone out. You go out to your boat and get it ready for us to leave. Okay?'

'But what if you don't have time to make it out? They'll kill you.'

'Shh...take a deep breath,' said Iversen, gently patting Breland's cheek. 'When your father passed away, I promised him I would look after you. And that is a promise I will honour even if it costs my life.

If you don't live a life in service of a greater good, you've got to at least die in service of the greater good. You have grown into a wonderful man, Gustav. I only have one wish to ask of you. Please tell my kids and grandchildren that I love them and that I will always watch over them. Would you do that for me?'

Breland's eyes were filling up with tears as he acknowledged Iversen's words. His bonus dad, trusted counsellor, chief purser and good friend had made his decision, and there was nothing he could say to change his mind.

'I will,' he replied, drying the tears from his eyes.

'Good boy.' Iversen patted his head like he used to when he was a kid. 'Now, run, kiddo, and never look back.'

Breland nodded and began sprinting towards the mansion's back door. Iversen heard the main entrance door being kicked open and quickly went into his private room. There, he pulled open his drawer and reached for his engraved Magnum BFR single-action revolver with custom mother-of-pearl grips. He took a gander at the gun before loading it with five bullets.

'It's me and you now. Show me what you're good for,' he muttered, ready to face the intruders as he climbed the winding staircase.

From below, he could clearly hear people getting gunned down in their rooms. Their agonising screams were heartbreaking to hear. His aim was fixated on the staircase as he waited for the gunmen to reach the mansion's top floor. Iversen's heart was pounding hard inside his chest, but he was at total peace with the decision he had made. The world needed a Gustav Breland, young and ambitious, who could change the world, not another old man in his last years with declining health.

As soon as the screams of people dying had turned silent, he heard military boots moving up the stairs. With a firm grip on his Magnum, he pulled the trigger, aiming for the chest of the first gunman who came in sight. His Magnum sounded like a hand cannon, and the bullet pierced the gunman right in his neck, causing blood to gush out like a geyser. Soon after, another guy reached the top floor, and Iversen gave him a third eye with his next bullet.

Shocked by the resistance their squad mates had received, Cheng's crew stopped moving up the stairs. Cheng signalled for three people to move at the same time to catch their target off guard.

'Please, come closer. I'm not afraid of you at all,' Iversen taunted his opposition.

When Cheng lowered his hand, the three members of his squad started moving up to the last floor in perfect synchronisation. Iversen had anticipated this move because of their sudden halt in progress. As the three gunmen poked their heads up the stairs, Iversen lined up his shots, taking the three of them down in a matter of seconds. As a flurry of emotions rushed through his body, he continually squeezed the trigger until the Magnum's hammer clicked on an empty chamber. Realising this was the end, he threw the gun on the floor and smiled, feeling like his childhood hero, John Wayne.

'Leave him to me,' Cheng said when he figured that their target had run out of ammo.

'Well, well, well, old man,' he said, clapping ironically. 'You sure have a good aim. A pity you did not have enough bullets,' taunted Cheng, stroking his shotgun.

Iversen did not say a word as he was grabbed by his shirt and dragged across the floor. He tried to fight back, but it was pointless. His adversary was built like an ox. Cheng dragged him out to the balcony and asked him to stand up. His teary eyes noticed Breland standing on the deck of his yacht.

'Breland, look! This is what happens when anybody works for you or even remotely cares about you.'

Cheng waited for Breland to look towards the balcony before pulling out his pistol and aiming at Iversen's torso. He pulled the trigger four times in quick succession, making the old man kneel in pain. As smoke exuded the pistol's muzzle, he pointed the gun right on Iversen's forehead, touching him with the heated metal.

'Good night, old man. That's one bullet for each of my men you killed.' Cheng pulled the trigger, causing Iversen's head to disintegrate into brain matter and splatter blood all over his black clothes.

Breland watched in despair and quickly turned on the yacht's engines. No one had made it out alive from his mansion, and it was time to flee. As he adjusted the ship's direction, an orange light caught his attention. He looked behind his shoulder to see his mansion, the dream house he had built for himself, engulfed in flames. Five gunmen were standing on the dock and looking out towards the bay. Their black shadows contrasted with the fiery orange backdrop of the menacing flames. One of them was waving him goodbye. It was a harrowing scene that would forever be imprinted in his memory.

Realising that the old man hadn't given up without a fight, he had a small, sad smile on his face – the first of the night. Although he knew this had been the right thing to do, he couldn't help thinking what he could have done differently. The scenes he had witnessed tonight would forever haunt him for the rest of his life.

After leaving the bay and entering the open ocean, he had only one thing on his mind: he had to contact Santini. The OMIA crew were the only ones who could offer him some help. He grabbed his satellite phone and dialled Santini's number. As he was about to press the 'call' button, he let out an agonising scream of pure desperation, unaware of what had just happened in his energy plant.

41

NICK, JASON AND Helen had just changed into their normal attire when Santini's satellite phone buzzed on the top deck table. He was quick to respond to it and was met with a pretty shaken Gustav Breland on the other end.

'It's me, Gustav. I... I... just witnessed my mansion go up in flames. A group of people dressed in black k–k–killed everybody. I'm the only one who got out alive,' he said, stuttering as he shivered with fear.

'Hold up, Gustav. That's pretty serious. Please stay calm and tell me where you are and whether you are in danger. We will do our best to help you.'

'I will transmit you my coordinates. I'm safe for now. I took my yacht and sailed away from Savo Island. A seaplane passed by a couple of minutes ago and was headed to my mansion, probably to pick up the ones who did all the damage and destruction. I hope they don't follow me out into the open sea.'

Santini checked Breland's transmission and sent the RV Solander's GPS coordinates.

'If you stay on a southwest course, you will find us. We've docked five nautical miles northeast of Honiara.'

'Do you have any clue who did these heinous actions?' Breland asked.

'I'm afraid we have found the root of all evil, Gustav. From what Nick and the others gathered earlier tonight, a Chinese spy called Lei Cheng, a prominent black market arm's dealer named Samuel Samani and the local rebel force, GRA, have partnered up to pull off a coup d'état. The puppeteer manipulating them is Honiara's biggest entrepreneur, Moses Sikua,' Santini explained, leaving out all the information about how the World Discoverer had been used to ferry one of the biggest underwater drug shipments for a more appropriate time.

'What?! He's behind all this!? It would have never crossed my mind!

I considered him a decent man with lots of good ideas for the future of his country.'

'Looks like he's a man of secrets in the end.'

'That's one way of putting it.'

'These attackers who burnt your mansion, are you sure they did nothing else while on Savo Island?'

'Gosh, my geothermal energy plant. How could I forget? I'll have to call them and see what's the status there.'

'Hold the line, Gustav. I'll get Nick to do it,' said Santini, snapping his fingers to get Nick's attention.

After receiving the contact information from Breland, Nick began calling every number on the list, but he was sent straight to the company's voicemail.

'Boss, ask him what's his security company, and I'll try to reach them instead.'

'What's the name of the security company you use, Gustav?'

'Oh, why? Couldn't Nick get through to any of the people I sent you?'

'It doesn't seem like it.'

'That's not good,' whispered Breland, fearing the worst. 'We use EyeQ Surveillance.'

Nick quickly searched for the company's 24/7 call line and contacted them. When the operator answered his call, Breland's worst fears had been confirmed in the most horrific way possible. Flabbergasted by the operator's information, Nick whispered the news to Santini. He didn't want to shock Breland with what he had just heard.

'Everyone's dead, Boss. They broke in and killed everyone who was working tonight. Their live feed went down for ten minutes, and when it switched back on, all they could see were bodies upon bodies piled up in the corridors and offices. The facility is flooded with the blood of innocent people. Sikua has to be stopped.'

Santini debated whether to convey this information to Breland. He ultimately waited until he would cast anchor next to the RV Solander. A distressed man on his own at sea is a man capable of highly irrational and emotional decisions. He didn't want Breland to do something stupid out of despair.

When Santini finished the call with Breland, he looked at everyone who had gathered at the top deck. Everyone who had worked on the World Discoverer case was gathered there and waiting for the next words that would come from his lips.

The sudden entrance of Captain Spencer Clark, who had burst out on the deck, turned everyone's heads.

'That arse-wipe has gone completely mental! He's unleashed hordes of GRA rebels in the capital. It's all over the news.'

Everyone began talking and speculating until Santini and the Admiral intervened with a loud clap to get their attention.

'I want everybody's undivided attention right now. We are amid a national crisis that can have serious rippling consequences on the continent's geopolitical landscape. We are the only ones who can save this country from spilling its own countrymen's blood. I think we have a responsibility to step in and capture those who sank the World Discoverer, those who poisoned another country with seven tonnes of illicit drugs, those who killed hundreds of innocent lives at Savo Island, and those who fuelled their local community with weapons and radicalised their own people to turn against each other for the last twenty years.'

The Admiral nodded and took over from Santini.

'Santini is right. We can't let a madman decide the country's fate and disrupt the balance of the entire region. By all means possible, we must stop Sikua. As soon as the GRA wreaks havoc inside Honiara, the MEF will respond. Surely, a bloodbath will ensue on the streets of Honiara. We can't let that happen under our watch. I propose we divide and conquer with two squads. The Alpha squad will focus on Sikua's mansion, while the Bravo squad sets their eyes on his casino. Sikua has to be in one of those two places with his accomplices. No way is he gonna risk himself by being out in the open. He can't afford to be linked to this coup d'état. It will jeopardise his candidacy if the government collapses.'

In no less than ten minutes, they concluded by enlisting the help of RSIPF officer Ramo, who had excellent knowledge of the city's layout and a means of transportation with his trusty old Toyota RAV4. The Alpha squad would comprise of Nick and Jason, and they would go to Sikua's seaside mansion, while Helen and Ramo were Bravo squad and were assigned the Queen of Hearts casino.

Jason took control of their RIB and switched on the electric engines to approach the beach closest to Sikua's casino. They dropped off Helen, who kept to the shadows and would meet up with Ramo in a secluded back alley. When Helen informed through her molar mic that she had made contact with Ramo, Nick and Jason returned to the open sea and sailed on a northbound course.

'Let's go full throttle, Jason. We have little time left.'

'Aye, aye, Nick.' Jason pushed the throttle stick all the way forward.

Nick could clearly make out smoke signals and flares going off in the distant skyline of Honiara. In a matter of minutes, the flares were replaced with Molotov cocktails, grenades, pockets of fire and the rebels' battle cries. The crackling of machine guns and rifles intensified as they sailed along the capital city's coastline. The muffled sounds of warfare turned silent as they neared Sikua's mansion, which was situated eleven kilometres away from Honiara's city limits.

42

THE MANSION WAS perched on a seaside cliff overlooking Iron Bottom Bay, an aptly named sea passage stretching between Guadalcanal and Savo Island. The locals had come up with the name post-war due to the innumerable planes and ships that populated its seafloor after the Battle of Guadalcanal in World War II. Now, everything lay in a state of decay, serving as time capsules for future generations of underwater explorers.

A dock where Sikua's seaplane was moored was interconnected with the rest of the property by an elevator carved into the cliffed coast. The option of a winding stone staircase hugging the cliff was also available for those who preferred the more scenic route up to the mansion.

Sikua's private sanctuary from the business world was a single-story house adorned with ample glass to allow for plenty of natural lighting. A generously sized communal area in the centre of the floor plan included a merged living room, kitchen and dining room. He had selected vaulted ceilings and expansive windows to create a comfortable living space where people would naturally want to gather.

The six hundred and thirty-one square metres of the floor were tiled with Calacatta marble, sent directly from quarries in the Apuan Alps of northern Tuscany. Sikua's hired interior designer had also splurged on furniture and accessories from Farrington Interiors, a bespoke luxury shop in Hong Kong's buzzing retail district in Causeway Bay.

Facing the sea on the mansion's south side was a pool area, where he entertained guests and mistresses. He had also built a tennis court and garage fifty metres north of the mansion. Inside the garage, Sikua stored his private car collection of vintage automobiles that he had curated during his years of going to Sotheby's auctions all over the world.

When Jason and Nick finally saw the mansion's lights in the distance, they killed the RIB's engines and cast anchor. Nick checked their chest-mounted Triton rebreathers, while Jason scoped out the premises with his night-vision binoculars.

'Doesn't look like there's much of a guard presence at the moment. I only see one down by the dock, watching over the seaplane,' Jason observed.

'Maybe everyone has moved up to secure the villa.'

'Could be, especially if he is holed up in there. Wouldn't fault him, though; the place looks spectacular. I feel like a pleb just looking at it.'

'Alright, my destitute partner. Here, grab your French-made rebreather to support some good old-fashioned European consumer capitalism,' Nick said, tossing him his rebreather. 'I will go straight for the guard and kill the lights at the dock.'

'Thanks. I'll target the seaplane and work my magic on it,' Jason replied, rubbing his hands. And by magic, he meant sabotaging the engines to prevent any heroic escape attempts from Sikua.

'Alright, let's saddle up and dive, my friend,' said Nick, donning his mask.

They both slipped into the black sea as gently as possible and gave each other a thumbs-up signal, confirming their compact rebreathers worked as they should. It wasn't a particularly long swim to the dock, but they wanted to do it as stealthily as possible. This time, they didn't use their fins, so it took them a little longer than usual to cover the two-hundred-metre distance.

When they reached the dock, Nick ordered Jason to wait underwater and keep a safe distance. Then, Nick continued his swim until he had reached the edge of the dock. He grabbed a rusty ladder and pulled himself out of the sea. Checking if the safety was off on his Beretta 92X Compact pistol, he attached the silencer. He slightly lifted his head to peek over the dock and locate the guard. At the moment, he was smoking and wandering back and forth. Nick waited until the guard had his back towards him.

When the guard had finished his smoke break, Nick closed his left eye and aimed at the light bulb over the elevator entrance – the only light source at the dock. The moment his sight was aligned with the light bulb, he pulled the trigger. It instantly shattered into a myriad of small glass particles.

The guard, startled by the sound, cursed in frustration that he would have to change the lightbulb. As he trudged along towards the elevator, unmistakably annoyed, Nick tip-toed behind him, clobbered him in the back of his head with his Beretta and knocked him out stone cold. He then stowed the body behind some fishing equipment.

'Coast is clear,' Nick reported into his molar mic.

Jason's head soon broke the surface next to Sikua's seaplane. He pulled himself up onto the right-hand seaplane float and began tinkering with the first of the two Pratt & Whitney PT6A-34 single-stage, free-turbine engines. Nick kept a close eye on Jason, trying to see if the seaplane's door was open. It opened without a hitch.

'Seems someone forgot to lock the door. I'm going to look inside,' Nick informed, stepping into the cabin.

The seaplane was a Canadian Viking Twin Otter Series 400. Nick estimated the cabin to be a little under six metres long. Fifteen to seventeen people could easily fit inside it. Nick began to look around, but when nothing caught his interest, he circled the plane and opened the other cabin door to see how Jason was progressing with sabotaging the engine.

'How's it going, partner?' he asked as he peeked around the seaplane's fuselage.

Before Jason could respond, Nick heard a loud gunshot from the dock, throwing Jason off the seaplane float and into the sea.

'Noooo!' Nick yelled as he watched his partner drift away into the darkness.

'Don't make a move or I'll blow your brains out! Hands up where I can see them, and drop your weapon.'

It was Lei Cheng. Nick disposed of his gun and turned around to face the barrel of Cheng's gun. A look of grim satisfaction was painted all over Cheng's face.

'I just knew that our paths would cross again. You're a real troublemaker, Mr. Nikolaou, or should I say, Mr. Diamantis,' Cheng sneered.

'It's over, Cheng. Soon, you will have a group of Australian SAS operators raining on your parade and making a complete laughingstock of your GRA rebels.'

'Oh, really? Last time I checked, the closest Australian Navy ship was in Papua New Guinea,' said Cheng, calling his bluff. 'Enough chit-chat. Move into the cockpit and sit your ass down.'

Nick walked into the cockpit, getting extra annoyed each time Cheng poked him in the back with his gun to get him to hurry. Cheng then started tying him up in the chair with a rope going around his chest. The rope was tied so tight Nick had trouble properly breathing and had to resort to really quick breaths. He tried to wriggle out of it, but he had no chance of freeing himself.

'Let me take you on your last journey,' said Cheng as he began powering up the seaplane's engines and running the necessary pre-flight checks. 'I've heard of your affinity for the deep seas.'

The seaplane roared to life, with Cheng focusing hard on maintaining the proper pitch angles to avoid porpoising during the take-off run. As soon as the seaplane reached a speed of twenty-seven knots, he transferred the right amount of back elevator pressure from the seaplane floats to its wings. The plane smoothly lifted off the sea and soared into the starlit night sky.

Aware of Cheng's malevolent intentions, Nick braced himself and waited for an opportunity to make a move. He would not let up without a fight, though, no matter how small the odds for survival were. He had to do it. If not for him, he had to do it to honour his good friend, Jason.

He grappled with the idea that they would never have a conversation again. Or that he would be forced to tell his wife that her husband had been killed in action while he was there to supposedly protect him. Everything seemed so surreal. One minute, you were there fully present and alive, and the next moment, you were gone forever. It didn't feel fair, and right now, the stakes had gone up a notch. It wasn't an eye for an eye anymore. No. Thanks to Cheng's actions, Nick was beyond that point. Now, it was a life for a life and every man for himself. Simply wiping the smile off Cheng's face was not enough. Only killing him would numb the pain of his friend's loss.

43

RAMO NERVOUSLY TAPPED his left foot while keeping his right hand on the ignition keys. He was constantly checking his mirrors to see if anyone had been curious enough to check on his illegally parked RAV4. Helen had left the car and was hidden behind a palm tree. She was using her binoculars to observe Sikua's office and the main entrance of his casino.

In the not-so-distant background, they could clearly hear the unmistakable sound of guns going off. Throughout their twenty-minute stakeout, the sounds of warfare grew louder, and the battle was slowly moving to their part of the city. When a lot of movement started happening in the casino's foyer, Helen returned to her co-driver seat.

'I think Sikua is getting transferred back to his mansion. I see a lot of activity now in the main entrance.'

Ramo twisted the keys in the ignition and shifted the car into gear.

'You think he's afraid of the rebels moving too close to the casino?'

'Yeah, I think so. He isn't willing to risk waiting it out in his casino. He's a sitting duck should they choose to move the fighting here.'

'Okay, let me bring the car closer so we can have a better visual. What's the plan?'

'If we can confirm it's Sikua, we'll trail him to wherever he goes and arrest him.'

'Sounds simple enough.'

Ramo slowly brought the car around as Helen zeroed in on the people exiting the casino. In front of the entrance, three cars had lined up. A Jeep Wrangler Rubicon 392 was sandwiched between two blacked-out sedans, standing out conspicuously.

'There he is; I see him! He's entering the blue SUV in the middle. Don't let him out of your sight.'

'I won't. I'll show them what this old baby can do,' assured Ramo, patting the dashboard of his car.

With all the fighting going on in the streets, Sikua and his guards had to improvise on the fly when looking for the best possible route to get themselves out of Honiara. For the moment, he and his guards were moving down Kukum highway, with Ramo and Helen maintaining a respectable distance from them. When they were about to cover the bridge over Mataniko River and enter Mendana Avenue, they faced the first rebel roadblock.

Sikua had no option but to turn left and cut into Chung Wah Road, which split Honiara's Chinatown in two. Since the roads were tighter, Ramo stepped on the gas pedal and increased his pace, speeding through the neon-lit street and catching up to the black sedan. As soon as Sikua reached the next crossroad, he took a hard right and crossed the bridge running over the river. The rebels hadn't set up their roadblock there yet, so they zigzagged between some abandoned cars.

Suddenly, the windows of one sedan rolled down, and two of Sikua's private guards peeked out from either side. By the time Helen realised what they were up to, their RAV4 was being peppered with bullets. Ramo attempted to make them a more challenging target by driving erratically. It instantly helped as most of the oncoming bullets were missing their intended target. Still, a lot of bullets had left their mark on Ramo's car.

Helen wanted to retaliate, so she leaned out of her window to get back at the shooters. 'Keep her steady, and I'll aim for their tires.'

Ramo dried his forehead and gripped the steering wheel harder as Helen started shooting at the black sedan. They were passing by the Ministry of Infrastructure and Development when they finally made visual contact again with Kukum highway.

Right before they were about to enter the highway, Sikua and the other black sedan pulled away and turned left onto Mbokonavera Road. Ramo and Helen were so occupied with the other black sedan that they followed it straight onto the main highway.

'We've lost them. We have to turn the car around,' Helen shouted in agony as she saw Sikua's blue SUV vanish behind some buildings.

'Don't worry. They can't get back to his mansion by going that way.

They will have to return to Kukum highway at some point. Focus on taking down the other sedan in the meantime.'

'Get the car at a forty-five-degree angle from them. I think I can hit them from there.'

Helen steadied her aim, while Ramo followed her instructions and positioned his car right where Helen wanted.

'Hurry, before they get a clear shot at us. My car is not bulletproof.'

Helen concentrated and pulled the trigger, emptying her newly re-loaded magazine. The right rear tire got ripped into pieces, and suddenly, the black sedan was leaving a huge trail of sparks on the asphalt. The shock of losing control of his rear tire forced the driver to fight with his steering wheel until he succumbed to the forces at hand. The black sedan abruptly swerved to its right and began barrel-rolling out of control until it smashed into the gas pumps of a roadside gas station. Helen looked behind to see the crumbled chassis of the sedan getting swallowed up by a gigantic explosion. The ensuing flames would keep lighting up the area in an orange hue for the rest of the night.

'Look, there they are again!' Ramo yelled, pointing at Sikua's SUV.

They had done exactly as he had predicted and re-entered the Kukum highway. Ramo tried to push his RAV4 to its limits, but it was becoming increasingly difficult to keep up with Sikua. His car was simply superior to Ramo's. As the blue SUV disappeared into the distance, Ramo and Helen readied themselves for another standoff against the second black sedan full of guards.

Soon, another set of Sikua's gun-toting guards started firing at them, forcing Ramo to drive to the edge of his limits. Helen, in the meantime, was trying hard to come up with a new way to dispatch their adversaries.

'John, try to stay as close to them as possible and wait until both of them have to reload their guns. At that moment, floor it and let me do the rest.'

Ramo nodded and kept the car in range, all the while dodging the bullets being fired at them.

'Now!' Helen screamed as soon as she saw the two gunmen retreat to the backseat to reload their guns.

Ramo pushed his RAV4 to its maximum speed. The car was catching up, and when it was almost parallel to the black sedan, Helen had a clear line of fire on all three occupants inside the sedan and began unloading on them. All three of them turned limbless in a matter of seconds, painting the insides of their car red with blood. The sedan began slightly turning over on the highway's median grass strip until it came to a complete stop when it smashed into one of the many lamp posts lined up along the road.

'Alright, now we're talking!' Ramo exclaimed as he looked at the wrecked remains of the black sedan in his left rear-view mirror. 'Time to catch up to Sikua. We already know where he's headed.'

Both of them continued down the road until they got out of Honiara's city centre. They were now on the coastal road circling the island and trying to navigate the treacherous roads in the dark. When they drifted around a tight left hairpin, they could see Sikua's car lights in the distance. Eager to catch up to him, Ramo upshifted and began driving much faster. When he was about to shift into the next gear, his engine made a strange noise.

'No, no, no, don't do this to me,' Ramo muttered.

'What's happening?'

'I think the engine must have picked up some damage from all the shooting. The car is not reacting to my inputs.'

The car continued moving forward until its lack of momentum brought it to a stop. Ramo exited the car to examine the engine, but what he saw troubled him even more. When he popped the hood, smoke trails ghosted their way upwards. Ramo covered his nose to avoid inhaling too much smoke.

'This can't be temporarily fixed. I'm sorry,' said Ramo, utterly deflated.

'Don't worry. I'll check my GPS to see how far away we are from the mansion.'

The GPS indicated they were three kilometres from their destination, which meant a thirty-minute walk along the coastal road. They pushed the car to the side of the road and grabbed a pair of flashlights from the trunk.

'Hopefully, Nick and Jason have better luck than us tonight,' said Ramo.

'Same, I just hope we can make it in time.'

Both of them wondered what was going on with Nick and Jason down at the mansion.

44

FROM THE COCKPIT, Nick had a clear view of both Honiara and Sikua's mansion. Cheng had put the seaplane in a holding pattern, allowing Nick to observe only the illuminated areas in their vicinity. They hadn't interacted since take-off, but Nick wanted to extract some information from him.

'So, what's the meaning of all this? I mean, you've gone to extreme lengths to accomplish Sikua's plan.'

'Sikua's plan? Ha! You really don't have a freaking clue,' Cheng responded patronisingly. 'Since I'm talking to a soon-to-be-dead man, maybe I'll grant you one last wish and tell you exactly what's going on.'

He pushed on a few buttons before turning his attention back to Nick.

'To make things absolutely clear, Sikua is just a pawn in my government's scheme.'

'Oh, so you're not some kind of rogue double agent?'

'Hilarious! No, I'm not. I am a spy for the Chinese Ministry of State Security, as you can clearly see.' Cheng proudly flashed his badge. 'And I would appreciate it if you didn't interrupt me unless you can't wait to reach the afterlife.'

Nick nodded, understanding that pushing his buttons further was pointless.

'Our plan was to find a potential candidate we could ally ourselves with. As you know, the Australians and the West have had a firm grip on this country since 2003. When Sikua popped on our radar, he checked all of our boxes. He was the first to understand the vision we had for his country.'

'So you basically promised him the reins of his country in exchange for his help along the way with your various dubious activities?'

'That's correct. But we ensured he felt like he was the one in charge during the entire process.'

'Clever. You boosted his ego so that he wouldn't suspect anything.'

'And we wanted to test him to see if he could get his hands dirty for our cause.'

'Aha, so this is where the World Discoverer and the drug smuggling come into play?'

'Of course. We killed two birds with one stone with that one. He showed us he wasn't afraid to dip his toes in illegal activities, and we made enough untraceable money to fund this operation.'

'Not bad. I assume you plan to take control of anything you can in the South Pacific, the same way you did in the South China Sea?'

'Definitely. It's the only way to expand our maritime borders without engaging in full-blown combat. It's genius.'

'What's next for this country and your plan for the future?'

'As soon as we bring down the current government, Sikua will win the snap elections. I suspect we'll start with the most important bureaucratic stuff to bolster the alliance with China. You know, security agreements, plans for a naval base in Tulagi and permanent severance of the umbilical cord with Australia. The most important aspect, though, would be funding and improving the country's GDP and infrastructure. When their neighbouring countries see what China can do for their economies, it will be easier to get them on our side.'

'This sounds like an alternative version of the Belt and Road Initiative, but with a focus on navy and maritime borders. Interesting. It could potentially block the American and Australian naval presence in the region with time.'

'That's right. If Palau, Nauru, Tuvalu and the Marshall Islands follow the same model we're establishing with the Solomon Islands, which is highly likely because of their smaller size and geographical locations, then Taiwan will run out of regional allies supporting their independence from China.'

'Leaving them politically defenceless against the intentions of your government. Not bad.'

'Indeed. That will completely sideline the Americans and leave the Australians with a small base in Papua New Guinea. Meanwhile, we can have full control of most trade routes and the biggest maritime borders in the area.'

Nick tried to visualise a world where this plan unfolded. It looked like a bunch of big countries were trying to brainwash a lot of minor countries to follow their lead by promising them an enticing and prosperous future. He was also a part of the equation now, making him just another man among a long line of foreigners who had tried to leave their mark on these countries. Even if he took down Cheng, nothing good was certain to come of it. The Solomon Islands' future didn't rest on his or OMIA's shoulders. No, only the local population itself had the power to steer this country in the right direction. However, if Cheng's success solely rested on his demise, he would do whatever he could to keep the spoils of victory away from his reach. How he didn't know yet, but his mind was busy working on it. Nick's own life mattered more to him than any geopolitical conspiracy.

The right engine rudely interrupted his next thought with an explosion. That sneaky devil Jason had had enough time to sabotage it. The seaplane began to gradually lose altitude when he heard a second bang. At that moment, the right engine caught fire.

'Well, it seems I have to move on to the next phase of my plan. Enjoy your trip to the deep sea.' Cheng stood up from the pilot's seat and grabbed a parachute. 'See you on the other side,' he said right before jumping out of the cabin door.

Nick instinctively panicked before trying to get a hold of the diving knife Helen had gifted him. It was perpendicularly strapped to the inside of his right ankle. Since the plane was plummeting from the sky and shaking profoundly, it made the surgical precision of Nick's escape attempt even harder.

He pressed with his left heel on the release button of the knife strap and released the knife from its secure position. Then, he quickly moved his left foot a few centimetres up, to apply pressure to the diving knife and stabilise it there. He followed it up with the same movement from his right foot until he was holding the knife between his two feet. After that, he carefully began lifting his feet until his left hand could grab the knife. He then started cutting the rope that bound him. In a matter of seconds, he could move again. Nick was relieved to be breathing properly again, but he wasn't out of the woods yet.

He moved over to the seat from which Cheng had controlled the seaplane. Time was limited, and he didn't have enough of it to jump out with a parachute. But that suited him well since he despised heights. Instead, he grabbed the steering wheel and turned it as hard as he could to the right.

The plane moved away from land and into the middle of the Iron Bottom Sound strait. His heart was beating in his mouth by now. When he glanced at the plane's altimeter, it showed he was at around a height of one thousand feet. The plane sluggishly replied to Nick's inputs and began turning. When he could finally see Sikua's mansion again, he straightened the wheel and let the plane continue on its downward trajectory. All the while, he could hear the flames eating up the plane's right wing and smell the smoke seeping into the seaplane's cabin.

Various warning signals and alarms went off as the seaplane descended. Nick braced for impact when he noticed how close they were to the sea. With a tremendous splash, the plane crashed into the sea so hard that its seaplane floats broke off from the rest of the fuselage. Nick braced as hard as he could, but the impact was so hard that he got thrown out of his seat.

Water began entering the cabin fast, so he had to pull himself together and find a way out of the sinking plane. Fortunately, his earlier manoeuvre had helped the plane land parallel to the swells, offering him a slim window of opportunity before it sank. In the cabin's rear, he spotted his Beretta before water covered it. Nick waddled through the water inside the cabin to retrieve his gun, and by the time he picked it up, the water was up to his neck. He put the gun in his holster and took a deep breath before diving.

Nick used one of his hands to touch the wall of the cabin and guide him towards the open cabin door. The moment he got out of the door, he began swimming as fast as he could up to the sea surface. The last metres were excruciating as his lungs burned, yearning for oxygen. But he didn't cave into his body's demands until his head broke through the water's surface.

Nick gasped for air and coughed violently, trying to orient himself with his surroundings. He could taste the seawater inside his mouth. One of the two seaplane floats was floating five metres away from him. He swam towards it and used it as a support to catch his breath and keep him afloat effortlessly.

Just then, something caught Nick's attention when he looked up at the sky. It was Cheng in his parachute. He couldn't be more than fifty metres over the sea surface and was moving towards Sikua's garden to land. It's time for you to pay, Nick thought. He climbed on top of the seaplane float and grabbed his Beretta before carefully aiming his gun, considering Cheng's momentum. The first two bullets whizzed by Cheng, clearly making him fearful of what was coming next.

Nick, stubborn as he was, refocused himself and held his breath. When he felt everything was perfectly aligned, he resumed shooting at Cheng. Jackpot, he thought when Cheng flailed his arms frantically and writhed in pain as some of the next bullets hit their mark. Nick kept going until his magazine was empty. Hopefully, that would be enough to silence him.

'He who laughs last, laughs the best,' Nick said to himself with a satisfied smile.

Sitting on the flotsam, Nick noticed that their RIB wasn't too far away. He waited for a few minutes until he had recovered enough energy to swim the seventy-seven metres that separated him from the RIB. The mansion would be his next stop as he had to see through his mission. Fuelled with adrenaline after escaping the plane wreck and injuring Cheng, Nick began his gruelling swim with the moon as his sole light source. When he was halfway there, he mentally commended JFK for his swimming abilities, who had done exactly the same for many nights straight, trying to locate help for his brothers-in-arms.

45

AFTER PULLING HIMSELF over the RIB's gunwale, Nick looked for some ammo to reload his gun. He then strapped his Beretta in its holster and took control of the RIB. Soon, he was occupied with tying it to the dock where Sikua's seaplane had once been.

When faced with the decision between the elevator and the stone staircase snaking its way up the cliffed coast, he was torn. Since the elevator was bound to be noisier, he finally chose to move up the stairs. When he got to the garden, everything was dark except for one room in the mansion that seemed to be illuminated. He cautiously approached the pool area, constantly checking around for guards.

Some metres away from the pool, he spotted Cheng's crumbled parachute. A crouched guard was attending to him and checking if he was alive. Nick hid behind the pool bar and waited to hear if he was alive. When all he could hear was the guard's voice, unanswered by Cheng, he stood up and approached the crouched guard.

'Hand where I can see them. Now!' Nick advanced purposefully with the gun in his hands. 'Don't make me do this.'

The guard ignored his calls and reached for his AK-47. Nick sighed and rapidly pressed the trigger of his gun. The guard slumped forward, landing dead on his stomach. Nick silently moved from where the bar and cabanas were and reached the spot where Cheng was lying. The man was dead and had bled out in the garden, lying in a pool of his own blood. Nick crouched and closed Cheng's eyelids.

Attack him when he is unprepared; appear when you are not expected, Nick thought as he stood up and observed the lifeless body. That was something Jason liked to quote whenever they discussed military stories from their past. Nick listened intently for any sounds or voices indicating more people were around. The eerie silence gave Nick the chills as he opened the sliding glass door leading to the living room.

The floor was all marble, making it difficult to muffle his footsteps.

To his left, muted slivers of light peeked through a half-open door leading to one of the hallways. Nick decided to enter the room with his gun held high, curious to see who was in there. He tiptoed with his back against the wall until he was next to the door. With a swift kick, he pushed it open and barged into the room with his Beretta, ready to fire at any guards hiding in there.

What he saw caught him by surprise. Sikua was sitting in an antique ornate chair, enjoying a drink and looking out at the sea. The room must have been his library or private study since all the walls were covered in art or bookshelves.

'Hell of a night, ain't it?' said Sikua, taking a sip from a fancy whiskey glass. 'You know, this was supposed to be the night where the fate of this country would change for the better. Right now, though, I'm not so sure that's the case.'

Nick slowly approached with his gun still pointed at his target. 'Let me see your hands.'

Sikua stood up and turned to face him, with only a glass in his right hand.

'Whatever existed between us is over now that you've stepped into my library instead of Cheng.' Sikua brought forth a bottle of twelve-year-old Macallan Scotch whiskey. 'Care for a drink?'

Nick thought about his offer and studied the look in his eyes. 'Alright,' he finally replied, lowering his gun.

When he had finished pouring him a glass, Sikua offered him his drink.

'I had this imported from Scotland. I'm more of a Baijiu man myself, but I thought that tonight seemed fitting for something with a little more class. Please take a seat. I'm not going anywhere.'

Nick grabbed his glass and settled into a matching chair opposite Sikua.

'Not bad,' Sikua commented after taking a sip from his whiskey and eying his glass.

'It's good, but I'd still prefer a negroni over this.'

Sikua's gaze wandered for a few moments before he pulled himself together and started talking again.

'At what moment did you know it was me?'

'When you commented on Breland's ship being unsalvageable back at the stadium. No one knew about the ship's ultimate sinking except for those in OMIA.'

'I slipped up, damn. Good on you for noticing that,' said Sikua, acknowledging his mistake before looking Nick straight in the eyes.

'What's your biggest fear, Nick?'

The question took Nick by surprise, so he dug deep before answering. 'My biggest fear is failure. Not being able to help the people around me and disappointing them with my actions.' Nick paused for a moment, the pain of losing Jason weighing heavy on his chest. 'What about you?'

'Interesting you should say that. From the outside, you seem like a really confident and steadfast person. My own fear is that I believe I am powerful beyond measure. And I believe it is never our own darkness that frightens us; it is always the light. We, as humans, always ask ourselves, "Who am I to be brilliant, gorgeous, powerful?" In reality, we should be asking, "Who are you not to be?" Playing small doesn't serve the world, Nick. There's nothing enlightening about shrinking so that others won't feel insecure around you. We are all meant to shine. Never forget that as we are liberated from our own fears, our presence automatically liberates others. Unfortunately, none of our political leaders share my mentality, and that's why we've always stayed hidden offstage as a country.'

'Seems you've done some soul searching. When talking about your goals, however, do you think the end justifies the means?'

'Good question. Listen, when I give food to the poor, these people call me a saint. But when I ask why the poor don't have food, they label me as a communist. The above saying epitomises what is happening with us in this country. When we give our land for the benefit of the government and that of the nation-state, we are called generous. When we ask why we have not benefited from that, they ignore us. When we start shouting, wanting to be heard, they call us troublemakers. When we start taking up arms to ask for what rightfully belongs to us, they call us militants. When we become angry when foreigners trample on us, they call us the hot-headed youth. Those are the names they use to justify their disregard towards us, Nick. Soon, they will call us the GRA guerillas or, even worse, terrorists. One thing's for certain, though – they will never get rid of us. I know for a fact that someone out there will continue my work if I'm willing to sacrifice myself. A lifetime in prison is no way to spend your time on earth.'

As Sikua spoke, Nick spotted the faint glow of flashing police lights in the background. It had to be Helen and Ramo.

'They're here, aren't they?' Sikua asked without looking back.

Nick nodded.

'Okay, then it's time to finish this.' Sikua pulled a Desert Eagle from his drawer and placed it on the table in front of Nick. 'Here, take it and finish this off. You'll get your revenge and become a hero, while I become a martyr for my cause. Both of us win. What do you say?'

Nick picked up the gun and pointed it towards his head.

'Do it, pull the trigger!' urged Sikua, getting more paranoid with each passing second. 'I said do it! Listen to me, goddammit!'

'No! These islands have had enough of death and spilt blood. I won't give you the easy way out,' said Nick, removing the magazine from the Desert Eagle. 'You will just have to man up and face the consequences of your actions.'

He pressed the small levers on each side of the gun and slid the barrel off its slide rack, dividing the gun into two pieces. Nick also removed a couple of springs and a piston that held those springs in place. When he was finished, he placed all the parts on the table, except for the gun's magazine.

This one, he held proudly in his hand until he pushed the bullets out one after another, letting them fall and scatter all over the marble floor. Sikua's manic screams drowned out the metallic sound of them clattering on the floor.

As Nick looked down at him with a stoic gaze, Ramo and Helen entered the room and promptly handcuffed Sikua. They quickly dragged him out of the room and took him towards the police car that had picked them up along the coastal road. Ramo had called in a last-minute favour from his partner, Michael Kere.

Nick took a last look at the insides of the majestic mansion, coming to terms with the fact that this was the end of Moses Sikua. He was hoping all of his efforts would have felt more fulfilling. But at the moment, he was just feeling empty. Like he hadn't really achieved anything at all. Just like Sikua had mentioned, when his story got out, it would most likely inspire someone else to accomplish his vision. And the vicious cycle of good vs evil would continue for eternity. History always had a habit of repeating itself, especially with criminals, or we wouldn't need all those national and international law enforcement agencies.

However, amid all these confusing and rather depressive thoughts, one positive note stood out like the North Star in the night sky. If there was one job he could carry on doing with pride for the rest of his life, it was that of a marine investigator. It was liberating to know that from this moment on, he would no longer have to worry about finding out what he was destined for. Since his teen years, he has been looking for the one thing that would make his life meaningful. He hadn't been able to find it during his time in the Norwegian Navy or his short-lived tenure as a scuba diving instructor in Greece. Right now, though, after coming all the way to the Solomon Islands as a marine investigator for OMIA, he had received some clarity.

He wanted to dedicate the rest of his life to solving the mysteries the seven seas held and catching the ones committing crimes against them. He saw himself pursuing this mission until it was his turn to be laid to rest, alongside the dearly departed who had shared the same ambitions as him. This simple thought released some of the tension that had burdened him during the long night, and a small smile slowly formed across his face.

46

'HEY, HOW ARE you holding up?' Helen asked as he exited the mansion.

'If the guilt doesn't eat me up, I think I'll be fine. I just wanted Jason to make it out alive as well. I mean, why not me? I have nobody waiting for me back in my apartment. He has a wife waiting for him to come home. I don't think it's fair at all.' Nick's mind was in turmoil, trying to process everything that had transpired in the last few hours.

'Life is rarely fair. I can see you're deep in thought. Follow me, I have someone who wants to meet you.' She ushered him towards a police car and an ambulance parked outside Sikua's garage.

'What happened to your car? You always spoke so highly of it.' He asked Ramo, who was resting on the police car's bonnet. Nick attempted to lighten his mood by poking a little fun at the expense of Ramo's missing car.

'You know what, don't even mention it. A couple of guys shot my engine to pieces. No big deal, though; we still made it in time to save your skin and bag the bad guy. I called in a favour from my partner and he picked me and Helen up as we were walking to the mansion.'

'What are you talking about? I had full control all the way. Did you see a plane in flames up there?' Nick pointed up towards the moon.

'I thought it was a shooting star.'

'Stop messing with me,' said Nick, putting his arms around Ramo's shoulders and patting him. 'It's good to see you again. Thank you so much for all the help we got along the way. I won't forget it; remember that.'

'Anytime. I have to thank you and your team as well for trusting me and letting me be a part of something this important.'

Helen stepped in to grab Nick's attention and usher him into Sikua's garage.

'There's someone waiting for you inside the garage.'

Nick obliged and walked inside, only to be surrounded by an array of vintage automobiles ranging from a 1906 Stanley Steamer to a 1965 Corvette Stingray. Santini was busy admiring the art déco hood ornament on a 1932 Auburn Boattail Speedster.

'Pretty impressive to have all this automotive history gathered in this secluded part of the world,' Santini said. 'I have a guy up in Arizona who'd kill for this lot. Maybe I should give him a phone call about this opportunity. Really nice guy, spends all of his time diving and writing books.'

'I do the same, except for writing. I enjoy reading them instead.'

'Maybe on the next trip abroad, I'll give you one of his books from my collection,' Santini said, walking over to cordially greet Nick. 'You've grown a lot these past days. You should be really proud of yourself and what you accomplished on this job. Rousseau wanted me to pass on his congratulations as well. We stressed him out, but we brought it home in the end.'

'Thank you, Boss. Couldn't have done it without you guys. It's a team effort through and through. You know, that's what we do in OMIA; we leave no stone unturned until the bitter end. I have one small question, though – what happens next with Breland and the Solomon Islands?'

'Breland is safe and sound. He reached the RV Solander and is already working on doing everything he can for the families who lost loved ones. As for the country, the Australians are flying in a sizable group of SAS operators to dismantle everything that is left of Samani's weapons smuggling network and the remaining rebel cells in Honiara. I think Ramo and his partner Kere are also involved from the local police.'

'Good. How do they plan to address the current problem with all the corruption?'

'They sadly did not disclose that to me. We'll just have to wait and see.'

'Okay, and what about the elephant in the room? Did we arrange for the extraction of fuel from the World Discoverer? The folks back in Hideaway gave me a hard time about that specific issue.'

'Ah, yes. The Admiral came through as promised with everything we would need to extract the fuel. I think the ships with the necessary equipment will arrive in ten hours from now. In a day or two, we can consider ourselves fully finished with this assignment.'

'Phew, that's fantastic. It's crazy how everything played out. The last couple of days feel like weeks.'

'I know, Nick. Save it for the debrief tomorrow. I'm curious to know how all of you did it. By the way, follow me. I have something that will cheer you up.'

Santini closed the door behind them and had Nick follow him to the ambulance.

'Go on and look inside.'

Nick climbed in, only to be greeted by Jason's smiling face.

'Cheer up, partner. You're not staring at a corpse. I'm the first human being to dodge the three stages of rigour mortis.'

The immense feeling of guilt on Nick's shoulders melted away when he saw his partner patched up and alive on the stretcher. One by one, he let go of all the repressed emotions that had been consuming him, allowing his soul to embrace forgiveness and self-acceptance. The weightlessness that followed felt like the first breath of fresh air after a thunderous storm. Nick felt hopeful now that he would be able to move forward from these recent events, not only with a renewed sense of clarity but also a lighter heart.

'What?! You've got to be kidding me?! I'm so glad to see you, partner.' Nick greeted him carefully so as not to hurt his bandaged shoulder. 'You've gotta tell me how you made it.'

'Thankfully, the bullet went straight through my shoulder. My body drifted over to the beach, south of the mansion. In fact, Helen spotted me when they were walking along the road with Ramo and called for an ambulance. To be honest, you have to thank her. Without her, I would have rotted on a sandy beach.'

'I might have to do that.' Nick winked.

'I'm really interested to hear what happened after I passed out.'

'Then you're gonna love tomorrow's debrief. Next time, however, make sure you stay in the game so that we can finish our assignment together.'

'You bet. I can't have you rubbing it in for the next few years. It will be intolerable coming to work just to be bullied by you. Next time, I promise I'll have your back.'

They both shook hands and agreed on that. When the medical personnel asked Nick to give them some space, he exited the ambulance.

He was beginning to feel much better than he had when he had walked out of the mansion and could feel a sense of relief and pride washing over him. After a couple of minutes, he began thinking about his apartment in Frogner and how amazing it would be to sleep in his own bed and enjoy some privacy again. The toils of the last days had clearly left their marks on his body and mind. It would definitely take some time to immerse himself in all the numerous impressions he was left with from this trip before allowing them to weave together into the vivid mosaic of his past experiences. One thing was for certain, post the Solomon Islands, Nick would never be the same person again.

'Ay, Boss, when do we get to go home?' Nick asked reluctantly.

'Soon, Nick. Real soon.'

47

NICK HAD JUST touched down on Norwegian soil, after being stuck inside Breland's supersonic jet for over ten hours. His back cracked loudly when he stretched his body, and he hungrily breathed in the fresh Norwegian air. Outside the spacious hangar, a black limousine was parked, looking mysterious with its tinted windows. It looked like someone important was onboard, but Nick paid no mind as he was just waiting to get his luggage from the ground handlers and go home. He reckoned it was there to pick up Breland.

After some waiting and small talk with some of the jet's crew, he grabbed his luggage and headed to his Alfa Romeo. The doors of the limousine swung open the moment he was about to walk past it, and he was greeted by Jacques Rousseau, along with an older gentleman dressed in a Royal Norwegian Navy uniform, who also stepped out of the limousine. Based on the distinctions on his shoulders, he had to be the new Commander-in-chief. They asked him and Santini to join them for a quick chat, and they could not turn it down.

'Gentlemen, what a pleasure to have you back in Norway,' said Rousseau, stepping into the car. 'Please, come in. I picked up someone special along the way who wanted to talk to you.'

As they got comfortable in their seats and exchanged pleasantries, the Commander-in-chief broke the ice.

'I want to extend my profound gratitude for an excellent job in the Solomon Islands. You went above and beyond your call of duty, and on behalf of the Norwegian Navy and our NATO allies, we are really thankful for your services.'

Nick and Santini smiled politely and nodded in acknowledgement.

'To show our appreciation, we'd like to discuss a potential avenue for cooperation between OMIA and the Norwegian Navy.'

Rousseau stepped in to decrypt the Commander-in-chief's ambiguous statement.

'What the Commander means is that we may receive warnings about jobs where plausible deniability may come into play,' said Rousseau, putting extra emphasis on those words.

'Exactly. Jacques, you've hit the nail on the head. We will, of course, provide you with access to the tools of our trade and our global network.'

'I think it's beneficial to both of us. Don't you think so?' Santini asked.

'I think so too. A little extra work hurt nobody,' said Rousseau, shrugging his shoulders.

'Yes, and sorry for interrupting, but I just have to give my two cents as well. Personally, I have nothing against spending more time at sea than behind my office desk,' Nick chimed in, the events from the Solomon Islands still fresh in his mind.

'I think that sums it up, Commander,' said Rousseau, giving him a satisfied smile and a firm handshake.

'You're totally right. I think I've heard what I needed to hear. Thanks for your time again, and you may hear from me when you least expect it,' said the Commander, tipping his hat.

Interestingly, their case involving the World Discoverer had reached the upper echelon of the Norwegian government. Nick got a taste of what his OMIA job could offer, and he couldn't wait for his next call from Santini or Rousseau. Doing the dirty work of the Norwegian Navy without adhering to the endless red tape was like a balm to his heart.

Enough of work, thought Nick as he closed the door of his Alfa Romeo 4C and gripped the steering wheel. It was time to get home, have a warm shower and sleep off this jetlag in a bed with fresh sheets.

48

The doors of BEWA Cruises' boardroom had just closed behind Nick when a familiar voice caught his attention.

'Hey, Nick, do you have a spare minute?' a panting Breland asked after bursting out of the boardroom.

'Of course. What's up? I hope we didn't forget anything important in the meeting.'

'No, absolutely not. I just had an epiphany of sorts. Since it was your idea to name our new cruise ship "Einar Iversen", I wanted to grant you the honour of christening our ship when the time comes. How does that sound?'

Breland's gesture startled and touched Nick. He had taken a liking to Iversen during their time together on their flight from Oslo. It was a real shame he had been killed, but the man fought like a true Viking until the end.

'Of course. I'd love to do that. It would be an honour. Just tell me when and where, and I'll be there.'

'Terrific! Let's say August 2024 in Genoa. I think you know where the Fincantieri shipyard is, right?'

'Sort of. If not, I'll just hit up Santini.'

'Excellent. Well, Nick, this is where our paths part for now. I hope you enjoy your vacation, and whatever you may need in the future, I'm only a phone call away,' said Breland, mimicking the hand signal of a phone. 'By the way, where are you planning to elope to for your vacation?'

'You're a funny man. I'm taking a week off and going to Switzerland. Lausanne, to be more specific.'

'Oh, a fine choice indeed. I spent many years there as a student. I would never have expected that from a Mediterranean guy like you. I thought you were ready for Mykonos or the Athenian Riviera.'

'Don't forget that I'm half Norwegian as well.'

'Damn, I keep forgetting that. Alright, my friend, take care!'

With that obligation out of the way, Nick was free to spend his evening as he wished. He had already packed his luggage in the morning so that he could chill by himself at home that night. He had gone grocery shopping the previous night and had all the ingredients to make himself a bucatini all'amatriciana, the Roman way, with a Greek salad on the side. The only dilemma for the evening was whether to watch a rerun of Tarantino's "Inglorious Basterds" for the umpteenth time or restart watching season 1 of Miami Vice. He would wait until he got home to decide, but the idea of escaping into the neon-lit streets of Miami in the 80s for just a night was particularly enticing.

49

THE SUN WAS shining brilliantly across the spotless sky over Lac Leman, a semilunar-shaped lake squeezed in between Switzerland and France, overlooked by the awe-inspiring Swiss Alps. Nick's iPhone showed it was twenty-eight degrees in Lausanne. The fresh-water lake was acetylene blue and had attracted myriads of locals to its coastline, who were either swimming or getting grilled by the UV rays while cruising on their recreational boats.

Nick had just swan-dived into the lake from the gunwale of a Riva Aquarama Special 774 and was holding his breath underwater. He kicked himself forward for a few metres and pushed his head out to replenish his lungs with oxygen. He dragged his hair away from his face and floated on his back, listening to the distorted sounds of the water. When the sun began burning his eyelids, he adjusted his body to an upright position, looked around to take in his surroundings and started swimming back to the boat. He then pulled himself up and grabbed a towel to dry his upper body and hair.

Helen was lying on her stomach in a baby blue bikini, soaking in the sun. Nick admired her enchanting curves, appreciating the tan lines that had formed on her luscious body during their week-long trip together. They had been really lucky and gotten the most out of the heat waves ravaging Central Europe.

'Was it cold?' she asked, turning back to look at him through her Prada sunglasses.

'Ah, it was just perfect. Not too cold and not too warm. Have you had enough sunbathing?'

'Hmm, yeah. We could return to land and find something else to do.'

'I know exactly what we can do, and no, I'm not thinking about what you assume I'm thinking about.'

'Knock it off and don't get too cocky now.' She hit him playfully on his arm.

'Alright, madame. Your wish is my command. Back to land, it is.'

He brought the Riva back to the small promenade next to the port of Lausanne-Ouchy. They held hands as they walked the short distance back to the hotel where they were staying – the Hôtel Beau-Rivage Palace, a mainstay on the city's waterfront since 1861.

Nick couldn't help but imagine what mysteries these walls had been privy to, listening in on the debates of pioneers signing important international treaties, stories from all the artists who had sought refuge there to get their creative juices flowing, and the secrets of the royal families who had stayed there during their vacations. He was sure this place guarded a lot of secrets, although Helen didn't share the same enthusiasm. She was more preoccupied with the unique aesthetics of the historic hotel and the exquisite selection of amenities at the spa.

Since it was their last day in Switzerland, they had a steamy shower together and changed into some much more elegant outfits for their evening dinner at the hotel's two-star Michelin restaurant, the Anne-Sophie Pic. All of their mouth-watering dishes were prepared under the watchful eye of the restaurant's chef de cuisine, Kévin Vaubourg.

Their meal began with an appetiser featuring Fera, the local whitefish of Lac Leman, which was smoked and marinated with spruce buds and ground ivy. A sea fennel mousseline sauce was strewn over the plate, the same way a painter delicately applied his brush on a white canvas. Green beans and oscietra caviar completed the dish. When their appetites were built up for the crescendo, they got served a roasted lamb rack from the Alpstein mountains, marinated with fig and cherry leaves. They ended their dinner by sharing a small plate of white mille-feuille.

When they went out for their customary walk after dinner, Nick came up with an idea. He wanted to take Helen to a special place where they could enjoy the sunset. Since they both knew this could be the last time they saw each other, he wanted to give her a fond memory she could look back on and hold on to dearly.

'You know what, I'm feeling kinda inspired tonight. Let's take the car and go somewhere special.'

Intrigued by the idea, she agreed, pulled him closer and gave him a warm kiss with her tender lips. As they neared the car, Nick looked through his pockets for his keys. Through Breland's contacts, he had borrowed one of the most collectable Italian cars of the 60s, a red convertible Alfa Romeo 2600 Spider. Carrozzeria Touring had built its chassis in Milan, and it was the last Alfa Romeo to sport an inline six-cylinder engine with twin overhead camshafts. This car held a poetic allure for Nick. as it was launched at the Geneva Motor Show in 1962, the same place where he and Helen had started and would end their vacation together.

After tipping the hotel's valet, he followed the coastal road of the city, driving past Parc Olympique, a park dedicated to the Olympic Games, and cruising at a steady speed so they could enjoy the ride along Avenue Général Guisan. When they had driven past the small marina of Lutry, he knew they had reached the outskirts of town. Nick turned on his headlights and took a left onto Route de la Petite Corniche.

This was the scenic route through the slopes of Lavaux, an area formed during the ice ages when the massive Rhone Glacier melted fifteen thousand years ago. The roads were winding and undulating as they carved through acres of terraced vineyards. Nick slowed down and parked the car in the main square of the picturesque village of Aran in Villette. He then opened Helen's door for her and gently closed the door behind her.

He held her soft arms and led the way as they walked through the village's tight streets. The destination he had in his mind was the François Joly Vineyard and its perching garden, where they could sit, drink wine and enjoy the breathtaking views of Lac Leman. After they found a secluded table, he ordered a 70cl. bottle of Châtelet Blanc that had been properly chilled at around ten degrees Celsius. When the first sip had kicked in, their conversation began flowing effortlessly. Nick was always fascinated by the fact that wine, good company and beautiful surroundings could turn everybody into modern-day philosophers.

'What are you planning to do when you get back home?' he asked.

'I still have some time off, you know. Maybe I'll lie low for a while, waiting for the next assignment.'

'You deserve that. Oh, and before I forget, when you see Ramo, send him my regards. I hope his family is settling in nicely in their new home.'

'I will. I've heard only good things about him from my old colleagues at the PD. Everybody is thrilled to have him as a member of the force.'

'He deserves a chance to chase his dreams in a less toxic work environment. I'm really happy for him.'

'And for you,' asked Helen, 'what does your future hold, do you think?'

'Hopefully, some exciting work and more travelling. I know I'm nearing my thirties, so the fatherly instinct is begging to grow inside of me. However, I need to suppress these thoughts because I am in no position to settle down and start a family. I don't have a fixed schedule to go by, so everything in my daily life is free-flowing. I wish I could have what Jason has with his wife, but I realise that if I want to pursue this career, I'll have to meet a special one who can put up with my lifestyle and get to grips with the fact that there is a possibility I may never return from one of my assignments.'

'I feel you. It's like we live two different lives – one at work and one where we have to function like normal people and do regular stuff.'

'Yes, and we are so set in our routines that we find it challenging to include other people.'

'No matter what happens to us, I'll always remember our time together. You're a good man, and I hope you'll realise when it's time to take a step back from work and focus on what really matters here in this life.'

'Me too. I enjoy spending time with you. It's a pity that our lives are moving in two different trajectories. Maybe, in another life, you and I could be more than what we've had this past week. I'm not gonna lie; I'm slowly warming up to the idea of opening my heart to someone,' said Nick, beginning to channel his inner Humphrey Bogart. 'And remember, we will always have Lausanne,' he said, kissing her.

Helen glowed with rapture.

When their bottle was emptied, they both sat in silence, enjoying the sunset until it was almost over, like watching the sand run out of an hourglass. Suddenly, Nick's iPhone vibrated on the glass table, startling them. He turned it over and saw it was a cryptic message from Santini:

'Meet me tomorrow, 11:30 at Place Bourg-De-Four in Geneva if you are interested in a dive. Demi Lune café. The job pays well.'

Helen recognised the look on his face and didn't have to ask what it was all about. She just knew.

'Seems like I have to prolong my stay in Switzerland after all,' said Nick, placing his phone down and looking back at her. 'But that doesn't mean we shouldn't have a good time tonight,' he whispered, kissing her passionately.

NICK DIAMANTIS WILL RETURN

Konstantinos Gustad Padazopoulos (b. 1994) grew up in the port town of Athens, Piraeus in a family brimming with seafaring legacy. Even before he had turned old enough to join kindergarten, he had gone along with his father onboard a lot of ships, exploring various ports in the eastern Mediterranean. When other kids his age spent time in the local playground, Konstantinos was busy exploring the insides of cruise ships and fast jumbo ROPAX ferries, listening to all the daring maritime adventures the crews had to share with him.

A voracious reader with a knack for detail, he took a particular interest in English literature during his teenage years devouring anything he could put his hands on. After a move to Norway in 2012 and hundreds of books read later he finally decided to merge his passions and start spinning his own adventure yarns. You will find him writing in the most unexpected places possible in Oslo, enjoying his long walks along Akerselva or reading a book in the shaded part of a Greek beach.